PRAISE FOR

FLIPPING THE CIRCLE

"Michael Leppert offers an informed and detailed account of the good, the bad, and even the ugly of government and politics and how it works. His insights, enlightened by his years in the Indiana political arena, reveal how fragile yet strong the democratic process is, and how the fight for good is often disadvantaged but can ultimately prevail."

—**ANDREW STONER**, PhD, author, and professor

"If any of this has a 'hint of truth' it's time for Hoosiers to start paying attention to what's going on at the Statehouse. This gripping story should be a reminder that you don't need to go to DC to 'drain the swamp', voters can begin in their own State Capitol/ Capital. I can't believe this is happening. Living proof why one-party control is BAD. Alarming, shocking, and educational, but sadly, I'm afraid this is what's happening in too many of our States."

—**JOHN GREGG**, former Speaker of the Indiana House of Representatives

"A wry and tightly drawn portrait of how big money and special interests work in small, big cities across the Midwest."

—**ADAM WREN**, National Politics Correspondent, *Insider*

FLIPPING

THE

CIRCLE

FLIPPING

THE

CIRCLE

A POLITICAL THRILLER

MICHAEL LEPPERT

RIVER GROVE
BOOKS

Published by River Grove Books
Austin, TX
www.rivergrovebooks.com

Distributed by River Grove Books

Design and composition by Greenleaf Book Group
Cover design by Greenleaf Book Group
Cover photo by Steven Van Elk on Unsplash.com

Publisher's Cataloging-in-Publication data is available.

Print ISBN: 978-1-63299-437-0

eBook ISBN: 978-1-63299-438-7

First Edition

For Marlene, Vince, and Bryan

All life is a circle.

—ROLLING THUNDER, CHEROKEE

1

Offtrack betting parlors are dreadful places. They are often smoke-filled, dirty, and depressing. If the smokiness or filth doesn't bring you down, the fact that almost everyone in the room is losing money will.

The Winner's Circle was a little bit different than the standard OTB, though. It was new, and it was clean. Okay, it was clean *looking*. The smoke filtration system was better than those of the old days, when most gamblers just didn't give a shit that they smelled like the bottom of a dirty ashtray. There was an actual menu with actual food on it. Expensive wine and scotch were available, presumably for the big spenders or big winners, not that many visited very often.

With its downtown Indianapolis location, the overhead was high. The gaming available didn't attract crowds the way a craps or a blackjack table or even poker room might. Most of the food spoiled before anyone bought it. And anyway, the regulars preferred a hot dog with their cheap Smirnoff vodka or Miller Lite.

After a year or two, the casual observer might wonder how the generic place stayed in business. But there was a reason it remained. A few reasons, really, and only a few people knew what those reasons were.

To passersby, it's just a bar like any other bar. It's on a city street like any other city street. Anonymous, really, and all by design.

It was the scene of the crime. People don't often think of corruption or white-collar crap having an actual crime scene, but the Winner's Circle was the scene of such a crime. If I had to point to the spot, this would be it.

The bar was a playground, a place for the executive of the gaming company who owned it to hang out and get drunk and entertain his buddies. He stocked the bar with his favorite snobby wine and kept it on the shelf to impress people. Every staff member in the place, from the host at the front door to the after-hours cleaning crew, knew who their most important customers were. There weren't too many to remember.

I never actually met Karl Satterfield. I was around him dozens of times, but we didn't shake hands once. Everyone considered him one of the guys even though he was also thought to be the owner of the gaming company that owned the Winner's Circle as well as the two casinos that were strategically located about an hour outside of Indy in different directions.

He wasn't either. Karl was a grifter of sorts, a quick-buck artist from the suit-wearing crowd. His colleagues back at the gaming company wore tailored suits and an ensemble of accessories. They used a bit too much aftershave, and they wore a gold bracelet on one wrist and some expensive Rolex-type watch on the other. They owned casinos, but they were venture capitalists and Wall Street types who only bet on sure things. They were not the stereotypical wise guys of Rat Pack Vegas lore.

Karl's job was to find, create, and—most of all—protect those "sure things" for his bosses. Sometimes he might find or create one for himself along the way, and why shouldn't he? This was America, after all.

In Indy, he was a big deal. He acted like he owned the gaming company and people rarely asked if he did or not. I'm sure when they did, Karl lied about his status, but I don't imagine he had to very often. He was surrounded by people who wanted to believe that he was a big deal.

The Winner's Circle had a VIP section like every other casino does. This was Karl's wing of the joint. He would wine and dine people there when he was bored or when a boss from the mothership told him to. But mainly, the VIP section was ground zero, the control center, home base of all of his evil little schemes that were the next great sure thing.

One Thursday night in January of 2012, long before anything inside seemed unusual to anyone, six or seven youngish white guys in cheap suits—for the most part—were sitting at a table in the VIP section. Their ties were loosened and their beers and cocktails were on the table as they watched college basketball on an oversize flat screen. This was Indiana, after all.

These guys were all members of the Indiana House of Representatives. They came over from the Indiana Statehouse, five blocks away. Across town, they were referred to as Representative Smith or Representative Jones. Maybe even Mr. Chairman or Your Honor. But at the Winner's Circle, they were just Joe or Bob.

Karl and his chief lobbyist, Pauly James, and two other suits, lawyers from one of the firms in town, were sitting at the table behind them. "There really is only one extremely important thing that we must have for this thing to get done," Karl said. "We have to make sure there is no legitimate lobbyist in the Statehouse who is available and willing to fight us on it."

Pauly James jumped in. "We have to find a way to clear the field, but it has to be cheap. We can't go hiring every contractor to stand down. We have to give them a reason to stand down on their own. That's why we want them all to buy into the business."

The first suit spoke up: "What the hell do you mean, 'buy into the business?'"

"Just what it sounds like," Pauly said. "We're going to sell shares in the business that will only exist if the law we want these guys to pass actually passes. And we are only going to sell these exclusive shares to the people we need out of the way."

The second suit interrupted: "Sell these so-called shares for what?"

Karl leaned back in his chair in a huff. "Who gives a fuck? They'll be paying us! We'll offer a hundred shares of Company X for sale. We'll say the shares are worth $1,000 each, maybe $10,000. And when this million-dollar company is worth a hundred million, these guys will feel like they hit the jackpot. But most of all, they'll stay out of our way in the Statehouse while we get the bill passed."

"So what do you need from us?" the first suit chimed in again. "Just the organizing structure, shareholder rights, all of that?"

"Yes," Pauly said. "And the details on how we define the security firm but presented in such a way that no one can understand it."

"That's a piece of cake," suit two said. "Convincing the entire Statehouse lobbying corps to buy into this shit will be the hard part."

"Really? You overestimate these guys," Pauly said. "They'll line up to get in on this before I'm done. Keeping it secret is the real work."

"No shit," Karl added. "Secrets are the keys to the kingdom. As usual, I guess. Lawyers are supposed to specialize in this crap. I expect your work to help." With that, he got up and joined his young legislator guests at the basketball viewing party, one table over.

That was how it started. It was the first meaningful meeting. Without the meetings that followed, it would have been harmless. If someone along the way had given any of these grifters a compelling reason to stop, they probably would have. Looking back, it's hard to believe no one did.

But any advice to stop was likely only given in an attempt to keep them out of trouble, or jail. Not because what they were trying to do was just wrong.

Right and wrong. Often the difference between the two is simply a matter of perspective. These crimes were like games to those committing them. To everyone else, not so much. Too often, nothing defines the difference so that it is clear to everyone.

Especially in my world.

2

On the far west side of town, on that same Thursday night, in the basement of a large Christian church, a dozen metal folding chairs were arranged in a circle. Seven or eight of the chairs were taken by a range of some pretty simple, average folks.

It's a church basement like any other church basement. And it's in a suburban neighborhood like any other suburban neighborhood.

Through the entrance of the door, a timid, good-looking, fortyish-year-old man appeared, seemingly uncertain if he was in the right place.

I was that man.

Okay, "good-looking" was a bit of a stretch. "Reasonably presentable" might have been more accurate. And "fortyish" was code for forty-three. I was legitimately in good health, though. The daily workouts and no-junk-food diet were the main causes of that.

The commoners in the chairs stopped their banter and looked up at me. A woman who appeared to be about seventy-five years old spoke up: "Come on in, honey. You must be Will."

"How did you—"

"Greg told us you might show up," she said. "Enough about that, it's time to get started. Find a seat."

Some might say that I was going through life changes at the time. They might cheer the things I did. Plenty of others would scorn the choices I made. But most people don't know—or worse, remember—that any of it happened, even those it happened in front of.

During my decade and a half as a consultant (which is a code word for contract lobbyist), I had a business partner or two, and I hung up my name plate in a law firm or two. But in the game of lobbying, clients don't hire firms or partnerships so much as they hire people. After a decade in the hallway, my reputation—and therefore my value—was pretty much set in stone.

My name is Will O'Courtney, short for William, like my dad, and his dad, although both of them went by Bill. You may have noticed by the names that I am Irish American. I stayed that course when I named my older son William, so we could call him Liam, and instead of naming my younger son Thomas, we named him Tomas.

But we aren't just Irish, we are also Irish-Catholic. Mainly American and Irish, but sort of Catholic.

I never thought much of church. It might be because of my dad's falling out with Catholicism when I was ten years old. For some reason, Dad seemed to blame the church for his life not turning out as he thought it should.

Church is a funny thing in America. Even for a guy like me, who had come to believe that religion in general was all just a bunch of nonsense, the God thing can be hard to avoid sometimes. It is all around us in the heartland.

There are two small towns where I spent—and now blame for—my youth. The first one is deep in the heart of Appalachia with a Baptist church every mile or so. The evangelical element of the culture never sat well with my transplant parents for the ten years we lived there. Dad used to say, "Show me a born-again Christian, and I'll show you a liar."

I came to learn that Dad was not always right and that some of his hostility toward the South had more to do with his own, self-generated unhappiness than any flaw in others. But as a child, I took his words literally, and I believed him.

When my teenage years started, we relocated from the Shenandoah Valley to Indiana and lived in a small town that was almost exclusively Catholic. Dad had already left the church, but Mom was still going. My older sisters and I became part-timers with her. All our new friends were there anyway. I grew from an awkward thirteen-year-old to a wannabe-cool kid at sixteen, and Saturday evening mass became a gathering spot for planning that evening's debauchery. Jesus really didn't have anything to do with it.

Of course, that was the scene where I found my first wife. People married young in small Indiana towns. It happened so often that it didn't seem odd. And like so many of us from that small town, odds were that of every new young couple teaming up for that first life mistake, at least one of them would be Catholic. That's how the church survived: inertia. I grew to believe that most of us knew the whole thing was bullshit.

But my first wife was a believer. Still is. Because of that, we raised our two sons in the church. I didn't have a counterargument to make on that front, except for a godless one, which wasn't all that compelling. The boys went to Catholic school. I mostly played along like a bunch of other sheep disguised as grown men. I coached youth sports and went to all of the church festivals. We hung around with other parents from school, who by definition were also Catholic. The groove was perfect for the wife because it was her choice. It was imperfect for me, though the people we spent time with were as fine a group as any other.

While I was somewhat Irish and sort of Catholic, I was excruciatingly Midwestern. After college at Indiana University, we were dug in on the west side of the big city. At the time, the big city was Indianapolis. I giggle when I think about how big I thought this town was. The skyline had a couple dozen buildings with more than ten floors, a half-dozen with more than twenty, and three with more than thirty.

Indy has an NFL team. And in the young, white, Catholic culture of the early '90s, the NFL might as well have been its own religion. As that character in the old Albert Brooks movie said about the league, "They own a day of the week. It used to belong to God. Now it's theirs."

That's what the Colts were for me. Success in my life was having a man cave, which was decorated with Colts gear signed by all the greats, mainly from the Peyton Manning era. I had a great collection of otherwise worthless shit that made me feel like I was more a part of the team than my friends were. Of course, these friends were exactly equal to me in our complete lack of influence on the game.

When I walked into that Christian church basement on the west side of town, the divorce from my first wife was final. I'd recycled all my business partners and ended up at what I vowed would be my last firm. I'd quit smoking and drinking. I was exercising every day and eating healthy food. Hell, I'd even lost interest in gambling. I was starting a new way forward with all of the aforementioned virtues. The only thing left in my life that might have been in conflict with what I referred to as my soul was my profession.

I wasn't convinced I could keep doing it. If I kept at it, I wasn't sure what kind of clients I could continue to take—or would take me. But I had gotten used to my income, and my kids were getting ready to go to college, and well, you know how this part of the story goes.

Lobbying wasn't fun for me like it used to be. Maybe I was getting old, or maybe I was growing up.

At lunch one day with Greg Bryant, one of my old friends from the west side, I told him how I didn't know if I could stay the course professionally. Greg didn't know the first thing about politics or government or lobbying.

"You need to quit bitching and whining about your rotten lot in life," Greg said sarcastically. "You've got it so fucking bad; I don't know how you get out of bed in the morning."

A horrifying-looking man, Greg Bryant stood six feet four, was bald-headed and beard-faced, and both of his arms were covered in ink. He was one of the Catholic mafia whose kids went to school with mine. He was the one friend who survived my divorce, but only because he was getting dumped at the same time. For the better part of a solid bad year, we really didn't have anyone but each other.

We got together once a week or so. It was a routine that started as a chance for us to bitch about our ex-wives, but that got old pretty fast, so we used the time to bitch about anything and everything else.

Greg told me he knew about a support group or a Bible study group—I can't even remember what he called it that day. A group of people working on their spiritual journey met in the basement of Grace Memorial Episcopal Church.

He'd attended a few meetings the year before, but his shift at work changed, and he wasn't able to continue so he fell out of the routine. He thought it was a group of otherwise sane people who got together once a week to talk about God, and how to improve their contact with him . . . or her . . . or it.

It wasn't just for Christians. Even one of the group leaders was Jewish. Weird.

"The folks at Grace Memorial will come up with some great ways to teach you how to shut the fuck up," he said.

"That's just what I'm looking for, a group of people to run their mouths at me," I said with a dismissive huff. "I get freed from the one person I couldn't listen to anymore, and your genius advice is to replace her with ten strangers?"

He laughed at me and said, "Don't be such a pussy. Trust me. Just sit there and listen for a meeting or two. How exactly do you plan to find your soul on your own when you don't even know where to look?"

"All right, smartass. Next week. Two weeks tops. I'm an expert at bullshit, you know. I won't need any more than that to decide if it's worth a third. You, on the other hand, are so damn dumb you wouldn't know the difference between BS and the gospel," I uttered with a defeated tone of agreement. "I just show up?"

"I'll let them know you're coming, and yes, just show up. That will be a miracle all by itself. I'll see you in a couple of weeks."

And that's how I ended up in the doorway of that church basement. I looked lost because I was. I needed career advice, but there I was at a church support group. Someone worse off than me sent me there, and by the looks of it, the people gathered there were as bad or worse than he was.

The good news was that at first glance, the group looked almost perfectly diverse. There were a couple old folks, a couple of young women, a couple of black people.

The old lady who told me to come in said, "We're gonna pick up where we left off last week. Will, we were talking about how people are born with a concept of God. That concept may change a lot over time, and it may change for a lot of reasons, but for most people, some concept of God is always there."

Oh my God! That was my immediate thought. But I was already in a chair.

Then a young lady started talking. She was maybe twenty-five, wearing faded blue jeans and an oversize hoodie that she probably hadn't washed in the last ten wears. She could be pretty, but she wasn't trying. It looked like she had combed her shoulder-length hair straight down right after a shower and let it dry. No makeup. Her fingernails were elaborately painted, each a different color. And I couldn't take my eyes off her flip-flops.

It was cold outside. Why flip-flops? I then started to notice everyone's footwear. There were work boots, New Balance tennis shoes, some overshined Italian leather shoes that belonged with a tuxedo. I wondered why I was suddenly looking at people's shoes.

I was hanging my head when I was supposed to be pretending to listen. Weird. That wasn't me. I needed to get it together. I had to consciously get my head up and focus on what the young lady was saying.

"I don't think the God my parents wanted me to worship was the one who belonged to me," she said.

What the hell did she say? Why was everyone nodding at that? I became curious in a frustrated, angry kind of way, but curious all the same.

The longer she talked the more I listened. The longer I listened, the more mature and pretty she seemed to become. Whatever she was saying had quickly turned into hypnotic noise, as if there weren't any actual words coming out of her mouth. There was something about the way she spoke. It was slow and deliberate but not tense or anxious. "Easy" is the best word for it. She spoke with an easy gait. Until she ended with, "And I've gotten into the habit of thinking about my God immediately, whenever I'm faced with a disturbance of any kind."

In about ninety seconds, she transformed from my first impression of "might be pretty" into an expanse of overwhelming curiosity. I wish she hadn't stopped talking. And I wasn't even listening to her words.

This young woman was reason enough for me to come back next week.

3

After college, I didn't have a long list of job opportunities, but I ended up working for the State of Indiana. With a base salary of $15,000, that job was enough at the time. I had no five- or ten-year plan on the career front, but looking back, showing up and giving a shit coupled with above-average intelligence was a pretty potent combination for success in government service.

By the time I was thirty, I was running a state agency and rubbing elbows with the most important people in government. I had not arrived on that scene through politics, which was an advantage and a handicap at the same time. It was an advantage in that people assumed I had gotten the job because I was smart, not through connections. But the main reason I had risen was because I possessed the most valuable skill: communication. Being able to speak publicly or write coherently are things few people do well. I didn't know that at the time.

My lack of a political connection was a handicap in many ways. For one, the upper echelon of the Democrat party never really trusted me. I wasn't one of them. I hadn't worked on campaigns. I didn't come from money. I was never targeted as a campaign contributor, and so the money I now spent was "new money." New money is less politically reliable than old money. And I had one major flaw: sometimes I disagreed with a partisan stance if I thought it was a stupid idea. That, specifically, was a dangerous thing for someone who had no built-in protection from having their ass fired for popping off in the wrong room at the wrong time.

That Democrats even controlled the governor's office seems crazy now, a dozen years later.

Getting canned for speaking up was always a possibility for me, and there were a couple of times that I know of when that very discussion took place among the lower-level staff in the governor's office. But let's face it, most politicians are punks. Firing someone who might be smarter than they are takes balls, and most of them don't have balls.

I'm a big believer in firing people who step out of line. So is the entire private sector. But bureaucrats are just weak souls usually. Which was another reason a guy like me could rise so quickly.

Ten years into my government career, I was making $75,000 a year, and I had gone as far as I could. The governor was two years away from retirement, and whoever replaced him would not keep me.

In 2002, I had a chance to become a consultant and finally make some real money. That's how I ended up in the hallway, as we referred to it. Some people called it the lobby, but in the Indiana Statehouse, it was the hallway.

In the hallway, I often was the guy who would come up with a client's or a campaign's story. Why would a company need a tax break? Between you and me, it was so they could make, keep, or save money. But the story was always more along the lines of "so we can reinvest in the community" or "so we can train more workers so their families can improve their incomes" or "because there are safety and security needs that cost money, and we want to protect the public."

You get the point. There was always some reason why a company or an industry needed a law tweaked. If I couldn't come up with some believable BS spin for why I was asking the Indiana General Assembly to change a law, then I was worthless.

Or, heaven forbid, the idea was just that bad.

The story had to be short so it could be repeated and repeated and repeated. The stories were much like slogans or marketing pitches. "Make America Great Again" or "It's the economy, stupid" are good examples of political slogans that became pitches. But in our world, they were lobbying stories. The more often they were repeated, the more believable they became.

Guys like Karl Satterfield tended to be the idea men. They were also almost never seen in the Statehouse. He was the type that would come up with the brainchild of new laws and regulations to make himself and his partners rich—or richer.

Coming up with the story was a strategy older than I was, but it turned out I was pretty good. But Pauly James was the best in the business.

Pauly specialized in sins—literally. He made his fortune in the contract lobbying business by advocating for alcohol and gaming interests. And he had grown into looking the part over the years. Spending one's days in support of more booze and betting usually leads to a transformation of one's soul and one's appearance. He could lose fifty pounds and still be round. If he wore a three-piece suit, he might look like a casino boss—or Boss Hogg.

Without the suit, he looked more like Tommy Boy. He was everything the average American thought of when the word "lobbyist" was used. He looked like a Bubba. As stereotypes go, as a young man he was the guy in the fraternity house winning the beer bong contests and thumbing his nose at campus rules. He was the guy supervising the all-night poker parties before poker was cool. He was the guy who only lost money so he could make the rest of the patsies at the table think the game was legit.

As a grown-up, he was still a partier. But he'd started making a fortune as one, so life was grand.

In addition to representing Karl Satterfield, Pauly also represented the liquor distributors. That business has always been as predictable as the sunrise. Drinkers drink. They drink in a good economy and a bad one. They drink in celebration and in sorrow. Again, those outside of the business miss something here: when there is a monopoly on who can sell the liquor to the liquor stores, bars, taverns, and restaurants, the only important part of the business is protecting the monopoly. That may sound easy, and it is easier than competing every day like in a true market, but Pauly and his clients did work at it. That work would look pretty sleazy to people on the street, though.

In Indiana, there are no limits on what a lobbyist can give a legislator—no matter if it's a case of scotch to take home or a $500 bottle of wine at a Tuesday-night steak dinner. There are reporting requirements if the value of any gift or entertainment goes over a certain amount, but complying with those rules really didn't matter much in Pauly's world.

The reporting requirements were part of a self-reporting framework established by the legislature years before Pauly appeared on the scene. Self-reporting is very much like asking the fox to report to the chicken farmer how many hens he ate last night, and then having the farmer believe it. It's a lot like those college poker games Pauly used to host. Guys like him reported just enough of their entertaining and gift-giving to make it seem like they were reporting everything. But of course they weren't. Why would they?

Unless someone was trailing a lobbyist and busting them picking up tabs and giving away unreported gifts, there really was no way to find out what kind of goodies were changing hands.

Pauly was the best at this, though it was hard to describe it as an actual skill. It was mainly a simple willingness to provide a gift, favor, ticket, plane ride—you name it—to keep legislators and anyone else happy.

The liquor guys have been greasing the legislature since Prohibition was repealed. Actually, they've been doing it on both sides of the Prohibition date. And it isn't just an Indiana thing. It goes on everywhere.

It is also important to point out that I once did smaller versions of virtually everything Pauly James did. I guess I just tired of it sooner than he did.

Pauly was an exception in the hallway. So was I. I didn't break laws like he did, but to the casual observer in and around the Statehouse, it would have been hard to tell the difference.

4

Monday nights when the legislature is in session is an easy night to find something going on. There usually is a get-together, a cocktail reception, or a big steak dinner, something fun or social, or even occasionally something a little unique to do for legislators. Guys like me are always part of the host committee for whatever industry group that is sponsoring.

When a lobbyist or a legislator has nothing better to do, showing up at the Winner's Circle is always an option. There is almost always a familiar face from the Statehouse there.

In 2013, one cold January Monday in the first month of the legislative session, I ran into Charlie Alderman and his new friend, a freshman senator from just west of the Ohio state line, named Matt Borden. It was tempting to mispronounce it and refer to him as Senator Boredom, but our relationship was too new for that. None of us knew if we liked him or not yet. They didn't have any plans later that night—at least not plans they wanted to have. They were both members of the Senate, and they both had the same evening reception to attend. They were looking for an excuse to get out of there early.

"You two are a couple of social wack jobs," I said. "Don't get me wrong, I would rather eat a dead rat than go to the economic development reception you guys are committed to. But how hard is it to shake ten hands and then tell them you have to leave to meet a constituent who is in town?"

"Why don't you show us how, Mr. Know-It-All?" Charlie taunted.

"You got it, smartass. I'll meet you both at the Marriott at 6:00, and if we aren't out of there by 6:15 and at the Winner's Circle by 6:30, I'll mow your grass this spring."

"Never mind that, Will," the short one intervened. "We'll meet you at the Circle at 7:00, and you won't have to embarrass us."

Even two young, type A elected officials didn't want to be made to look weak-kneed.

"Okay, but I don't want to have to give you my seminar on how to escape a bad party in three easy steps, so don't be late," I said as I headed down the sidewalk on Capitol Avenue.

Typical. These two guys more likely would show up with five friends looking for all the free food and booze they could handle than they would flat-out stand me up. Legislators are known for standing up lobbyists for a date like this because lobbyists' invites keep coming anyway—and these guys might get three other offers before 7:00. When I was younger and newer to all of this, anything other than these two showing up by themselves and on time would have pissed me off. I got over it when I realized that whatever the tab was, it was being paid for with someone else's money, a mantra we all lived by. After I stopped partying so much, I'd go home when that 7:00 game was over no matter what.

The days of killing a couple of hours and then going out for a giant steak at 9:00 and then on to some after-hours place or even a

19

strip club with guys like these were way behind me. I did that for a decade and, honestly, I was over it.

I build and protect my relationships on the "small dose plan" now. That means I will gladly spend ten minutes with any of these guys small-talking in search of a connection, but not a three-hour, sit-down dinner. That large dose can turn into torture real fast, when the date says something stupid or offensive before the waiter has even taken our order. If a legislator showed up an hour late for dinner, I'd be eating dessert as they sat down. Tough shit. Be on time.

By 6:30, I'd parked myself at a table designed for six in the VIP section. The staff knew I was one of Pauly's friends and that the sky was the limit on my budget. They also knew that others would be joining me soon enough. At 6:45, in walked my dates.

Charlie Alderman was my buddy. Of 150 members of the general assembly, having 30 one can refer to as a buddy was more than enough. Though he was younger, we partied together when he first got elected and before I stopped partying. He put on a conservative front because it served him politically, but he was a pretty normal guy otherwise. He was the pretty-boy type all of the ladies liked, and he didn't do much to quash that stuff, even though he was married. He lived an hour and a half away from Indy, so when he was in town, he might as well have been a million miles from home.

We spent a lot of time together, and he carried some of my clients' bills the last couple of years, so he was one of my guys. When anyone in the hallway wanted to know what Alderman thought about something, they'd either ask me or Pauly. A smart lobbyist would ask both of us because Charlie was known for telling people stories that were not exactly—oh, precisely identical.

"Damn Charlie, you must have outdone yourself getting out of that reception!" I said.

"Shut up, smartass," he responded. "If anyone asks, you're a Baptist minister from Attica, Indiana," he said with a proud giggle.

The younger, shorter Senator Borden politely smiled, showing his nervousness about even being in an OTB. I decided to ignore him until I didn't have to, which would likely be sometime after he got reelected the first time.

The waitress came over and before she could say anything, I announced, "Get whatever you want, we have at least two hours to kill with this ball game on. But pace yourselves."

Charlie ordered a Dewar's on the rocks with a twist, and his little buddy ordered some kind of beer-snob IPA, and we settled in.

Pauly James was across the room at another table with some members of the House. Karl Satterfield was at the table with them with his back to the corner. Pauly waved our way, and I knew he would be over to visit soon enough. Knowing him, he'd pick up the tab too.

Karl acted like he didn't even notice we were there. But he knew.

"How long are you going to keep up this 'no drinking' thing?" Charlie asked me as I sipped a cup of coffee.

"Why do you care?" I said. "No one is judging you for being a lush. Just because your body isn't a temple, doesn't mean I have to be godless. As a Baptist minister, I know about shit like this." They laughed. "Besides, I can look after you better when I'm in the throes of sobriety."

"I don't start making bad choices till much later, as you well know," Charlie responded.

"I'm sure Pauly will be here for you on the night shift," I said as Pauly approached the table. "Pauly! I'm shocked to see you here!"

"Will, the bullshit never ends with you, does it?" Pauly said. "I came over to say hi to your guests and ask them why they would be seen with someone like you."

Charlie chimed in first. "Pauly, I didn't know there were any upstanding citizens in here. Point those guys out for us right quick if you don't mind, and we'll change tables," he said with a laugh.

"That's no shit, Senator. Everything good over here?" Pauly asked.

"All good, pal. I'll check in with you later, after the Boy Scout here goes home for his early bedtime," Charlie said with a shoo-away wave.

As Pauly headed back to his group across the room, Charlie asked, "Are you working with him on his iPad gaming idea?"

"I have no idea what you're talking about," I said.

"Don't worry, he or somebody in that bunch will be coming to see you about it soon enough. It sounds like a pyramid scheme, but it's not. It seems like a legit idea to me, but I can't get involved with it. You know, I am in the Senate after all."

"You're in the Senate?!" I half yelled with fake surprise. "Jesus, I forgot. It's so hard to tell sometimes. No one would ever know; I mean, you hide it like a champ!"

"Fuck you, Will. Don't forget about the iPad gaming thing. They've been working on the concept for about a year, and they'll be ready to roll it out soon. You don't want to miss out on it."

"I have really been meaning to ask you," Charlie said, "do you miss the partying we used to do? Things haven't been the same since your good, clean living started." He turned to his sidekick and said, "He used to be the last guy standing. He might have been wobbling or staggering, but he was definitely last."

"All right, all right," I interrupted. "And no, I don't miss it. I feel so much better these days, and all I ever got out of those late nights with guys like you was . . . hell, I can't even remember what I got out of it." I looked at the new guy, leaned over the table, and said, "Do not follow Charlie's lead. He is truly the gatekeeper to Hell."

"Yeah, yeah," Charlie said. "I'm the Devil, but when I need to find a way to get around the rules in the Statehouse, bring a dead bill back to life, or say, change the effective date of a law . . . the Devil goes looking for Will to come up with the plan."

"Come on—I'm the baddest apple in the basket now?" I asked.

"Remember that property tax problem one of your clients had a couple of years ago and you had the chairman of Appropriations change the effective date of the tax structure back four years so your guy could get the tax break? What did that save him? $200,000? I think maybe five people even know you did that. That's the kind of shit this guy does."

"It was a simple misunderstanding, Charlie," I explained. "That's all."

"Uh-huh. Don't believe this guy's bullshit. He's a snake in the grass, and he smiles while he's biting you. The only way to protect yourself from him is to make him your friend."

"That part is true—at least about the friend part," I said. "You guys gonna eat or what?"

It was another typical night at the Winner's Circle. I only went there every now and then because nothing good ever happened there. And I knew that one mistake of reliving those good old days for one night could turn into a year or two before I knew it.

Pauly and Charlie could seem like the Devil in that regard. Eventually, they would either want me to get back all the way into the Circle or get the hell out. I was dancing on a pin with the half-assed act I was doing.

You see, Pauly and I were kind of frenemies. We had never fought over anything, but we had represented different gaming companies over time. Since I met him, he'd had Karl Satterfield as a client. I had two other casino companies at two different firms. They all seemed the same to me. Whatever the issue, it was a fight over market share, and whoever your client was, theirs was the story you pushed.

Mainly, I thought I made Pauly nervous. He was a Republican and I wasn't. I think he didn't feel he could trust me, and he was right about that. I always thought he was dirty, and although I never told him that to his face, I'm sure he knew me well enough to know that I did have at least a little respect for laws, rules, ethics—you know, the little things.

I thought like him before my divorce and when I was out and about like the guy Charlie Alderman missed. After all the things I did to clean up my act, it seemed easier to be committed to goodness, even though that wasn't really why I cleaned up. I was in a weird spot; I was an insider but without the gluttony. I didn't really want to be around that stuff, though I didn't bitch about it when I was. But I learned that most hedonists aren't comfortable around people who play life straight. I remember feeling that way.

We shared too many secrets with each other in places like the Winner's Circle. It was awkward, to say the least, for any one of us to stay in the mix without being *all in*. The others felt they were being looked down on by someone who used to be one of them. That wasn't really what I was doing, but that's what I'm sure most of them thought I was up to.

5

By the time Charlie Alderman asked me if I missed the good old days that night at the Winner's Circle, I had been spending every Thursday night at Grace Memorial, or just Grace, for a good solid year. Spending time every week on my spiritual health had become my routine, and the things that the routine had impacted in my life were starting to become noticeable.

I didn't really join the spirit group to help me keep from drinking or smoking or gambling. But without even paying attention, I had simply lost interest in those kinds of things. Don't get me wrong, I wasn't walking around with a Bible or a Koran under my arm. The bad things in my old life just had no logical or rational place in my new one.

Every few weeks in the group, someone would share part of their personal story. It was sort of a "tell me how you got here" session even though most of the stories didn't have much to do with spirituality or religion. The stories were limited to ten minutes, so people shared only part of their history.

It was a bonding exercise to some extent, and it helped make clear how the spiritual lessons we'd discussed could be applied to improve our daily lives. Sometimes it worked and was obvious. For me, it was a slower, more subtle transformation.

A couple weeks after that evening at the Winner's Circle with Charlie and his friends, it was my turn to share with the group.

"I know you're still new to this, honey," said Dottie, the boss lady, "so don't feel like you have to tell the whole thing tonight." That was her way of telling me to keep it brief and that she would cut me off in ten minutes no matter what.

"I talk for a living, but I'm not selling anything here, so if you start to feel the urge to buy something from me, please interrupt," I said to a few giggles.

"One thing I wanted to share first in the vein of how I got *here* would be about growing up in a couple of places and not feeling like I belonged *there*. Don't get me wrong, I might be able to go back to either place now and live a happy life, but when I was growing up in a house where my parents hated the town and even the region of the country we were in, it was hard not to let that get into my head."

Renee, the young, flip-flop-wearing beauty who motivated me to join that first night interrupted: "Why did they hate it?"

"That's a good question," I said. "When I was younger, I took their words seriously. They would bitch about small-town people having no ambition, that those folks didn't see a world beyond the small town. They would complain that none of them went to college or even aspired to go. Therefore, of course, everyone there had to be stupid.

"When we lived in Virginia, it was the Baptists they hated. We were in Appalachia as y'all know it. And it's pronounced App-A-Latcha, not App-A-Lay-cha. It took me about a month to quit saying 'y'all' after I moved to Indiana, even though I still smile inside every time I hear someone else say it. The kids here made brutal fun of my hillbilly words when we moved here. Still, after I visit there, or even have a talk on the phone with my sisters, I can hear their accents creeping back into me and then coming out of my mouth."

"So what did they hate about Indiana?" Pretty Renee was more interested in this than I thought she would be.

"I never thought you would be so interested in the reasons people hate. That's interesting. Oddly though, the things they hated were pretty much the same. Though now the whole town was Catholic, so I didn't hear much about the Baptists anymore. But as I have thought about my parents more over the last year or two, I don't think they hated those places so much as they were just unhappy people. It wouldn't have mattered where they were. They would have found a way to hate it.

"And that's the best thing I have learned since I got here in this group. I think about it all the time, maybe even every day."

"What? You learned what?" the curious young lady inquired.

"That the things around you have less to do with your own happiness than you might think. That everything Mom and Dad bitched about were things they could leave behind anytime they wanted. And most of all, that the responsibility for my own well-being is all mine. I can't expect someone else to give a shit about it or contribute to it. True happiness, or misery for that matter, doesn't come from the conditions that surround us. We have more control over all of that than we seem to think."

"And so you're completely happy now?" Dottie asked. "How good it must be!"

I chuckled at her sarcasm. "I'm happi*er*. Every day, I'm happier than I was the day before. At the rate I'm going, I might be unbearable to be around soon."

"And all of that happened here from this little gathering?" Dottie asked.

"Oh no, just from you," I joked. "Actually, when my divorce

started, I made a decision to try and take better care of my body. That got me pretty far down the road before I ever walked in here. Spending this hour every week and everything I'm learning from you people keeps me headed the right way. You guys wouldn't even recognize who I was two years ago. And my ex-wife wouldn't know me at all."

"Time's up, Will," said the boss. "See everybody next week."

Sometimes the things a person says out loud become a promise not to the people who are listening, but to the person doing the talking. Taking care of myself in every way I could was the promise I made to myself that night. Another promise I made to myself that night was that I would get to know Renee better.

I started calling Renee "Flip" in my head shortly after the first night I met her, and before I knew her actual name, because of her flip-flops. It took me a year to start calling her that to her face. She was beautiful, and cool, and smart. But she was young compared to me.

She made me nervous. As the lessons of the group were doing for me what I thought they were supposed to do, I found myself thinking about her more than I think I should have. She didn't waste time or energy with purposeless words, and she always seemed to be listening intently. I didn't want to feel like a creepy old man, uncontrollably drawn to the only beautiful woman in my life who also happened to seem above my creepiness. I felt like she was rating me each week, trying to decide what she thought of me.

I worried about what she thought about me. I wish I didn't, but I did. In all likelihood, she didn't think about me at all.

As this slow-moving transformation, which many could callously refer to as a midlife crisis, was taking hold, almost every other aspect of my life went on uninterrupted. I never paid much attention to people who left our business or our cliques within the business. At least not when I was partying my way through every day, I didn't. I didn't venture back to the Winner's Circle until later that year for a party celebrating the end of the 2013 session. Again, it was like I never left.

· · ·

"Damn, Will, it must be a special occasion for you to come stomping in here by yourself like this." Pauly stood to greet me at the entrance to the VIP section. This area of the parlor sounded more special than it actually was. There was an open entrance with wood columns bordering the walkway into it with a small hostess lectern positioned at the opening to keep any undesirables out. The furniture was a little grander, a little more comfortable, and the TV screens were a little bigger and brighter. All of these subtle upgrades, and that there is always a place to sit, is all visible from outside of it. That too is by design—enticing people on the outside. All it takes for a customer to enter is for them to obtain a player's card and pay for some barely noticeable pricing upgrades.

"Stomping? I do tend to act like I own the place, no matter what place it is. But if I owned this place"—I looked around—"I would break every record in the book on how fast I could sell it," I said as I shook his hand.

"Just don't cause any trouble in here with your smartass remarks," he said.

"Really, Pauly? Of all the things you should worry about, my smartass remarks shouldn't rank very high."

The place was absolutely jammed with people from the Statehouse, which was good for me. I set out to take my lap. I glad-handed and backslapped every person I could without getting too locked into any debate or bullshit session. On my way out of the VIP section, Pauly stopped me.

"Did any of the guys talk to you about my mobile gaming company?" he asked.

"Someone mentioned it to me awhile back, but no real details," I answered.

"Well, if you're interested in investing in it, come and see me when the dust settles after the session is over," he said.

"You got it. I hear you guys are hosting a bunch of fundraisers here this spring."

"Yeah, these fuckers have to have them somewhere, I guess it might as well be here," he said like it was no big deal.

"I'm sure I'll see you at some of them, with check in hand. See ya later, PJ." I slapped him on the shoulder and headed for the door.

The guy was unbelievable. He knew that all it would take was one complaint or one press report about legislators having fundraisers at a gaming facility and he would be back in the paper for it. I'm sure there was a way to host those events legally, but he wouldn't bother with covering those tracks. He would just thumb his nose at the obvious appearance problem it created and work to fix it later if he needed to.

Like I said, the law that prohibited gaming companies from contributing to Statehouse campaigns was stupid. It was probably unconstitutional and could be manipulated in so many ways that it was mainly useless. I sometimes thought Pauly broke the rules on purpose—although I don't know what the value in doing so would have been.

This is also just how he did his job: volume. Don't get me wrong, he was the Devil. But legislators couldn't see that they were making a deal with that Devil over and over again. I never saw him mad. Never. His style was so nonthreatening that it was like he lulled them to sleep in his dirty little dream world. If he had to divvy it up, he probably would have spent ninety-five percent of his time with legislators and regulators bullshitting and wasting time and about five percent of it actually asking them to do him a favor.

I bet those same percentages applied to how much legislators even understood what it was he was asking of them. He wanted comfortable and selective ignorance from them, and that's what he usually got.

The politicos all ran for office for some reason that was at least theoretically rooted in goodness. They never saw themselves as the future tools of guys like Pauly or even guys like me.

Now that I think about it, they probably couldn't tell the difference between us. A couple of years ago, I couldn't have either.

6

The Indiana Statehouse is a grand structure. It took a decade to build beginning in the 1870s. It used to have basement stables for legislators and other VIPs to park their horses and carriages. There are still parts of the stables in the building's lower level where the brick shape of the walls leave evidence of them.

Today visitors marvel at the beautiful rotunda and its breathtaking stained glass. Sometimes tourists will make it upstairs to the third floor where the House Chamber on the east and the Senate Chamber on the west reside. They are beautiful rooms, particularly in the House, which features an enormous chandelier with a hundred lights on it that signify the hundred elected members of the body. It also features a mural that tells a story of Indiana through its paintings of mining and farming and manufacturing characters.

It's an American castle. Like many Statehouses, it can be an intimidating place the first time or two one visits. But as much as we think our Statehouse is the most beautiful Statehouse around, I have now been to a few others across the country. It turns out our Statehouse is just like every other Statehouse. Of course, each one looks unique, but they feel similar. Each one I have visited is a grand structure, often intimidating in its grandness, and apparently by design. They often lack modern functionality but attempt to make up for it with marble and limestone excesses.

That is certainly the case in Indiana. In the winter of 2015, nothing out of the ordinary should have occurred. Both chambers were controlled by the Republicans. The state was halfway through its third consecutive gubernatorial term also held by a Republican. It was a political climate built for yawning.

But two things were about to happen that legislative session: the state was going to be thrust into the worldwide spotlight because of a profoundly stupid idea called the Religious Freedom Restoration Act, and Pauly James and Karl Satterfield were going to make a move that had been part of a plan that started three years prior.

While the whole world was watching our state stupidly try to elevate religious—or more accurately, evangelical Christian—rights, Pauly and his team were using the legislature to monopolize a new market.

. . .

I was walking through the Statehouse one morning doing my thing, bebopping along and saying good morning to anyone who would listen, shaking hands, slapping backs, and making people smile. I only had a few clients with some small issues for me to fill my days piddling around with, so I was on cruise control.

While I was prancing toward the bathroom on the second floor, I had to pass by Room 233, a Senate Committee hearing room where the Senate Commerce Committee was meeting. I didn't have any business in there, but I was going to stick my head in and smile at a few folks to let them know I was on the job, and then saunter out like a cool breeze. I called it a flyby.

But on this day, Thursday, January 29, 2015, the hallway outside of the hearing room was jammed with people. But they weren't a bunch of suits like me. They were what lobbyists call real people, what most others would call citizens. These folks showed up at the Statehouse for ceremonies or as part of a convention at the convention center a block away. There might be a high school state championship team, a veterans' group, or, occasionally, celebrities and their entourages.

Lobbyists generally don't want these people around, unless they're there because they belong to a lobbyist's interest group. In the influence profession, these individual humans are known as grassroots. If organized properly, grassroots campaigns can be a difference maker. But sometimes grassroots folks collectively don't amount to much influence, and the public would be amazed at how legislators can find ways to ignore them.

The people outside of Room 233 looked like they'd just come from a biker bar. They were clad in denim and a little bit of leather. More than a few of them had chains connected to their wallets like there was something in the wallet that was chain-worthy. All of them had piercings and tattoos. Greg Bryant would have fit right in. They were wearing matching red T-shirts with white lettering that said "I Vape and I Vote."

I'm no square. In fact, I'm so confident in my coolness that if I see a gathering like this in the political sandbox I spend most of my time in, I am completely comfortable jumping right into the fray and asking what the hell is going on. So I did.

I walked up to the nearest couple and said, "What the hell is going on?"

The couple smiled at my curiosity and then glanced at each other with a bit of nervousness. How could they know if I was just some suit off the street or if I was a member of the Senate? They couldn't.

The man spoke up first. "These guys are trying to pass a law that will put me out of business," he said, his female companion nodding along.

"How so?"

"This new law is making up all these regs that we won't be able to do, even if we could afford it," he answered. "We'll have to close our shop if it passes."

"I'm sorry, what kind of shop do you have?"

The woman chimed in: "It's a vape shop, you know? We sell juice and components people use to vape. It's like a smoke shop but for vapers."

"You guys aren't regulated now?"

"Not yet," she said, "and no one will be able to comply with the shit that's in this bill."

"Is it gonna pass?" I asked.

"Hell," the man said, "we don't know how any of this works."

"It's early in the process," I said. "Keep doing what you're doing. These guys will cave at some point. Good luck!" I walked away.

The Statehouse sees a lot of protests—so many that they blend into the rest of the noise almost like the marble. There were probably about seventy-five people in the vape crowd. That's not enough to get people who are there every day to even notice. It's not enough to get most people to even ask what the hell was going on, like I did. And if I had been busy, I wouldn't have asked either.

Furthermore, they didn't look like they had a clue about lobbyists or what might make a difference in their fight. They had passion, and sometimes that's enough. They weren't making noise or being disrespectful as near as I could tell, which led me to assume that someone had coached them a little.

I had my own stuff to worry about. I hopped onto the elevator around the corner and headed up to the third floor.

. . .

When the legislature is in session, the third floor of the Indiana Statehouse is a lot like a big cocktail party—without the cocktails. There's about 150 feet from one end of the hallway to the other that stretches in front of each chamber. The rotunda, the trademark dome that Hoosiers can see from the outside, separates the two chambers. And there are large marble catwalks that connect the two sides on the north and south of the rotunda. The dome rises up through the third and fourth floors, creating large amounts of cubic space and visibility from a variety of angles.

The drop from the bannister on the third floor down to the second is significant. Double it from the fourth. In the world of Indiana lobbying, it is common to say "throwing someone over the rail," which means destroying an enemy with certain death by shoving them off the elevated balconies to a hard landing on the marble below.

An old mentor of mine told me of a suicide attempt that took place in the seventies when someone jumped from the fourth floor. They survived the fall, which I find hard to believe.

When standing in front of the glass windows looking into either chamber, you can turn around and look right through the open space under the dome and see the window of the other chamber. You can, that is, when there aren't so many lobbyists milling around and blocking the view.

The glass windows are kind of a funny feature all by themselves. I guess they're useful from time to time, but with modern technology and cameras mounted for internet broadcasting of the sessions, there isn't much need for either lobbyists or real people to be outside the chamber with their noses pressed against the glass. Plus both chambers have galleries for people to sit in that anyone can get into from the fourth-floor entrances on both sides.

The third floor is like the elementary school playground. This is "the hallway." It's more of a square wheel with spokes extending off it, but that's what the place is called. It's where all of the suits show up. It's where we make ourselves available for the thirty-second exchanges with members of either body on whatever idea we are pushing that day, week, or month.

In many ways, it's more important that it is where the lobbyists lobby each other. It's full of senseless cliques and some meaningful ones. Some discussions or relationships make perfect sense, and some don't. If anyone is spending more time with someone than they should, guys like me start working on figuring out why.

Forming new friendships is often how new deals get made. Sometimes they can be just natural friendships that spring up; lobbyists are still human beings, for the most part. Or they can be corrupt professionally, which is always concerning to the rest of the crowd. The really good new connections are sexual—or adulterous—because that gives guys like me something to share or snicker at.

If someone has been in the hallway for any length of time, they have been the talk of the grapevine for one reason or another. I know I have. But after my divorce and my departure from my early business partners, I think the hallway got tired of whispering about me. I became one of those guys who had lots of friends in the young crowd of thirty-somethings and the old crowd of sixty-somethings. I knew a little bit about everyone and everything.

I liked to justify my gossiping by pretending that the shallow judgments I cast on people actually helped our industry err on the side of goodness. Really I just enjoyed bullshitting about people who might be pushing the envelope dangerously in one direction or another. My transgressions from my younger days were behind me, and I needed drama from others to fill the time that all lobbyists waste standing around waiting to do their jobs.

. . .

The elevator opened on the northwest corner, and out I bopped like I'd just been let into a nightclub past the line of wannabes who had no business there. Of course, there was no one waiting. It's a public building, and there are plenty of real people there every day who think they are participating in their government.

We looked past them for the most part, especially on the third floor. And that's good for them, because this is the capital of infinite bullshit.

"Hey smartass, when's the last time you took that suit to the cleaner?" I popped off to the first random suit I came across—a forty-something white guy who looked like me.

"Fuck you, Will. I'm working on something," he yell-whispered back at me while covering the phone he may have been pretending to talk into.

I gave him the yikes-I-didn't-mean-to-interrupt hands-off ges- ture like I was truly sorry, followed by a subtle flash of my trademark middle finger. I love flipping people off. I do it so much that it's almost code for "good morning" coming from me. If I don't give you the finger from time to time, then we aren't really friends.

There was a huddle of the youngster crowd on the corner, and it looked like they might be swapping last-night stories that I needed to hear.

"I can't tell if he's seriously trying to get laid, or if he knows it's so ridiculous that he can just say whatever," a young blonde woman lobbyist said.

The male version of the young woman snapped back, "Oh, come on. You know he's casting a wide net just waiting for someone to say okay. That old man is the dirtiest whore around. Ask Will."

"Who we talking about, people?" I asked. They were talking

about Senator Johnson, of course, a name I giggle at every time I say it. Yes, I'm that immature.

"My advice is to not turn your back on that old man," I said. "A rule that applies for both the boys and the girls. He doesn't like talking to Democrats though. I think they make him feel stupid. Anything fun happen last night?"

"Same old same old," another young male colleague reported. "The Pacers game had most of us scattered around the Fieldhouse with our dates, including Johnson."

"Did we win?" I asked rhetorically.

"Who cares?" the young lady said. "We were in the suite watching the IU game."

"I don't want to talk about that," I said. "Have I told you what I think about Tom Crean? See you in committee tomorrow. Ready? Break!" I said and left the huddle to toss my briefcase in its designated spot by my designated bench.

I stopped and turned back to the group. "Hey, any of you guys hear of this 'I vape and I vote' bunch hanging around down by 233? Look down there." I pointed to the corridor below, visible through the rotunda.

The group looked below to see the small gathering for a moment, and then collectively shrugged with intense apathy and returned to the huddle. They clearly didn't know a thing about it, and they clearly didn't care.

That was a typical glimpse of a five-minute flash in the hallway. One out of ten times, the conversation matters. Okay, maybe one out of twenty. But like the aforementioned Senator Johnson, we all are in the business of casting a wide net. The more friends we have, the more often we might glean something of value in our little exchanges.

There's a whole set of protocols and appropriate distance to keep when approaching people in the hallway. A pro has to know when an actual meeting is taking place or when it's safe just to join in a huddle. Conversations with legislators, as an example, are private unless an invite has been issued.

Someone talking with a legislator while holding a piece of paper, for instance, and pointing at it periodically is in a hardcore meeting. The paper serves as a "do not disturb" sign.

We are communicators. And after we get beyond each other's salaries, political juice, sex partners, etc., we ultimately rank each other on the good or bad scale from this perspective.

Being a good communicator is a broad description. In the hallway, it is often just the ability to get along and make friends with others. But in the actual profession, it is often all about one's ability to tell their client's story effectively. I'm the guy who is constantly reminding people in the communication business that half of the skill comes from one's ability to listen and observe others.

People tend to forget that last part more than they should.

. . .

In most legislatures, the sessions are divided in halves. The first half is when the House and the Senate deal with all the bills that have been introduced by their members the first time—or not. In Indiana, in odd-numbered years, the session lasts from the beginning of January until the end of April. The first half of the session is usually scheduled to conclude by the end of February or the beginning of March.

The second half of the session is designed for each chamber to deal with bills that were passed by the first chamber. Or not. This second half is actually a little shorter than the first, since so many of the bills have already been killed by the first session. They die by not receiving a committee hearing, being voted down, or simply by being abandoned. There is a long list of ways a bill can die. There are only a few ways a bill can pass.

After the second half is a period that lasts a week or two called conference committees. That stage is when any differences between legislation that is still alive get negotiated between the Senate and House members—or not. I tell you this now, because of a very important unwritten part of the process.

Between the first half and the second half of the session, the two chambers take a long weekend. The legislators might claim that the break is designed to give them a little extra time in their districts to reunite with constituents. Or they might claim that the break is there so they can catch up on their businesses or pay attention to family matters they have been neglecting while serving in Indianapolis.

For lobbyists, it's spring break. Most of us who are able go to Florida, Cancun, Arizona, or some other warm locale for some adult wintertime fun in the sun. As a golfer, three rounds are a minimum standard on this trip. Four is a true success.

7

It was February 26, 2015, but just barely. The Indianapolis International Airport is an early-morning airport. There are countless flights that leave between 5:30 and 7:00 a.m., and this Thursday morning was no different.

Indy is proud of its airport. Its new midfield terminal opened in late 2008, and it wins awards from the trade publications that rate airports, whoever reads those. But Indy is not a hub of any major airline, so it is way busier in the morning because there are so many connecting flights to catch. At the crack of dawn, it's crowded here. Security lines are long. Starbucks lines are long. It's a good mix of people sleepwalking because of the hour contrasted with those excited to get the hell out of here.

Right before getting on the 6:10 direct flight to Phoenix—the direct part being a true gift from heaven—I received a text message from a lawyer friend in Chicago: "Do you represent any tobacco clients?"

I replied that I didn't, and he shot back: "I have one for you. He'll call this morning if that's okay."

"Okay? That's awesome. Even though tobacco almost killed me. I got bills to pay. LOL."

By the time I was on the ground in the desert three hours later, I had a voice mail from another lawyer from Chicago: "My name is Tom Athens, and I have a legal and lobbying practice in Chicago. I represent a national tobacco company, and they have a little problem in the Indiana Statehouse. Our mutual friend, Richard Fairbanks, says you're the guy who can fix it in Indiana. Can you give me a call back ASAP? I fear it's time sensitive."

That was one way to start my grown-up spring break. My pal Richard Fairbanks is a healthcare lawyer who relocated to Chicago a few years back. He's a good lawyer I suppose, but to me, he's mainly a Cubs/Bears fan now.

I returned the call while waiting for my golf clubs at baggage claim. "Hey Tom. This is Will in Indiana. Hang on. I don't want to open with a lie, so let me start over. I'm Will from Indiana, but I'm actually in Arizona. What can I do for you?"

"Thank you so much for calling me back. You out there on business or pleasure?" he asked, with a slight touch of nervousness in his voice.

"We're out here playing as much golf as we can in three and half days while the legislature is on its halftime break. We'll be back at it on Monday. What's up?"

"I'll get right to the point. I'm working with a number of national tobacco companies to form a new trade association. The association will be made up of companies that manufacture vapor products. These guys are a group of tobacco manufacturers that are changing their businesses or adding divisions to provide products to customers who vape."

I hadn't thought much about the "I vape and I vote" people since the day I met them a month ago. They'd been back in the building a few times, but they hadn't been in my way.

"Are you dialed in on what's going on there in the vapor space?" Tom asked.

"A little bit. It looks a little like a mess, to be honest with you."

"Are you talking about the T-shirt crowd?" he asked, again with a little nervousness in his voice.

"You know about them? Yeah, that's what I was talking about. But I don't know anything about the bill or bills themselves. I hear there are bills coming out of both houses."

"Yes, there are two bills," Tom fired back. "They basically say the same thing. And either one of them will run my new association members out of the state. I need to know if you think you can slow them down, get them tweaked, soften the blow, whatever you call it. If you can kill them, that's great. But I know I'm calling you awfully late in the process."

"Well, I'm free—I mean, I'm available. I don't have a good sense for what you're facing, but I'm not intimidated by anything in the Statehouse. I don't have a conflict with any other clients, which is the main thing, so all I need to know is the background and I can be ready on Monday."

"Good, good. You're going to get a call from Bethany Cramer in the next hour or so," Tom said. "She's the general counsel at Tobacco America. She can work out the contract with you and give you the rest of the details. She doesn't mess around, so be prepared."

"How much can I prepare between the airport and the hotel, you think?" I sarcastically added.

"Just do your best. Richard assures me you're the guy. Good luck." He hung up before I could respond with a good-bye of my own, like he was the one on vacation, not me.

I picked up my baggage and golf clubs and got into the car rental line. As I waited, I scrolled through my phone for the bills Tom was talking about. For guys like me, it was almost always more import-ant which legislators were the authors of the bills than what the bills actually said. I checked the Senate bill first, since I'd met the T-shirters outside the Senate hearing.

Good news: the Senate author of the bill was none other than my buddy Senator Charlie Alderman. My man! This was blind luck for me. Regardless of the issue, no one had better access to Alderman than I did, even though we didn't party together like we used to. He and I hit it off right when he came to the legislature a term and a half earlier. That's six years in Indiana. He plays golf, which is how we met the first time. Even he would have to admit that he plays better courses since he got elected, and I am a big reason for that. But our friendship is really based on the fact that we speak the same language. Sarcastic, sharp, profanity-laden rhetoric does not always translate well. But when two people are speaking it every day in rooms where no one else is, those two smartasses end up together. That is Charlie and me. We don't just talk that way. We think that way. And when two people can read each other's minds, even on trivial little things, it's hard to avoid bonding.

Bad news: the House bill was being authored by a guy I didn't have any relationship with. This kind of thing happens, but it was my fault on this one. Representative Chris Miller had been around about the same amount of time as Senator Alderman, and he had risen fast in the House. He was the chairman of the Government Oversight Committee where the vape bill was heard and fast-tracked.

I knew I should have done something to meet Miller at some point over the last three or four years, but I got lazy about it. Now I'd have to start from zero with a guy who probably thought I'd been ignoring him for some shitty reason. I wished that were true, but it wasn't.

I was halfway to the hotel and halfway lost when I received a call from the 202 area code—DC. I assumed it was the Bethany lady Tom mentioned.

I'd never met anyone my age named Bethany. I didn't want to

prejudge, but I knew a little bit about women regulatory attorneys who were ambitious and—given her name—young.

They were the most hard-working, no-BS types in the business, and they seemed to love being attorneys a little bit more than they should. It didn't matter if it was taxes or Medicaid, utility rates or tobacco regs. They tended to know the legal issues, the operational issues, the history, and anything else that might matter to their clients better than anyone else around. They didn't seem to sleep. They were usually the only woman, or one of only a few, in their field, and they were constantly made aware of it. I loved having them on my team. I worried a little when one was my boss though. Over time, I learned what BS I could skip and what corner I could cut. These women didn't cut corners and didn't tolerate subordinates who did. Good old boys didn't mind that crap, and novices didn't know better. I doubted Bethany was either.

I predicted that Bethany was even more no-nonsense than Tom had described her. And guess what? I nailed it.

"Will, my name is Bethany Cramer, and I am the general counsel with Tobacco America. Tom Athens spoke to you earlier on my behalf."

"Yes. I have caught up on things a little bit this morning," I said, "but I'm traveling this weekend and being remote is a disadvantage."

She dove right in. "I need to work out the terms of an agreement for your assistance, so we can get busy planning immediately."

Wow! She was exactly what I expected. I followed her into the deep.

"For me to give you all of the attention I can for the two remaining months of the session, I would charge you $10,000 per month or $20,000 total. But if you think you may have a need for assistance beyond the session, I think it would be a better plan for you to enter into a one-year agreement for $50,000."

This was where she pissed me off: "I think the annual agreement makes the most sense. Can you send an engagement with the rest of the necessary terms in it today? If so, we can discuss the time-sensitive problem I have."

Every time you throw a number out on the table for a contract and the client immediately says okay without a moment of hesitation, the number was too fucking low.

"Of course I can email that to you today. What is the emergency?" I asked, knowing of course that to her, everything was an emergency.

"The Senate committee hears the House bill on Wednesday, and we need to give the committee a reason to slow down and rethink this whole thing."

I already knew that from the deep-dive research I did on my phone at the airport.

"I plan on being in Indianapolis on Tuesday," she said, "and would like you to arrange meetings with committee members on Tuesday afternoon to prepare them for my testimony on Wednesday."

Damn. I was getting curious what the hell she needed me for except to maybe carry her briefcase.

"Bethany, I haven't read the bills or done any real research yet. Your plans make sense, but I need to catch up."

"Do you know the authors and the people on the committee?" she asked.

"Absolutely," I replied.

"Well then, let's get the contract done today, and then I'll send you some information and you can catch up over the weekend. It's not that complicated. Oh, and have a good time playing golf. Tom said you're on a golf trip, right?"

"Yeah, yeah. We tee off in about an hour," I remembered.

"Email me the contract and your contact info, and go enjoy yourself," she said in a most insincere way.

I got her email address, and we hung up.

It was the easiest $50,000 deal I ever made, but I was already worrying that it probably should have been a $100,000 deal.

I did have a couple of immediate problems though. First, I'd been a heavy smoker for twenty years like most of my family. During my divorce four years earlier, after I had quit smoking and started running and lifting weights, the damage to my lungs reared its ugly head. The COPD diagnosis didn't happen till I had otherwise gotten healthy. I would be lying if I didn't admit to being bitter about the whole thing.

Lungs are supposed to heal when smokers quit. At least that was always what I thought. That was also how it seemed to be working until I got sick a couple of years after I quit. It's just a chest cold, I thought. My doctor did too. But after two weeks of steroids, that chest cold was still hanging on, and the doc wanted a chest X-ray. Now I know I won't ever get all of my lung capacity back. No matter how hard I work out, no matter how long I am smoke-free, the damage I did won't ever completely heal. And I'm mad about it. In other words, lobbying for tobacco was not really how I saw my future.

Second, Bethany wanted to fight legislation that had already passed both chambers. Yes, the House bill and the Senate bill were different in a small and trivial way, but both bodies had already voted to regulate vapor products in generally the same way. Killing the legislation now was going to take a small—maybe huge—miracle.

The annual contract helped, but I knew I was about to lose. And I was going to lose fighting for something I hated. I started working on my coping processes almost immediately. Doing so on the golf course for a few days under the Arizona desert sun would help, I guessed.

. . .

I played twenty-seven holes right up until sunset and the temperature dropped from eighty to fifty-five in about an hour. I couldn't wait to get to bed at the hotel on the property.

It was 8:00 when I got back to the room, which was 10:00 at home. If I had been home, I would have missed my spirit group anyway. But I couldn't help thinking about it while lying there.

Would they think it was okay for me to represent a tobacco company? They knew about my lungs, and more importantly, how hard it had been for me to take responsibility for what I'd done to myself.

Starting up with a new client becomes the most important thing in the world to me, and I quickly become numb to the impact of the policy debate and start seeing the issue purely from a win or lose perspective. That's what people pay me to do.

But it was hard to imagine being successful for Tobacco America and to know that one day I'd have to look back on what I'd done. I doubted I'd be proud of it. But losing? That's not what I do. Guys like me have a character defect. We hate losing more than we love winning. Maybe that's a sign we're playing the wrong games. I don't know.

If I could have created a god, like the one Flip imagined that first night at the group three years ago, would the god have wanted me to fight my ass off so tobacco companies could get rich on vaping? Would there be a silver lining there?

Yes, I still thought about her more than I should have, and whenever there was a blank spot in my brain, she filled it.

Our age difference was awkward. She was ten or fifteen years younger, but she had the air of maturity that I should have had. She had a calmness about her, a quiet manner, that made me want to ask her what she was thinking. A lot. I could almost always feel her thinking something when I saw her. Her silence was not apathy. It was deliberation. Or maybe it was restraint. Whatever it was, it was fascinating.

8

got back to Indy late Sunday night and was in the Statehouse early Monday. The legislators and the lobbyists slowly trickled back into the building late that morning after the long weekend. I took the opportunity to run to the downtown mall for some errands and a quick lunch before starting to stalk the senators I needed to see before Wednesday's committee hearing.

I'd just finished lunch when Pauly James called.

"Anytime I see your name pop up on my phone I immediately get nervous," I said. "Why is that?"

"Haha, smartass. I have an easy business proposition for you."

I'd known him for almost twenty years, and he'd never called me on business. "Well it may not be easy," I said, "but I'm sure it will be interesting. Fire away."

"How much do you know about e-liquids or vaping?" he asked.

"All that I know I learned from the 'I vape and I vote' crowd," I sarcastically returned.

"I'm happy to hear that, because that's exactly who I want to talk to you about. You got a minute?"

"Sure thing, hang on so I can get to a quiet spot." I walked all of twenty feet toward a window in the Circle Centre Mall, braced myself for some bullshit that would be delivered by the king of it, and said, "All right, Mr. James. Shoot."

"Here's the situation. I represent a developer who wants to build a manufacturing facility in Indiana that will make e-liquid, the juice that is used in e-cigarettes and other kinds of vaping devices. They want to be sure they know what the regulations will be on the product beforehand. That's why we're working on passing the bills that the 'I vape and I vote' people are against. We're setting up the regulatory requirements for the manufacturing of this stuff. These little mom-and-pop shops won't ever be able to comply with our rules and will end up not being able to operate, which isn't such a bad thing. They mix their stuff in the damn bathtub or the sink in the garage. It's not clean or safe."

"Interesting," I said. "What would a company like Tobacco America think about all of this? They called me at the end of last week about it, but I haven't met with them yet."

Pauly's tone changed immediately. "Oh really? Looks like I'm already too late. Never mind, I guess," he said as if I was somehow not available to discuss his proposition any longer.

"I haven't signed anything with them," I said, trying to keep the conversation going.

"No, I don't think this will work," Pauly said. "Thanks anyway." He hung up.

Later that afternoon, Bethany called to give me the details of her travel plans for the next day, and I told her about the call from Pauly James.

She half-interrupted me. "I know Pauly," she said. "He used to be our lobbyist."

"No shit? What happened?"

"Out of the blue last year, he called and said he wasn't going to be able to represent us any longer. It was odd that he canceled, but we didn't have anything going on in Indiana at the time, so I didn't think much about it."

"He has a client building a manufacturing facility here that is behind these bills you are trying to stop," I said.

"Is that a problem for you? I knew he was on their team, but I didn't think to tell you."

"Not at all," I replied.

"I'll see you tomorrow afternoon," she said in her very business-like way.

"See you then." She might have heard me say that before hitting the red button.

My head started spinning. I had negotiated a $50,000 contract with this national company in about ten seconds four days ago. Then I found out Pauly James had them on a recurring deal that he canceled last year. Why would he do that? I was considering talking him into bidding for me when he called. Nothing is better for the bottom line than that, and it doesn't happen in this business all that often. He put a stop to the conversation before it could, but it made me wonder what he would have paid me. Jesus, how much was this new client paying *him*? I was going to get killed on this project, but it was going to be fascinating.

First, I needed to meet with Bethany. I needed to get a firmer grip on what she really wanted. If the bill was about some competitor of hers wanting to build a plant here in Indiana, then Tobacco America should want at least some similar kind of regulatory oversight.

Second, I needed to get some members of the committee prepped for Bethany's testimony on Wednesday so they wouldn't be surprised that they hadn't heard any of the information during the first round of hearings six weeks ago.

. . .

On Tuesday afternoon, from the third-floor catwalk, I could see a young lady walking on the second floor with a designer bag on one shoulder and dragging a matching trolley of a suitcase behind her. Dressed in a classic Manhattan, DC Beltway, or San Francisco tan business suit and skirt combo, she was a dead giveaway even when I couldn't make out her face. I had already researched her face on social media, so I knew the face from close up, but not from the balcony.

I yelled down: "Bethany?"

She looked up immediately.

"Stay there. I'll come to you!" I shouted.

She was in her late twenties, early thirties at the oldest. She was in good shape, pretty with shoulder-length blonde hair. She was a little too attractive, especially for a woman so young. The Indiana General Assembly is still dominated by men, and most of them do not hide their sexist biases well. Legislators would probably not be able to overcome those biases and see how serious, knowledgeable, and no-nonsense she was, since she would only be here for a day or two at a time.

These crusty old men in the Senate would only see a hot young lady and then do a worse job of listening than usual. They would forget she was a lawyer, with a law degree from some snobby East Coast law school, as if that would help them take her more seriously. The DC types that fly in to spread their knowledge to the dumbasses in the heartland usually get a cold reception anyway. No one likes being made to feel stupid, and this body has gotten defensive about outsiders doing that to them over the years. New legislators quickly fall into this defensive behavior, almost as if the bias is in the employee manual.

I'd be willing to bet that she knew more about tobacco, vaping, and its relationship to all levels of government better than any of the jokers in the Indiana Statehouse. Even those who'd been working on it for months.

After exchanging the usual pleasantries, we went up to the third floor to start training each other.

"Tell me what your problems are with House Bill 1432," I said as a formal way of ending the small talk and beginning the dive into the weeds.

"First of all, every provision in this bill is different than any normal business practice or operating procedure of an e-liquid company. The bill is a re-creation of the wheel, and it doesn't make any sense why," she explained.

"Like what?"

"Let's start with packaging. There is an entire section in this bill that is aimed at preventing tampering with the product. Like any legitimate business in 2015 needs some state government to tell it to keep its product from being tampered with. I have reviewed what happened in the House and Senate hearings from the first half of the session, and these guys have convinced legislators that e-liquid is being tampered with and people are being poisoned, which is crazy."

"Why would anyone think that, and why did the committees believe that so willingly?" I asked with pure curiosity.

"I don't really know, but there's another section that requires the product to be manufactured in a clean room."

"What the hell is a clean room?"

"It's basically a laboratory like you would see at a pharmaceutical manufacturing plant. The workers would need to wear lab coats, and there would have to be high-end security monitoring. That's the part that gets really weird."

"I haven't heard the weird part yet?" I asked.

"All manufacturers, no matter what state their facilities are located in, will have to contract with a security company that certifies that all of this crazy lab stuff is compliant. *And* the security company will also need to monitor the employees' comings and goings, document the production, require the reporting of the output—"

"Wait, wait, wait! You're telling me that the State of Indiana is passing a law that creates state jurisdiction over all of this cleanroom, over-the-top security monitoring bullshit of manufacturing this liquid anywhere in the country? Are you sure that's what this thing says?"

With my "holy shit!" questions, I was making it blatantly clear that I hadn't really read the bill, but at the same time, I was hoping she had read it wrong. It was too goofy.

"Yes. That's what it says. Trust me."

"Well, why isn't every company in the country that does what you do going crazy over this?"

"For a couple of reasons. First, since we are the biggest, I think they expect us to do it. Second, they aren't all that sophisticated yet, and most of them aren't selling anything in Indiana. And finally, they're banking on the FDA preempting most of this state-by-state stuff anyway."

I'd dealt with preemption issues before, mainly with the Federal Communications Commission and the Federal Energy Regulatory Commission, so I knew how that went.

"Do you think the FDA will preempt?" I asked with a glimmer of hope that even if she got screwed by the Indiana legislature, the federal government would bail her out.

"I do. But they are a few months away from passing their rule, and I'm sure someone will sue them over what it says, no matter what they pass. I might even be the one suing them."

"I assume that's our message, right? That Indiana is sticking its nose into a national market and the FDA is the authority and will ultimately govern all of this, right?" I asked rhetorically.

"You guessed it."

This was the obvious play for a company that operated coast to coast. Lobbyists always opened with jurisdictional challenges in a situation like this. On its face, this legislation would result in lawsuits. The high-priced lawyers would argue that the law violated the dormant commerce clause. Pauly James and whoever was working with him knew that. They were willing to roll the dice. They might even be willing to lose, because they knew how long that kind of stuff could take.

But it was unlikely these "I vape and I vote" people were going to be suing anyone in federal court. They likely couldn't even afford to hire someone like me.

Bethany and I obviously didn't know the real story. Some of it was an obvious attempt to run people out of the business whom Pauly and his pals wanted out. He told me that on our brief call. And let's face it, if vaping was going to be a legitimate business going forward, these little local shops probably wouldn't survive anyway. I'm sure Tobacco America didn't care about them either.

But Pauly's client and Bethany should have generally lined up on a regulatory framework. The fact that they didn't was a huge warning sign. I doubted legislators had heard from anyone like her yet. Hopefully that would matter.

My first order of business was to communicate with committee members that TA was engaged on this thing and that there were big problems with the bill. Meeting number one would be with the ranking minority member of the committee, Senator Gene Anderson.

Senator Anderson was a former sheriff, and while he was a Democrat, he was as conservative as most of the Republicans. The Democrats couldn't be choosy, after all.

I knew him well enough, and he had a pragmatic streak in him. The problem with him on this, though, was that he had signed up to be the co-sponsor of Senate Bill 539, the Senate version of the same bill. To get him to reverse course was not going to be easy because that would be an admission that he was wrong on the other bill. Of course, that was going to be the challenge I would face with all of these people.

Bethany and I walked into his office after the receptionist waved us in following a "You got time for O'Courtney?" inquiry.

Like most offices in the Statehouse, Anderson's office had wood-block panel walls and a large conference table that was big enough for ten people. Framed pictures of former members of the Indiana Senate were scattered across the walls. Senator Anderson's office was bigger than most, however, because he was the chairman of the Democrat Caucus as well. That sounded important but it wasn't. The fifty-member Senate had forty Republicans; the ten Democrats who made up their caucus were like the Island of Misfit Toys.

Of course, most legislators were misfits in my eyes. I often wondered how many of them—regardless of party—got elected in the first place.

"Senator, I've got good news for you today!" I said with an enthusiastic handshake.

"Will, if I believed that I would be one happy man," he replied. "At least you brought someone with you this time who looks like she knows more than you."

"Meet Bethany Cramer. She's the general counsel with Tobacco America, and we need to talk to you about House Bill 1432."

"It is good to meet you, sir," Bethany deadpanned.

"What can I do for big tobacco today?" the senator asked, as if he didn't know why we would care about e-liquid legislation.

"Senator, House Bill 1432 has a long list of problems for those of us who sell vapor products across the country," Bethany said. "Have you not heard from any of my competitors on this?"

"Not a peep."

"You have got to be shitting me, Gene," I interrupted. "No one has been bothering you about this train wreck?"

"Those damn 'I vape and I vote' weirdos have been driving all of us crazy, but I quit listening to those characters weeks ago. You aren't working with them, are you? They're nuts."

"No, Senator, those people are not affiliated with my company," Bethany said. "Tobacco America manufactures and distributes tobacco products in all fifty states. We sell products in every sector of the tobacco market except cigarettes. We are heavily invested in the e-liquid or vapor market, and we are the industry leader in the nation. We are also not 'big tobacco' as you described. That is RJ Reynolds or Altria. We are a large company but not that large."

"Surely you've heard from RJR or Altria on this, right?" I asked.

"All they want is to be exempt from the bill and since they are, they don't care," he replied.

I shot Bethany a look that said, "What the hell is that about?"

"I understand that the bill does not regulate e-cigarettes or closed vapor systems," Bethany said. "That's what the big tobacco companies are selling right now. We don't think that will last, but that is what they sell today. It is important for you to understand, though, that the liquid in an e-cigarette is the same liquid this legislation regulates."

"Oh, I know, but that's different."

"I am planning to testify in committee tomorrow about how it actually is not different at all," Bethany said. "I also plan to show the differences between how this bill contemplates e-liquid manufacturing and how it really works. And then I will talk in detail about how the FDA is likely going to preempt the state's authority when its rule is implemented."

"Damn, Will. Where's the good news you promised me? Sounds to me like this bill is the worst thing we have ever considered," the good senator said.

"You don't have to move this bill, you know," I reminded him. "And what's the rush, anyway?"

"I'm not the chairman, as you know. But I will look over your stuff here, and I will be all ears at the hearing tomorrow. You know how I operate, Will. Have you met with Chairman Alderman yet?"

"Not yet, Senator. Sadly, he has been a little slow returning from the break."

"Well, he is in a rush with this one, so you better get in front of him. I gotta get going myself, I'll see you tomorrow. Nice meeting you, young lady."

Bethany and I walked out of there with little encouragement. It sounded to me like the bill was being fast-tracked. If I had to guess, the main reason was because the longer it lingered, the more likely companies like Tobacco America would show up and object. I'm sure that's what Pauly James was telling them.

Bethany had an evening full of conference calls and a couple in the morning as well, so we only had a window of about an hour before lunch on Wednesday to talk to committee members about our oppositional testimony. She brought handouts, legal documents, and talking points—all of which I needed to study. I would be providing them to every member of the Senate who would take them, even though these guys were generally not big readers.

If this hearing were next week, we could have scheduled meals with the senators, and I could have talked to every one of them in detail. But because it was scheduled so soon after the break, I hadn't had enough time to get into my routine.

I couldn't figure out why Bethany wasn't frantic. Most clients who are about to get rolled act pretty desperate. Maybe she thought her testimony the next day would knock these hillbillies in the heartland off their feet, and they'd crumble in the presence of her greatness.

I'm pretty sure that was not what was about to happen.

9

I spent Tuesday evening and most of Wednesday morning learning the actual words contained in the bills and reading the media coverage of what had occurred during the first half of session.

Bethany met me on the third floor outside of the Senate Chamber at 11:00 on Thursday. Senator Charlie Alderman was my primary target that morning.

His office knew I'd been looking for him, and so did he. I'd sent him text messages and emails. He'd told me he would see me when he got back from wherever he'd been, but he was acting unavailable. That is the way I'm sure he treated other lobbyists, but not me. He could have at least texted me back with something vulgar about getting off his ass—that would have been normal and oddly calming. I couldn't tell if he was preoccupied with his long weekend vacation or if he was purposely putting me off. Maybe it was both.

Bethany and I walked into the Republican office entrance on the right side of the chamber, and I announced my presence to the young man working as the receptionist. I said with a blend of sarcasm, humor, and seriousness: "Andy, I've been stalking Senator

Alderman for two days, and I am not leaving here until I meet with him. These guys should know by now that they can't hide from me."

"Will, I can vouch for you on that," Andy said. "It's just easier meeting with you than it is to try and avoid it. You got company with you today?"

"Meet Bethany Cramer from Tobacco America. Bethany, this is Andy Bauman. Behind that black beard and hipster do is the man in charge of Indiana. Unless he can't get me in to see Senator Alderman. Then he isn't worth shit."

Andy nodded. "Let me work my magic, Will," he said and turned his attention to the switchboard.

About sixty seconds later an anxious, blonde-haired, childlike young man came scurrying down the stairs behind Andy's desk.

"Mr. O'Courtney?" The kid didn't look a day over twenty-two.

"Don't tell me, young man, the senator can't see me now."

"He isn't here, and he won't be here until right before his committee starts. He told me to tell you that he would take care of you this afternoon and that you would know what that means."

"Well that's the worst bullshit story I've heard this week, young man. But I guess you're not a magician. You want to come to the committee this afternoon and see for yourself how he takes care of me?"

The young man looked petrified.

Andy came to his rescue. "Take it easy on him, Will. He's a new guy."

"Oh, all right, Andy, as long as the new guy knows he owes *you* one. Young man, tell Charlie I will see him this afternoon."

That was just a big show for my new client. No one there was scared of me or anyone else. Well, maybe that young man was a little.

Bethany and I had largely struck out on the pre-committee work, so we decided the best thing we could do was go to lunch.

It was shitty outside as it often is in March in Indy, so we took the tunnel connecting the Statehouse to the state government office building to the west. The Indiana Government Center South had a cafeteria that I thought she should experience. The South building was the newest one in the complex. I loved taking people over there, hoping they would say things like, "Man, this place is nice." That way I could respond with, "Yeah, Indiana government loves investing in buildings because it's cheaper than investing in people."

Bethany didn't walk into that one like most do.

We went through the line and found a table by the window.

"So what's your story? How did a young, healthy lawyer like you end up working for a tobacco company?" I asked.

She almost smiled through the half-mouthful of salad she was eating. "I bet you imagine that I get that question all the time."

Of course she did.

"I would bet a lot on that, but I don't gamble as much as I used to," I said and jammed an unruly forkful of my larger version of the same salad but smothered in ranch dressing into my mouth.

"The short answer is that I ended up at TA by accident. I was at a firm, and TA was a client. They needed someone in-house, and I thought becoming a partner at a DC law firm would take eighty hours a week for a decade, so the corporate track made sense. A merger or two later, and here I am. What about you? It's my experience that only a few people end up doing what you do on purpose."

As I dabbed the ranch from both sides of my mouth, I agreed with her. "Nice description of my story—I say those exact words to people who ask. I ended up here on accident. You're wearing a ring—what's the story there?"

"Both lawyers in different corporate jobs. No kids, one dog. Too much travel. We met in law school. I'm not sure the corporate gig has turned out to be any easier than firm life would have been. I'll be here for two days instead of locked in some office inside the loop, but either way, we won't be together tonight. I know, I know. Boo-hoo."

"Good lord, get ahold of yourself! You're damn near hysterical!"

"Thanks for asking." She laughed. "I bet you thought I was just some cold-hearted bitch," she tested me as she nursed her ranch-free baby salad.

"Maybe a little," I confessed. "But I want you to be a cold-hearted bitch. I'll worry about kissing ass around here. You need to be the expert, because that is what you are."

"I can be that. I need you to interrupt me when I'm going too far. Can you do that?"

"I will commit to interrupting you if you agree to try and push hard enough for me to need to."

"Deal."

. . .

Back at the Statehouse we went straight to the fourth floor for the hearing. It was being held in the Senate Appropriations Committee room, even though this was the Public Policy Committee.

The room had been renovated a dozen years earlier, and it looked more like a mini-congressional hearing room than any of the other Statehouse committee rooms. There were two rows of benches for the committee, with the back row elevated a couple of steps so the honorable members could appropriately look down on the peons below. There was room for eight people on the top row, reserved for the Republicans, and eight people on the lower row, where the Democrats sat with assorted committee staff. Mahogany panel walls covered the fronts of both rows, assisting in creating an image of power for those sitting in them, looking down on the peons in the public seating area. The design of it all is meant to elevate those in the big chairs and to intimidate those who are not. A table was positioned in the middle of the room facing the committee, where the presenters and witnesses sat and testified.

Unlike congressional hearings, there was no swearing in of the presenters and no penalties of perjury when people decided to tell tall tales. Guys like me quit counting the number of times people plopped down in front of those microphones and flat-out lied. Why let the truth get in the way of a good story?

Two rows of spectator seats are behind the testimony table. These used to be hard-sought-after seats when something dramatic was going on. Now the hearings are all broadcast on TVs out in the hallway and live on the internet as well. So the actual chairs aren't as important as they used to be.

I still liked being there to roll my eyes or shake my head with outrage whenever I could.

When we got off the elevator on the fourth floor, a full half hour before the hearing was set to begin, the "I vape and I vote" crowd had already packed the area.

Practically on cue with our arrival, the Senate staff unlocked the door to the committee room right after we got off the elevator. People flooded into the room to snatch up the fifty public seats. Bethany and I got two seats in the front row. After we put our briefcases on our seats to reserve them, we went back out into the hallway to greet any of the other committee members as they arrived.

There were about an extra fifty people from the T-shirt crowd out in the hallway as well. The lobbyists on Pauly's team and a smattering of others noticed my presence. I was a new entrant into this fray, and I'm sure some folks were curious about why I was there. I'd have to disclose to the lobby registration commission that I'd been hired, but I had fifteen days to do it. By then, everyone would have found out.

The ten members of the committee had to enter the same door as everyone else. I shook hands with each of them and introduced

Bethany. It was largely a meaningless ceremony. But as much as I knew I was an underdog, I also knew they didn't want to ignore me.

The majority of the committee was made up of seven Republicans, six of whom were men—white men. The one woman was probably the most liberal member of their entire caucus, which mattered a lot when the committee dealt with abortion or gun issues but not so much with tobacco and alcohol.

The other three members were Democrats. Two of them were black, and all of them represented urban areas, at least in part.

The last off the elevator was Senator Alderman, and I was the first guy he saw.

Before I could say anything to him, he said, "Will, goddamnit, I told you I would take care of you. Why the hell did you have to spook my intern like that?"

"Welcome home, Senator. Bethany Cramer and I were just all a-flutter waiting for the good news you're planning to give us."

"Excuse my language, young lady. It's a pleasure," he said to her with an apologetic handshake. "Will is one of my guys, but we need to keep this thing moving today. I'll huddle up with you all after the hearing, and we can start talking about what we can do to help. Don't worry too much this afternoon; we have two months left in the session."

"Not quite two months, Senator," I said.

Over his shoulder as he walked into the committee room, he said, "Will, that's more time than I can stand, knowing you're on the job."

The exchange caught the attention of my lobbyist friends, but it also caught the eye of some of the observant T-shirt folks. All of a sudden, there was a new suit on the scene who had a relationship that mattered. They were likely eager to find out whose side I was on.

Once everyone was seated, Chairman Alderman called the meeting to order. "Welcome to the Senate Public Policy Committee."

The chatter in the room stopped instantly.

"We have one bill for consideration today, House Bill 1432. I am the Senate sponsor of the bill. It is very similar to Senate Bill 539 that we heard and passed during the first half of the session. The bill author, Representative Miller, is here to present the bill. Welcome to the Senate, sir. The floor is yours."

Miller was already sitting at the table in the middle of the room. "Thank you, Mr. Chairman and members of the committee. I would like to show you a video that details why I am here before you today." He pointed the remote to his left at a big flat-screen TV hanging above a fireplace that hadn't been used in probably a century or more.

The video showed a young man leaning over a bathtub filled with dingy water. Next to him were a bunch of containers on top of a folding table. The sound quality was bad, but he was listing the chemicals he was mixing into the water.

The video cut to a different young man doing the same thing in what looked like a service sink in a garage. He had a shelf above the sink with a bunch of little bottles that looked like those cocaine bottles from back in the '80s.

With their beards, piercings, and tattoos, both characters would have blended in with the T-shirt crowd.

Of course, the T-shirt crowd gasped as much as anyone. That's what the video was for—to make the T-shirters look dirtier, more irresponsible, and more dangerous than they actually were. Mission accomplished.

Representative Miller stopped the video. "Mr. Chairman, this is what is going on in the vape world here in Indiana. Our children are buying liquid, or e-liquid as it is defined, from people like this. They are then putting that liquid in a vaporizer and inhaling it. Does that look safe to you? Of course not. It shouldn't.

"House Bill 1432 is my attempt to put an end to this kind of unsanitary, unsafe, and unsecured practice of e-liquid manufacturing. People are buying this stuff, and they don't have any idea what's in it since there is no label listing the ingredients. There is no childproof bottle or package. And there is no one responsible when someone gets sick from consuming it. Believe me, that's happening."

Representative Miller then read the list of regulations that would make all of what the committee saw on that video illegal. Of course, what he didn't discuss was how they were going to either catch guys like the ones in the video and arrest them or convince them to voluntarily stop doing what they were doing.

Bethany was expressionless the entire time. I checked—a lot.

Miller closed his comments and Chairman Alderman thanked him and asked the committee if they had any questions.

"Seeing no questions," he said, "I will begin public testimony on the bill. We have three people signed up to testify. Today I am going to let opponents of the bill go first. First up is Ethan Murphy."

While this Ethan person was heading up to the table, I leaned over to Bethany and told her the suspense was over. "Charlie's making sure this thing comes out of committee today. Letting Pauly go last is a setup. I'm getting more and more curious about how he is going to help me."

The chairman put the opponents up first so that Pauly's group could respond to anything guys like Ethan would say. But he, or whoever it was speaking for him, could also contradict anything we might say. That sucked. I preferred getting the last word.

Ethan Murphy was a relatively clean-cut man in his mid to late thirties. He had on a jacket and tie, but he didn't look like he wore that crap regularly. Brown hair and a light beard, unlike the ZZ Top–style stuff the others had. No visible piercings. No ink. I had seen him around a lot, and the fact that I recognized him at all I found interesting. The rest of them just looked like an anonymous blob.

"Thank you, Mr. Chairman and members of the committee. My name is Ethan Murphy, and I am here on behalf of the Hoosier Vapor Association. Our organization is made up of vapor retail store owners, manufacturers of e-liquid, and consumers.

"House Bill 1432 is designed to wipe out small businesses. Nothing more. I appreciate Representative Miller's concern for the safety and health of consumers, but I find it interesting that no consumers are supporting his bill.

"My members were able to start their businesses with investments of as little as $10,000 and as much as $150,000. All those investments will become worthless if this bill passes. None, absolutely none, of my members can afford to construct the clean room that this bill requires or install and contract with the security of that clean room that this bill also requires. There is no way to amend the bill and keep those items in place so that we can continue to stay in business."

Ethan Murphy spent the next several minutes explaining the details of the bill that required things that were not required in any other business. For example, there was a QR code that would be required on each bottle of vapor juice, but that code had to be able to trace the contents of the bottle back to the exact time the contents were produced. Furthermore, in conjunction with the security requirements, the Alcohol and Tobacco Commission would be able to determine who was in charge at the manufacturing facility the day the juice in that bottle was made and who else was working that day and anyone else who may have been present. All of it would have been documented on video surveillance.

I glanced over at Bethany, and she nodded and whispered, "That's the casino-style security I was talking about. That QR code and the security regs in the bill are a lot like tracing cash at a casino, except this is being developed as if it will prevent counterfeiting."

I'd been on a back-office tour of a casino before, and those places made Big Brother seem like the padlock on a high school locker. The security system in a casino is comprehensive. Those cameras record everything that happens inside. Everything. The cameras on top of the building can follow people who have left for a disturbing distance too. That's before we get the safes and the locks. Casino security is designed to protect against the *Ocean's Eleven* crowd.

When Ethan finished, Chairman Alderman asked, "Any questions for Mr. Murphy?" There were none. "Thank you, Mr. Murphy. Next up are Bethany Cramer and Will O'Courtney."

Bethany and I went to the table. I was mainly there to introduce her and to keep her from offending the committee. There was something about Statehouses and people who come from DC to testify. It was a big deal in Indiana, and I'd talked to lobbyists in other states about it as well. State legislators were instinctively turned off by people they associated with the federal government, or people who worked with the feds and thought they were smarter than everyone else.

In that way, I was there to serve as the bridge from the evilness of Washington to the purer, higher ground of the state. I had to make sure we didn't do any harm. Senator Alderman thought he was going to help me somehow, and putting on some big show or making the legislators feel like we thought they were stupid wouldn't help that.

I opened. "Thank you, Mr. Chairman and members of the committee. Will O'Courtney today on behalf of Tobacco America," I announced without letting anyone see how mortified saying that out loud and in public truly made me feel. "I have with me Bethany Cramer, the company's general counsel. My client is the largest manufacturer and retail distributor of e-liquid in all fifty states of America, and we don't want to have to change that number to forty-nine. But House Bill 1432 seems to be designed to do just that."

I got a few welcoming smiles.

"I am confident that you have not heard from anyone who knows more about the future of regulation of this product and its processes by the federal government than Ms. Cramer, who is with me today. She is actively involved in the rulemaking that is almost complete at the FDA, and she is confident that when it is complete, it will likely render much of what is being contemplated in House Bill 1432 moot. With that, I would like to turn it over to her."

The committee still may not have cared enough to change course, but I could tell by their posture and their expressions that they were curious what Bethany was about to say.

"I thank the members of the committee for their time this afternoon. Our headquarters is in Louisville, Kentucky, and while I am able to visit your state's neighbor to the south regularly, I do spend the bulk of my time in sinister Washington, DC."

This humorless, all-business woman actually listened to me about the DC stigma, or already knew it and knew how to kill that problem.

"I was born and raised in Kansas, so I am familiar with the heartland. I am familiar with the thought that our culture doesn't like to be told what to do by the folks in Washington. At the same time, the people who operate our company's manufacturing facility in California don't want to be told what to do by the Alcohol and Tobacco Commission of the state of Indiana. House Bill 1432 tries to empower the Indiana ATC with authority to regulate my company all across the country. No federal court will see that aspect of this bill as proper, but that is not what I came here to discuss with you today."

Very subtle move there. She was all but promising the committee that the bill would be struck down as unconstitutional in federal court, and then she was dismissing that fact as just one problem. That was usually the nuclear bomb of problems with state legislation.

"What I want to talk about today is the health and safety of your constituents as it relates to these products."

She spent about sixty seconds sharing research, most of it from the United Kingdom, that showed that vaping was less harmful than smoking cigarettes. She then said: "That's why our company has left the cigarette business entirely.

"The FDA is preparing to regulate everything House Bill 1432 is attempting to regulate. The rulemaking process at the FDA is a nine-step process, and seven steps of it are complete," she began, making clear that the FDA had more authority, expertise, and every other advantage to doing this instead of the state.

If testimony actually made a difference in committee hearings—and on occasion it actually does—Bethany nailed it. She confidently communicated that the bill was unconstitutional, that it would be ultimately preempted by the FDA, and that vaping was less dangerous than smoking. If any two of these three things were accepted as fact, there was no reason to pass the bill.

Chairman Alderman opened: "Ms. Cramer, welcome to Indiana. You predict that the FDA's rule could be in place as soon as June. Is that realistic?"

"That is optimistic, Mr. Chairman," Bethany replied, "but the rulemaking would be fully briefed in May, and then the only thing left would be the issuing of the rule. It *could* be as early as June, but it *should* be in place by the end of the year."

"Does the committee have any questions?" Alderman asked.

Senator Gene Anderson, the ranking Democrat, raised his hand. "Ms. Cramer, are you testifying that Indiana is the only state that is regulating this stuff?"

"There are two or three other states that are considering regulating e-liquid almost identically as cigarettes, but no state is doing anything like this," Bethany said. "There are children to protect in other states, and there are new small businesses starting up in this new market, but nothing makes Indiana unique in this space. Except this over-the-top regulatory framework."

Chairman Alderman glanced around the room. "Seeing no other questions, thank you Ms. Cramer for your testimony, and you too, I guess, Will."

He pulled the last appearance form and announced, "Last up, in support of the bill, is Bryce Baldwin."

Bryce was an asshole. He was actually the managing partner of the biggest law firm in town. His firm had offices all over the world and political connections at all levels of government in the States. Hell, they might have been connected everywhere on the planet for all I knew, but since I only worked in Indiana, they had my political world covered.

He worked with Pauly in the liquor distributing business, and he had gaming clients as well, but I could never keep track of which casinos belonged to him. He was also a master of the aw-shucks liar's act. For those who didn't know him, he seemed profoundly sincere. For those who did, not so much.

He looked average in every way. Gray suit. Business-cut, salt-and-pepper hair. Glasses issued to him by his law school. He's a white guy you wouldn't even notice walking by on the street.

I knew him well enough to know that he was going to go full "Vinny" on us.

The *My Cousin Vinny* treatment came from the movie when Joe Pesci walked up to the jury to deliver his opening statement and said: "Everything that guy just said is bullshit. Thank you." That was the entire statement.

"Thank you, Mr. Chairman. I appear today on behalf of Indiana

Tobacco and Liquid, LLC. My client is a new business in Indiana, and we plan to build an e-liquid manufacturing facility in central Indiana upon the passage of this bill. I do not have much to add to what Representative Miller presented. He did an excellent job explaining the bill. I do, however, take issue with much of what Ms. Cramer just stated."

Well of course you do, asshole. If you didn't, there wouldn't be a bill.

"Mr. Chairman, when was the last time you had confidence in the federal government? Ms. Cramer would have you believe that they will have regulations in place that will keep Indiana children safe this year. But imagine five hundred lawyers just like Ms. Cramer arguing, litigating, and suing the federal agency when those rules come out in any kind of objectionable way. That rulemaking is a lawyer's dream. It might be ten years before those rules are in place, but we are supposed to wait for them here in Indiana?"

Actually, he could be right about that one.

"And along those same lines, she all but committed to suing the State of Indiana if this bill passes. So let's see if that's true, Mr. Chairman. If our proposal is so over the line, why don't we just see if the courts agree with her? If the mere threat of going to court is a reason not to take proactive steps to protect the people of the state, we wouldn't ever take any of those steps."

Again, while a bit dramatic, the committee would agree with the asshole on that one as well.

"I just don't see a reason to delay implementing our own oversight today. If the feds or the courts want to modify or preempt later, there has been no harm to those we are trying to protect. There will only be harm to those who never cared about Indiana in the first place. My client is an Indiana company and always will be. We stand ready to be regulated and want to be a long-term partner. Thank you, and I will take any questions."

Chairman Alderman asked the standard question about questions. None were asked. The lawyer was dismissed. The chairman then asked, "Is there any committee discussion?" Again there was only silence from the other committee members. He quickly followed up with, "I will entertain a motion."

Senator Gene Anderson said, "I move the bill to pass." Two other committee members simultaneously followed in unison with "second."

Chairman Alderman said, "The bill has been moved and seconded. Call the roll."

The committee staff person read off the committee members' names one by one. And one by one they responded with "aye" or "yes."

Chairman Alderman announced the result by saying, "The bill passes 10–0. We are adjourned."

Groans and grunts erupted from the peanut gallery, and some murmurs of the same came from the hallway. The door opened, and people started filing out. Most of the people seemed unhappy but not surprised.

I took Bethany out into the hallway to get away from the crowd a little bit, but I kept the door in sight. I was waiting for the chairman and wondering how he was going to help me. I felt like I was losing control of the situation. There was a bunch of chatter, and some friends came up to me and tried to engage me in conversation, I blew them off with the give-me-a-minute sign. Then Ethan Murphy approached me, and I told him it was nice to meet him, but I needed a minute before I could talk. All the T-shirt people were giving me and Bethany the eye.

When the chairman finally came out, he walked right at me, ignoring everyone else in between. "Walk with me, you two," he said.

"Okay, Charlie," I said. "I'm dying to know how you are going to help me."

"So am I," he said nervously.

"What?" I fired. "I thought you had a plan!"

"No, Will. I expected *you* to have a plan."

"Jesus Christ, Charlie. Why the hell didn't you say that?"

"I know you. You'll think of something," he said with absolute confidence.

"All right. Here's what I need you to do. Just tell Representative Miller and Pauly that you are going to sit on the bill to give me and Tobacco America some time to work out a compromise with Pauly before the deadlines. If you will tell them you want us to work out a deal, we will get a deal done. Okay?"

He exhaled. "See how easy that was? I can buy you some time and give that ounce of leverage. But don't you think for one second that you can satisfy the tattoo crowd. Trust me, they can't be helped. You need to get what you can for Bethany here and move on."

I turned to Bethany. "Does that work for you?"

"It sounds like the best deal we are going to get this week," she said, "so I guess you should sign us up."

"Okay, Charlie. Thanks for your awesome idea. You're the best."

"I'll get it started, but we'll have to keep this a secret from those crazy asses. And then I want to talk to you in private about all this next week. You hear me?"

"Of course," I said.

"In *private,* Will. You hear me?"

"All right, Charlie. I'll get that chickenshit intern of yours to schedule a lunch for Monday or Tuesday."

"Good. See you later. Good luck, Bethany." He disappeared into the fourth-floor entrance to the offices above the chamber.

I knew I could get a deal to help my client at least a little, as long as Pauly and the rest of his criminal friends knew that they had to cut a deal with me. Charlie was right, though. He didn't even have to tell me about the T-shirters. What helped me was different than what they needed. I couldn't fix their problems, and why would I worry about them? They weren't paying me.

I loved knowing that Pauly would be trying to buy me off. He should have just written me a check two days ago. When Charlie told him about the deal he just promised me, he'd be wishing he'd written me twice what Bethany was paying me—all just for staying out of his way and shutting up.

Too bad. I suddenly wanted to win, and I had an opening that could lead to just that. All details aside, winning was everything. I was in the game. Game. On.

On my way out of the building on the second floor, the leader of the T-shirters was loitering, apparently waiting for me near the elevator. "Mr. O'Courtney," Ethan Murphy said, "can I have a moment?"

I tried to brush him off with "I'm running late, but here's my card."

He took it, and as I rudely tried to keep walking, he said, "Do we even have a fighting chance?"

I kept on walking half backward, so I could lie to him more comfortably. "It's too soon to tell. There's a lot of time left."

10

t had been two weeks since I had been to church. I liked calling it that, because technically it was true, but mostly because it made people feel awkward on those rare occasions that I had to explain to anyone where I was going on a Thursday night.

Thursday was usually a pretty free night for lobbyists in Indiana because the legislature had long ago adopted the practice of not working on Friday. The bulk of legislators left town after business was done on Thursday. But from time to time, an event or potential obligation would come up on a Thursday night. I loved telling people, "I'm out. I have a church commitment."

In politics, no one questions church stuff. But at the same time, insiders also think church commitments are bullshit. Though no one ever says that out loud.

In my case, people believed it even less.

My hipster giant of a friend Greg Bryant was back in the group, and over the last few years I had become close with Dot, the lady who seemed to run the place. She was actually a little older than my first estimate of seventy-five, but what difference did it make?

Her actual name was Dorothy. My grandma and one of my aunts were named Dorothy. Just like people named Bethany are always younger than I am, I don't know any Dorothys who are. And my new friend and my aunt both were nicknamed Dottie or Dot. I always giggled a little inside when I was a kid and someone called my aunt "Dot." Now, it's the coolest name I know.

Dot's husband, Danny, was part of the group too. He was a little younger and little quieter than she was, and he reminded me of an older version of me. His Irish heritage and the big family he came from made his stories sound familiar.

Dot and Danny were the two big reasons I'd kept coming to the group for more than three years. I didn't know why. Maybe it was because they filled the void my parents' detached approach to parenting created in me. Along with my ugly buddy Greg, they had become my best friends. I needed friends away from the Statehouse, though I wouldn't have planned to find them in these three.

And of course, there was Flip. She'd be eye candy for anyone, but she'd quit being just that to me a long time ago.

She was a single mom who was as no-nonsense or no bullshit as she needed to be. She never dolled herself up for the meetings, which only made her cooler. I guessed her natural hair color was brown, but she'd lightened it. She always was a little tan, but she never looked like she'd been tanning. She was maybe 5'2" and neither skinny nor heavy. She looked healthy, like she exercised regularly but wasn't psycho about it. And she had beautiful green eyes.

She didn't seem interested in hanging out with men. Plus, I was fifteen years older than her youthful thirty-one. I really wished neither of those things were true. It was hard for me to take my eyes off her at the meetings. I tried not to sit across from her, because when I did it was near impossible to not look at her.

Everyone else in the group came and went for the most part. There was never more than about a dozen of us in a group session.

Most people stayed with the group anywhere from a few weeks to a year, but the five of us—Flip, Greg, Dot, Danny, and I—had been regulars for my entire time in the group.

My lobbying and political network wouldn't give people like my group friends a second thought. But they were the treasure I hid from everyone else I knew. Neither side of that balance sheet cared about the other, so I didn't have to work too hard to hide my church buddies. Over time, they became the only ones I truly loved.

The week following the meeting I missed because of the spring-break golf trip, I slipped into the room just under the wire of the 7:30 start time, which had become customary.

"Jesus Christ! Will's here," Greg announced. "The weekly suspense is over—I guess we can start now."

I didn't even make eye contact with him while flashing him my middle finger and smoothly taking off my jacket to sit down.

"I missed most of you while I was gone last week," I said, "and so it's mostly good to be home."

"All right, you two," Dot chimed in. "We have a new visitor this week so give it a rest. When we finished the meeting last week, we were talking about God's will.

"Who wants to start?" she asked.

After a couple of awkward seconds, I asked, "I don't know where you were or what the context was when you stopped last week, but was the discussion about destiny?"

Danny said, "That is certainly an element of God's will in most religions, and it should be a part of our discussion. But we were talking more about God's intention in our daily lives. Like what would God do or have us do in a particular circumstance."

A regular attendee, a middle-aged white guy whose name escaped me, took the floor. "Every religion has its own definition or interpretation of the will of God. But I looked it up after last week's meeting, and as usual, it seems pretty similar across religions. Since in Christianity, God's ultimate will is to have a peaceful world dominated by love and compassion, I think everything we do should be aimed at that goal."

A few more awkward seconds passed before he added, "And that seems pretty hard to do for me. Damn near impossible!"

Agreeable laughter followed.

"Don't we, and when I say we, I mean humans, constantly manipulate what we believe God's will to be?" I asked. "You guys know where I work. The next right thing is sometimes hard to recognize there."

"Here's the deal," Danny said. "Over the years, I have learned to ask myself that silly 'what would God do?' question more and more. Sometimes the question is 'what would God think?' about what I just did. At my age, I have a pretty clear idea of what is right and wrong. We'll talk about destiny again later, but how much confusion do we really have as grown-ups on this? How often do we truly face a dilemma? For me, I am not confused by what I think God's will is. I just need to be diligent about evaluating my choices from His perspective. When I don't do that—I stop living well."

Danny was a man of few words, and he chose them wisely. To look at him, you wouldn't immediately think that he was overly cerebral. He dressed like a factory worker even though he retired years ago—and not from a factory. The more I got to know him the more I recognized his tendency to evaluate his day through a worker-like lens. You know, the type who asks, What did I get done today? That's a question I imagined him asking himself every night at bedtime.

I didn't know this to be true, but I bet Danny could fix anything, like my dad could. He kept his hair cut short, sometimes sporting the clean dome look. He read. He read a lot. He was curious. He listened. These were the things that were not obvious about him, but they were the things that impressed me.

"Answering your manipulation question is the real struggle, Will," he added. "Trying to identify the difference between your will and God's will is sort of the point of the discussions last week and tonight."

My mind started wandering. Religions give guidance on what God's will is. That's the advantage of religion. For a guy like me, believing in a higher power of some kind but not trusting religion made the answers to these questions less rigid and less clear.

Spirituality instead of religion was the path I was on, which was all well and good for those of us who didn't trust religions and didn't want to go to church on Sunday. But it did create philosophical quandaries fairly often.

Walking out the door behind Flip after the meeting, I said to her, "Did you get all of that tonight? I sure hope so."

"I'm a good listener, Will. The question is, did *you* get it?"

"I think so, but I'm going to have to give it some more thought. I do that, you know?"

"I wonder what you think about when you go into your little zones," she said.

"You shouldn't wonder about what I'm thinking. *Ewww, it's disgusting*—might be what you think about that!"

"Now I'm going to have to give *that* some more thought," she said. "See you next week."

Once again, she paralyzed me with embarrassing ease.

In between Flip fantasies, I thought about the "God's will" thing plenty over the weekend. I wasn't going to be back working on the vaping project until I met with Pauly and Representative Miller on Monday, so it was easy for me to set that aside.

I also ran a lot that weekend. I exercised every day, but I only lifted weights two or three times a week. The rest of the time I was on an elliptical, a Stairmaster, or I was running.

Besides the occasional run, the only real outdoor exercise I got was walking on the golf course. The rest of it was in the Downtown YMCA. It's the closest thing to an hour of pure thinking I get. The Downtown Y is inside the Athenaeum, a big old red brick building that was built in the late 1800s and is now a National Historic Landmark. It was originally called Das Deutsche Haus, but the name was changed in 1918 after the US declared war on Germany, and along with it, war on German culture.

Now it's just a sprawling gothic structure in one of the most historic sections of the city. Besides the Y, the building is home to the Rathskeller, a German restaurant that is popular for its sauerbraten, and the hot mustard that comes with the pretzels. But also for its beer and the Biergarten, a courtyard that turns into a great place to kill a summer evening and listen to live music.

Almost every surface inside is hardwood. So even though it's this huge red brick building that is reflective of the Germanic Renaissance Revival style, the place creaks on the inside like a haunted house.

Down the hall from the entrance to the Y is a large lobby area that went unused for many years where some young entrepreneurs opened up a coffee snob joint called Coat Check Coffee. Yeah, that's what the area was known for before these guys moved in earlier this year. It's a good place to hang out, has good WiFi, windows, and plenty of space. And I love high ceilings. The Starbucks around the corner is tiny, so the young guys running this place picked a great spot.

I drink water there more than coffee, mainly because of all the things I am a little snooty about, coffee isn't one of them. And the coffee at Coat Check is as snobby as I know. But I land there a lot, and it has become my home court. No one else from the Statehouse even knows about the place. Yet.

I wonder what God would think about a typical day in the life of a lobbyist. Is it possible to be godly and still be successful at lobbying?

I didn't lie to people. Not really. I guess I lied to that T-shirt leader yesterday, but what good would have come from me telling him the truth? It would have made my life more difficult without changing the result.

The guy and his friends were going to lose anyway. What difference did it really make if he lost in early March or late April?

The deist in me would say that God's will ended at creation and that anything that happened was exactly what God intended, without intervention. The longer I spent with my friends and the more faith developed in my life, the less I believed this bit. I felt guilt for the things I did that I knew were wrong. It wasn't really a dilemma like Danny said. It was more of an obvious choice to make or to live by.

I guess.

11

The first order of business on Monday was to meet with Pauly. Of course, that couldn't happen till the afternoon because he didn't do mornings in the Statehouse all that often. Even Mondays. Especially Mondays.

The second order was making sure Representative Miller knew that a negotiation was taking place. Since I didn't expect him to have a role in it, technically that should have been easy. But legislators instinctively don't like outsiders cutting deals on their bills, so I'd have to be delicate.

Pauly wasn't going to be thrilled at the idea of me holding up his bill. I hoped Charlie had told him the details of the deal he made with me. If he hadn't, it wouldn't be all that out of the ordinary.

The committee report on HB 1432 was adopted the day after that quick Wednesday hearing. That meant that the next business day, today, the bill was eligible for a second reading.

Second reading on the floor of either chamber in Indiana is the opportunity for a bill to be amended by any member of the body. A bill appears on the Senate agenda until it is moved from second reading to third reading. With Charlie's commitment to hold it until I could work out a deal with Pauly, HB 1432 would sit until it could move on to the third reading, which might be a month.

Normally bills don't stay on the second reading calendar for more than a day or two. And a bill that sits that long could attract a pile of amendments.

But that wasn't my problem. Working out a deal with Pauly was my problem.

Pauly agreed to meet me on a hallway bench around 3:00. I was happy he wasn't bringing lawyers with him, but I knew we weren't going to be able to get much done without one of those assholes. At least our first conversation could be frank.

Pauly came dragging around the corner right on time. The House and the Senate had already adjourned for the day as they had almost nothing on their calendars.

"Pauly, did you just get up?" I asked. "If that windbreaker were a bathrobe, I'm not sure people would even notice the difference."

"I was already mad at you before I got here, and that's your opener?" he said. "This is gonna be about as much fun as a colonoscopy—an amateur colonoscopy."

"Mad at me? What the hell for? I haven't even asked for anything—at least not yet."

"Just shut up for a minute, and I'll tell you what the deal is. Then you can start telling me what your ransom is."

"You got it, Pauly. Ransom. I like the way that sounds. I always wanted to kidnap someone, but I never thought it would be a hungover lobbyist. I could have done that to myself in the old days. Come to think of it—"

"Shut the hell up, Will. Step into my office so I can get this over with. I'm already sick of your bullshit."

We both sat down on that third-floor bench, and he took a deep breath. He was clearly collecting his thoughts, and he was clearly a little pissed that he had to buy someone off when he thought this thing was already a done deal.

It was also obvious, by his use of the word "ransom," that Charlie had told him to cut a deal with me. His bill had been kidnapped, held up until there was a deal. These weren't commonly used terms for me in the Statehouse, but it sure seemed like they were for Pauly.

"I know that you don't represent the small mom-and-pop shops," he said. "And I'm sure you know by now that I used to represent Tobacco America. I know what your client does and what they will want or not want in these bills. But the most important thing about all of this is to not confuse what your client wants with what these mom-and-pop shops want. Okay?"

"That's what Charlie told me," I confirmed. "I am here to take care of my client, Pauly, and absolutely nothing more."

"Good. Like I told you on the phone and like we testified in committee last week, we want to build an e-liquid manufacturing facility here, and we want these little independent shops gone. I know your guys operate and sell everywhere, and we are not trying to keep you out of the biz here, but these hairy tattoo folks have got to go."

"Do you mind if I tell you that I think that's weird?" I asked. "I mean, what sort of threat do these guys really present to your client or mine? Aren't we going to cream them in the market anyway?"

"Of course we are, but we want them gone right now. We don't want them hanging around and surviving while the market grows."

"You want to skip the steps my client and others like my client went through to become a player in this market by eliminating the low-level competition at the beginning?" I asked sarcastically.

"Jesus, Will. Since it's just you and me sitting here talking, I guess I'll say yes to that. But I'm convinced that your client will benefit from these guys being gone too. What we need to do is find a way to get your client in the position to comply with this new

Indiana law without letting the law get watered down enough so these leeches can survive."

"Some of the shit that's in this bill is off the charts, though," I said. "You know that don't you?"

"We'll be able to modify a bunch of stuff, but the tough stuff like the clean room, the monitoring, the security . . . all of that is going to have to stay in."

"The labeling, containers, and packaging crap in the bill has to be fixed," I said. "I have no idea why you seem to want your new facility to be a top-secret, nuclear-space-powered lab, but I'll let Bethany put some more thought into that part. But everything on the package is going to have to look more like national standards at a minimum."

"We can work on the packaging. I don't know if we can get our vision to match what you guys are already doing, but maybe we can."

"One more thing," I piled on. "The State of Indiana coming to California to inspect our plant? Really?"

"I don't know if I can fix that," Pauly said.

"I'm pretty sure federal court will fix that one for you."

"One thing at a time," he said.

"I'll get the packaging language changes from Bethany, and we can go over it on, say, Wednesday?"

"Works for me. I'll make sure one of my guys can be there."

"I bet you will. We can't have a meaningful meeting without a giant asshole in the room," I said as I got up.

"With you there, I guess that makes two assholes," Pauly said, and then he answered his phone.

As I walked away from him, I realized that what just happened was as good as it could be. He was going to give me something that Bethany couldn't get without me. No matter what the details were, I was going to win—something.

Objective number two was now upon me. I needed to hunt down

Representative Miller and confirm that he knew we were working on a deal at the direction of Senator Alderman. I'm sure he knew. What I didn't know was whether or not he was pissed off about it. If he was, he'd direct his anger at me.

In the world of lobbying, it is never a good idea to ask for something the first time one is meeting with a legislator. A good rule is to have at least two or three meetings or social opportunities before asking for some legislative favor. It is a terrible situation to be holding a legislator's bill hostage before the first meeting and to be doing it without his approval.

The doorman on the north side door of the House chamber called and told Miller I was there to see him and then told me to go on up. There were even fewer people milling around the building than when Pauly and I sat down. I find the Statehouse a little creepy when it's quiet. I always have.

I went up the stairs to Miller's office. Most of the House offices that were right off the chamber were reserved for those in leadership. Miller was a committee chairman, but I didn't know what other rank he also had. None of the lobbyists give a shit about that stuff. All we care about is who's in charge and who is the next man up. Rank inside a caucus goes about ten people deep, which is meaningless to us. I suspect it's mostly meaningless to them too. It probably equated to a roomier office, a better parking place, and an extra fifty bucks or so a week.

I knocked on the open door and tried to act a little sheepish and apologetic on my entrance. There would be none of my trademark sarcasm in this meeting. I was just hoping to make him understand that I knew I had broken protocol and that I was going to work to make sure my involvement was not going to make things difficult. At least not difficult for him.

"Come on in, Will," he said without much excitement. "I was wondering when our paths would finally cross."

"Mr. Chairman, let me open with my apologies for letting them cross like this," I said as I extended my hand. "I just got hired on this project right before the hearing or you can be sure I would have been here to see you long before now."

"Don't worry about it, Will. I know how this works. I just wish we had gotten to work together before."

"Me too. You would already know that what I am about to say is the absolute truth. But because this is our first rodeo together, I guess you can only rely on Senator Alderman vouching for me. Right? He did talk to you, didn't he?"

"He did. I'm not sure I fully understand what will be accomplished by all of this, but I'm happy to listen," he reluctantly conceded.

"I'm going to work with Pauly to modify the bill to more accurately match what is common business practice for us at Tobacco America. That should also make the bill more workable for other national companies who you haven't heard from yet as well. I only represent TA, but my assumption is that other national companies can be calmed a little by taking care of some of these problems."

"What kind of problems are you talking about?" he asked.

"Pauly and I just met, and he knows that the labeling, container, and packaging requirements in the bill are sharply different than what we do in our facilities now. Your ideas aren't better or worse, they are just different. For us to do it your way would cost us a bundle. And then when the FDA rule passes, we are going to have to change again. We want to avoid that."

"I'm not emotionally attached to that stuff," he said. "But the security stuff, the things that make sure the liquid is safe, not tampered with, and all of that is what matters to me. That's where the stuff is unsafe."

"Pauly said the same thing. I don't know what to say about that, but we will work it out one way or the other with them. And that's what I wanted to make sure you knew. The Senator has asked that I work out a deal, and that's what I will do. I am not asking you to negotiate or mediate this thing for me. Pauly and I will come up with something that you guys can pass. All I need is some time with him to straighten some of this out. When we are done, we will come back to you with what we agreed to."

"If Charlie says you can get that done, I trust him. As long as you know I have no interest in helping those crazy folks. They've been terrorizing me on Facebook and calling me names and writing letters to the editor. I've had it with them."

"I'm starting to sense a theme about the T-shirt crowd," I said.

"You don't know the half of it. I'm not helping them, and Pauly isn't either. I do trust him on that one."

"Fair enough. They aren't my client or my concern. Again, you can be confident that I will work out what Tobacco America can with Pauly and Senator Alderman, and then we'll get out of your hair."

"Good luck with that. I don't want this thing getting too bogged down, but Charlie is going to have to take care of that. Let me know how it's going if you can."

"You got it, Mr. Chairman. And again, I apologize for us meeting this way," I said as I headed for the door.

He jabbed me with the last words: "I'm watching you, Will."

As soon as I was out of his office, I texted Alderman:

Senator, I've had the first meeting with Pauly, and we have a plan on how to deal with all this. I just left Rep. Miller, and he knows what the deal is. You wanted to meet privately. How about lunch tomorrow?

He immediately replied, quicker than usual for him:

91

> I had a lunch scheduled for tomorrow, but I will cancel it.
> Meet me at Weber Grill at 11:30.

That's weird. I couldn't imagine what was on his mind that he would cancel any lunch to bullshit with me when he could do that any time of day, any day of the year. I responded:

> Canceling a lunch for me? I can't decide if I'm scared or honored. I think I'll go with scared. I'll be there.

He didn't reply.

. . .

After I got back to my townhouse that night, I called Bethany and gave her the update. She was already working on the packaging changes. She wasn't overly impressed with the opportunity I had arranged for us, which pissed me off a little. But in her defense, she had two pretty good reasons.

Fundamentally, she knew that TA and others would sue the State of Indiana if their manufacturing facilities in other states were subject to inspection. The idiot Indiana legislators had convinced themselves, through Pauly's work, that the state could dictate manufacturing practices outside of the state in exchange for the ability to retail in the state.

This would never survive a constitutional challenge in federal court, but why should anyone have to sue when everyone could see what the outcome would be?

The second reason was the clean room and strangely specific "security firm" requirements.

But in the short term, she would focus on the packaging language, and I would deliver it on Wednesday in my next session with Pauly.

. . .

The next day, I bopped into Weber Grill to meet Charlie for lunch. Weber was a popular spot because it was the first decent restaurant people from the Statehouse passed while using Indianapolis' elaborate downtown pedestrian tunnel system.

I was right on time, but Charlie was already sitting in a booth in the bar. Again, that was a little odd. "Legislator time" means tardiness, usually in the fifteen-minute range, especially for an 11:30 lunch. "Mr. Chairman, I gotta tell you, you're freaking me out a little bit lately with your rapid text responses, your promptness today, and what not," I said.

"Sit down, Will. I can't stay for lunch, but I want to chat before I have to take off for another meeting."

What the hell was this? What was with the cloak-and-dagger warning biz?

"You know I don't do bad news, Charlie. So, don't—"

"Shut up. This is serious. I just need to give you some advice. You need to get what you can for your client on this one, and then you need to run like hell in the other direction."

I'd never heard a warning like that.

"This is a bad one. I agreed to do it before I knew what it was about, and I need you to remember I told you that. Okay? You and I are friends, and I need you to remember that."

I nodded with what must have been a complete look of terror on my face.

"I can't tell you the details. You're going to have to figure all that out on your own. Maybe you won't have to figure it out. Or better yet, maybe the details won't matter to you and your client. But I can't stress this enough to you, keep your eye on the ball of what your client asks you to do. Don't go looking for anything more than that. And don't let those T-shirters suck you in."

That last part fired me up a little. "Why the fuck do you guys keep warning me about these real people who don't know shit about the legislature? You guys act like you're scared of them, and near as I can tell, they're about as important as a housefly buzzing around our heads."

"The reason why is that they are going to find out you're working on a deal, and they are going to try and get you to help them. We can't let that happen, because once that door opens for them, the rest of this thing will collapse. Just promise me to keep your eye on the ball, do your thing for your big client, and then run like hell."

"I don't understand, Charlie—"

"You don't need to understand. You weren't supposed to be in on this. None of you guys were. I gotta run. Remember what I said—but keep this lunch a secret."

"Jesus, Charlie, this lunch is so fucking secret, we didn't even eat."

"That's the spirit, Will. Keep me posted on your progress. See ya."

He fast-walked out of the bar door back into the tunnel. It was all of about 11:37 and "lunch" was over. There wasn't anyone else in the place, and the waiter hadn't even come to the table yet. I sat there feeling lost.

12

Wednesdays during the legislative session were set aside for committee hearings. The gatherings of lobbyists, legislators, and even the real people were scattered all over the building in their little groups and niches.

I was killing time until I had the privilege to sit down in the afternoon with Pauly and the lawyer, Bryce. While Pauly and I had been so-called friends, it was another story with Bryce. Maybe he knew that I thought he was a run-of-the-mill liar. I couldn't even remember what the guy did to end up on my shit list, and I didn't know if he even knew he was on it. I did know that he couldn't care less one way or the other. He was the managing partner of his firm's Indy office, and I don't think he was in that spot because he was the greatest lawyer around. It was because he generated business for the firm like no one else.

It was a little odd that he wanted to get in the weeds on a project like this. His firm had other lobbyists and lawyers who had plenty of juice and plenty of skill and who were perfectly capable of taking care of this for him.

For some reason, he cared about this seemingly little project in a personal way. I wished that wasn't feeding the paranoia that Charlie planted in my soul, but it was.

I strolled up right at 3:00, and those two were already sitting at the table we'd planned to meet at right outside the entrance to the House gallery. The promptness trend I was seeing on this project was downright strange.

I greeted them: "What a couple of eager influence peddlers I have before me today."

"Will, good to see you. Sort of," Bryce responded with a handshake.

"Sort of is a stretch, but if he says so," Pauly added.

"I don't know how you see this situation," I took a seat, "but this is how I see it."

They both sat back in their chairs with looks on their faces that said, "Who the hell does this guy think he is?"

"I assume that you guys have a bill that is on the floor of the Senate right now that you are pretty happy with, if not completely happy with. If the damn thing had been moved to third reading on Monday and voted out yesterday, that would probably have been perfect for you, right?"

"There isn't anything we need changed in it," Bryce said, "so I guess the answer is y—"

"That's what I thought. Let me describe this bill in my terms so we can get down to the three areas of trouble and prioritize our discussions for fixing them."

Bryce said, "There are changes you probably want that are off the table—"

"Don't get this off on the wrong track by telling me what you won't change before I even tell you if I need it changed. Like I was saying, there are three areas of the bill that we need to discuss. First, the packaging, and that includes the mixing and bottling of the liquid *and* the packaging of those bottles. Second, the jurisdiction of the state and the state's ability to inspect operating facilities in other states. And third, the goofy security requirements of the facilities that exist outside of the state. Which leads me to this completely crazy security firm definition from outer space and the requirement that we hire this crazy firm from utter la-la land."

Bryce tried to break in again, but I put my hand up to stop him. "Today I want to discuss and give you suggested language changes on the packaging. When we are done with that, I want to listen to what you have to say about the second and third items, because my client and I can't figure out what the hell you are trying to accomplish with them. At least we can't figure out anything good there. Now, dig in, Bryce. The floor is yours."

"Jesus, Will. Are you sure it's okay for me to talk now, or would you rather I just agree to let you rewrite the whole thing?" Bryce usually ran meetings like this, and he knew that I knew that I sure as hell was not in charge.

"You could agree, but I was hoping we could fight for a little while first, if you don't mind."

"No dice. I guess I can listen to your bit about packaging. Because the second and third things are probably not flexible for us."

I looked at him with a fake expression of surprise and shrugged my shoulders, my hands extended outwardly, like I couldn't believe he wasn't buckling to my demands.

"We'll see," I finally said. "Let's take care of the easy part first, and you'll enjoy it so much you'll want to keep dealing." That was painful BS that I knew wasn't true.

"What I'm handing you is a mark-up of the bill with what we do at our manufacturing facilities with the liquid and bottles."

Bryce and Pauly looked at each other like they didn't know I might be able to help them.

"See how easy and fun this can be!" I chuckled.

Bryce gave me the keep-rolling hand signal without speaking.

"Next, we can't figure out why you have used the concepts of childproof packaging and tamper-resistant packaging interchangeably throughout this part of the bill. In the industry, these are two very different things." I explained to them what the difference was and how it could be written in the law.

I got the same sense that they didn't know the difference and that they felt slightly embarrassed about their ignorance.

Bryce gave me the keep-rolling signal again, even though he was getting a little fussy about it.

"Next, what the hell is this crap about having a 'scannable code on each bottle, which may include a quick response code' really all about? My client already does this too, but this is written like . . ." and I swing my bat a third time at what appears to just be bad legislative writing rooted in their lack of knowledge of the industry.

"When did you get so smart?" Bryce said. "You know, like you said a few minutes ago, we're okay with the bill as-is and don't need you to help us. This is supposed to be helping you. Sure, we'll look at your stuff here and think about it. We aren't up and running yet, so I don't think this stuff is all that troubling. We may need to tweak it some, but the sooner this little get-together ends, the better off you will be. Trust me on that."

"Uh, don't forget the interstate problem with the ATC inspecting our facilities, Bryce."

"I don't want to talk about that today, since you guys are already planning to sue the state on that," he said.

"We will win that, and you know it."

"Whatever, Will. Are we done here?"

"Almost. I can't let you leave until you help me understand the security firm and all of the locksmith and surveillance BS."

"That stuff is off the table."

"You can't be serious," I said. "It doesn't make any sense. It's like you're trying to build a better mousetrap. Who fucking wrote this? It was one of your casino goons, wasn't it?"

"You're like Dick Tracy, Will," Bryce said. "But it doesn't matter, we aren't changing it."

"We can talk more about it later," I said, as if he was waffling. "You have plenty to look at there already. You want to regroup tomorrow afternoon?"

"I can," Pauly said, "but I don't think he should have to do this two days in a row."

Bryce added, "I'll be here if there's a reason to be here." He stood up and began walking away.

"What the hell does that mean?" I asked.

"I will be here at 3:00," Pauly said. "Bryce will be a game-time decision. I'm not sure it's good to put you two together again so soon." I gave him the sarcastic parade wave so Pauly couldn't hear me say what I was thinking.

As soon as their backs were turned, walking away with what appeared to be about a third of everything I had hoped to gain, I shot my middle finger at them. I always felt better after I did it, even though it didn't count if no one actually saw it.

. . .

I got home feeling pretty good about how things went with those guys. My update call to Bethany was typical. She acted unimpressed that progress had been made. She asked for details on the part of the conversation about the security scheme, which was pretty uneventful except for Bryce's unwillingness to change any of it. Bethany was baffled. So was I.

The next day came pretty fast. I showed up at the same spot right at 3:00 again. I expected to see Pauly alone, rolling in with a brutal afternoon hangover after entertaining his friends three nights in a row at the Winner's Circle. But once again, I was shocked to find Pauly and Bryce already at the table, ready to pounce.

"I can't believe I'm here on time, let alone you, Pauly. But to have Bryce two days in a row is like Christmas in March!"

"Save the bullshit, Will. Does it ever stop with you?" Bryce answered.

"Tell him, Pauly."

"No, Bryce, it never stops. He can go all day."

"The packaging stuff works for us," Bryce said. "We're going to write it up in three amendments and give it to Charlie over the weekend."

"And?" I probed.

"And that's it," Bryce said. "That's all we have for you."

"Well now, that's not a deal. The stuff I gave you on packaging was all for your own damn good. That's why you took it. We need to talk about interstate inspections and that goddamn security crap too."

"Nope," Bryce said. "We aren't going there, Will."

I decided to give Pauly a look to see if he wanted to play good cop or bad cop. To my surprise, he seemed to be playing good cop, which meant to me that I could have all of my packaging language like Bryce said and maybe another inch or two on the other stuff.

"I think, if you snakes don't mess up the language over the weekend," I said, "that we can start with this leg of the three-legged stool going into the bill on the floor."

Bryce started to act like he was getting up, and I threw one more thing out. "If I can get an agreement that the bill has to go to conference committee so we can keep talking about the other two legs of the stool, I'm sure Senator Alderman will agree to that."

Bryce immediately retorted, "No way!"

I looked back at Pauly.

"Let us think about that one, Will," Pauly conceded.

"Over the weekend?" I asked.

"Sure, Will. Nothing can happen till Monday anyway," Pauly said.

Bryce got up and walked away coldly but without stomping and pouting.

"He must be insane to party with," I said.

"He doesn't like the squeeze you're putting on him and neither do I. You need to quit having so much fun doing it."

"Oh, come on Pauly. You know I'm getting fucked on this bill without some of the other two things. And no matter how hard he tried to act like he was giving me something, you know I'm gonna be on the phone with Charlie in a few minutes to tell him I just need one more inch. You and I know he's gonna make you give it to me. Why don't we just skip the act and get right to the bottom line? Otherwise, your asshole partner there will have to keep meeting with me."

"You know that's what I want to do. Give me the weekend," Pauly said. He hurried to catch up with Bryce who was halfway down the hall already.

"Be good, Pauly," I said to his back as he walked away.

Two minutes later, I was on the phone to Charlie telling him where we were.

"So when they tell me they have a deal, that's not true?" he asked.

"I'm not telling you they'll lie to you, it's just that I need one more thing agreed to, at least in principle, before you move the bill to third reading."

"So it would just be easier to make sure they know I want your agreement before I do anything?"

"Exactly."

"No problem." It was all he needed to hear and then the phone went dead.

I planned to take the weekend off, but Pauly called me at 11:00 the next morning while I was in my luxurious high-rise office. I hated being there so much, I only went in on Fridays. As cool as I thought the view was when I first walked in, I never really adjusted to the penthouse feel of it. With the legislators already gone, I had no place else to go without looking like a homeless person who had just stolen a suit off the rack at Jos. A. Banks.

"Pauly, you have got to be shitting me! I didn't know you got up before noon these days."

"Will, please dial your shit down for once," he said.

"Fire away, sir."

"You got a deal," Pauly said with a weak attempt at enthusiasm.

"What? I haven't even told you what I want on the second and third things."

"No, you asshole. We have a deal on the packaging, tamper-resistant packaging, and scanning language, and an agreement that we can talk more about the other two things in conference committee."

"And you want me to tell Charlie for you?" I asked.

"Yes. Did I already call you an asshole once?"

"You did, and I will. Of course, Charlie will have to make a deal with Representative Miller too," I reminded him.

"I don't expect you to trust me, Will."

"I'll lay it out for Charlie then. I'll read the amendments when you have it ready Monday morning. There better not be any of your famous mistakes in it."

"There won't be any mistakes, Will. Bryce would explode if any-one made another one. You're under his skin, you know?"

"I sure hope so. I'll talk to you Monday."

. . .

On Monday morning, I got a chance to review the three amend-ments and was mildly surprised that they were written exactly as they should have been. I still didn't see why they needed to be in separate amendments, until the time came to present them on the floor that afternoon.

My pal Senator Alderman, who had filed all three amendments, only moved the first amendment on the floor and let the other two die without moving them. I was ready to explode.

I fired off a text message to Charlie while he was still on the floor:

What the fuck are you doing? What happened to #2 and #3?!

> Don't worry about it. Miller is taking it to conference, and we already have his word on that.

Really, Charlie?! Really?!

> I know what you're thinking, Will. We need the bill to be incomplete when it leaves the Senate or there is no reason to go to conference committee.

Charlie, they've already agreed to #2 and #3. I want the other shit in conference. That's why I wanted this crap in the bill now, so Miller can't just agree to the bill as it is. If he does that, I never get 2 and 3. Jesus, Charlie.

> Calm down, Will. We are going to conference. Trust me.

There were about twenty T-shirt people watching the proceedings through the hallway window, likely not really understanding what they were looking at. The amendments were filed right on the deadline at 11:00, so by the time the bill was called they'd had a chance to read the three amendments.

Ethan Murphy walked up to me and with a tone of pure ignorance calmly asked, "What the hell is going on? That can't be what you wanted to happen." It sounded as if he wasn't completely sure one way or the other.

"Not exactly," I replied, trying to get my game face back on. "Legislators are stupid people. Sometimes we forget that out here. We have to walk them through their own jobs pretty slowly some days. This is one of those days." I turned around and hurried away like I was late for something. And I was.

I was late for a truly uncomfortable phone call with my client. Bethany was underwhelmed when I did great things. I couldn't wait to find out how she acted when something surprisingly bad happened. Surprises are for losers in this business.

I couldn't figure out if the reason for Charlie's procedural explanation was given to him by some staffer or Senate leadership or someone else. It was total bullshit. That was another big divide between the members of the legislature and the hallway, especially old dogs like me and Pauly. We knew the procedure better than all the rank-and-file legislators. So, when Charlie told me he needed to do something different because of some procedural issue, he didn't realize that I knew he was wrong. The only question was whether or not it was his fault.

13

The Statehouse still has several old-school phone booths, four on the north end of the third floor, and four on the south. There's a couple on the second floor also. They are elaborate structures made out of wood from Indiana white oak trees. White oak was used for most of the wood framing inside the building, most notably the doors, which weigh a ton.

The pay phones have been gone for a while, but people still use the booths to make private calls. Inside the phone booths, there's room for one chair and there's also a small built-in counter that nowadays is used for laptops and tablets. The near-soundproofness makes people forget that they aren't invisible too. It is hilarious to see someone throwing a temper tantrum on a conference call, especially without the sound. A great bonus is watching the expressions of someone listening to some horrible client request or idea that is a total waste of time. People flipping off their phone or making other obscene gestures at people who aren't there can be great fun too. But the best is sneaking up on someone who is falling asleep and slapping the glass. That one is my absolute favorite—and my inspiration to stay alert when I'm in one of the booths.

After a long day, when it's hot in the building, these little ventless chambers of misery can start to smell like a cross between a locker room and a Porta Potty. But if a private call needs to be made, we just don't have any place else to go. I stepped inside one of the booths and called Bethany. "We've had a little procedural setback," I said when she answered.

"Let me hear it."

I gave her the "just the facts" description.

"What's the next move?" she asked without an ounce of emotion.

"I just need to get the commitment that we'll get the language from the other two amendments put into a conference report, and then get back to focusing on the security and interstate issues."

"Okay. Keep me posted," she said.

Needless to say, our approaches and range of mood were wildly different. I couldn't decide if she was an extremely cool customer or if she had low expectations. Either way, she wasn't letting on that she was enraged like I was. Good.

Right after I hung up a text came in from Charlie:

> You need to go see Rep. Miller this afternoon and explain what we need to do in conference committee. I want to know that we are all on the same page before I let the Senate vote this bill on third reading.

> Any reason to rush? You fucked this up once already, maybe it should sit on the calendar for a few days. You know if you had just followed my plan . . .

Oh, Will, I didn't fuck it up. But if you
want me to slow-walk it a little I will.

I'll go see Miller today, but let it sit on
the calendar just for a day or two to
torture them a little. Can you do that?

Yes, smartass.

I'll let you know after I have met with
him. But please don't take any calls
from Pauly while it sits on the calendar.
He can sweat a little.

I got it—I got it.

By the time I met with Miller in his office around 4:00 that afternoon, Pauly and Charlie had already briefed him. When I told him I
needed the other two amendments put in, he was already agreeable
to it, as long as Pauly and I were in complete agreement.

That was sort of what I'd thought. Miller was covering for Pauly.
Entirely.

Miller did commit to going to conference committee though,
which was what I needed. On the surface, all was well. I just didn't
trust anyone or anything by that point.

Charlie agreed to sit on the bill, and I'd make sure he did that for
at least a week before the Senate got their last vote on it. And Pauly
agreed to listen to our ideas about tweaking the security language.
I'm sure by "tweak" that he meant nothing meaningful, but the
more we talked, the better my odds.

Charlie called the bill for its vote on third reading that following Monday, and it passed on a 33–15 vote. I was a little surprised

at the number of no votes. I didn't know that many of them had any kind of problem with the bill. No matter. There still weren't nearly enough votes to defeat it, so I still needed to keep working on my deal.

For the next three weeks or so, they'd keep coming up with new excuses why they wouldn't budge further, and I'd keep making them look like unreasonable asses. Maybe they'd crack a little.

A week after the final floor vote, Representative Miller filed his dissent motion on the bill, which forced it into conference. That was exactly what I wanted, and it confirmed that Miller was keeping his word.

One member from each caucus makes up a conference committee. Senator Alderman would also be on the conference committee, and two random Democrats. This is the part of the session designed for negotiation to work out the differences between the chambers. But in this case it was all about me and Pauly, but on a tight time line.

The first thing I was able to get Pauly and Bryce to agree to was something they originally didn't want to. I got them to agree that the locking mechanisms and video surveillance equipment that may already be in an existing facility before July 1, 2014, or last year, *could* or *may* be approved by the ATC. The "may" and "shall" provisions of any bill become the most important part most of the time. Governmental discretion, especially regulatory discretion, is something lobbyists fight over every day.

In any case, this didn't fix the interstate problem obviously, or the crazy security firm language, but it might have been enough to keep TA in business in Indiana. Short of this change, the "America" part of the TA name was going to equal forty-nine states, not fifty.

It took a few meetings and plenty of approvals from both Bethany and Pauly's client, but we finally reached an agreement on the final version on Wednesday evening, April 15, 2015.

It was a little after 6:00 on that Wednesday night when Pauly and

I called "deal" on the bill. The amendments Charlie had neglected to call, and the discretionary and grandfathering language were to be added into the bill, and then we would be done. It should have been simple.

Then the morning of April 16 rolled around, a day I won't ever forget.

The House was scheduled to convene at 10:00 that morning. I was there with a paper copy of the proposed conference report to put in Representative Miller's hands. I had the doorman put a note on his desk on the floor of the House to let him know I was there with the hard copy. I could see him inside and the session did not gavel in immediately, but he was in no rush to come out and pick up the paper.

Finally, at about 10:30, he came out the main door in the middle of the House. I was standing right there to hand him the language.

"Will, I wanted to let you know that I've decided just to go ahead and agree with the version of the bill that passed out of the Senate. I'm tired of having this hanging out there and these T-shirt people are causing me trouble back in the district—"

"Whoa, whoa, Representative Miller. We have a deal! This deal I'm holding in my hand is the one we've been working on for over a month. You're not seriously going to renege on it now, are you?" I could feel the blood rushing to my head.

"Sorry, Will, we've run out of time."

"What the fuck are you talking about? I just sent you the deal last night!"

"I'm sorry it didn't work out, but that's what I'm doing." He turned around and went back into the chamber.

I could barely breathe. No one had ever done this to me. I had never even heard of anyone doing something like this. This was so unbelievable that I wasn't convinced it had actually occurred.

I stood there in the hallway, staring through the window, letting it sink in. Then I heard the Speaker of the House announce that Representative Miller's motion to dissent had been withdrawn and a motion to concur had been filed.

That made it real. He'd flat-out lied to me. He set me up. And I could tell by the way he told me and walked away that he thought I was going to simply accept it and move on.

That was a miscalculation he'd likely not forget.

After trying not to go completely postal for a few minutes, I decided to go get a drink of water and take a little walk. As I walked around the corner toward the Senate, I saw Pauly getting off the elevator.

I had to stop for a minute to keep from charging him and choking him right there in the crowded hallway. Miller didn't screw me on his own. I thought I was going to explode. Surprises are unsettling to most people, but the feeling that I had lost control was unbearable. This is the one thing that is hard for a player to accept, even with a warning. But when that control is taken from me, and by people who shouldn't be able to, it is enraging. I took two deep breaths, looked up at the stained glass above the rotunda for about three seconds, and went stomping up to him.

"What the fuck do you think you're doing, Pauly?" I yelled. Twenty or thirty people in the vicinity froze and looked over at us.

"Are you so fucking drunk or hungover to not even know what the hell is going on around here?"

I waited for him to reply, but he just looked at me. "Look at you—you're sweating last night's booze out and looking at me like you don't know what Miller just did! Did you think I was just going to let you fuck me right here in the Statehouse?"

By now, Pauly was breathing hard, as if he'd done something he didn't mean to. He was acting disoriented at my rage. One of his usual lawyers was sitting on a hallway bench not far from us. I looked right at him, practically inviting him to tell me to calm down, but all he did was subtly shake his head like he was trying to claim no involvement in whatever it was I was ranting about.

"What are you talking about, Will?" Pauly asked.

"Fucking Miller just pulled his dissent and concurred on the Senate version of the bill. Are you trying to act like you didn't give him the green light to do that? Fuck you, Pauly. No one is going to believe that bullshit—"

"Will, I don't know what you're talking about. Really, I don't."

"That's because you're a drunken mess. You know good and god-damn well that Miller didn't renege on me without your approval. I'm gonna fuck you up over this if it's the last thing I do. You finally made the big mistake didn't you, you fat fucking drunk."

Pauly looked rattled. I would be too if someone was ranting at me like I was at him.

"Will, we made a deal, and I plan on honoring it. I don't know what Miller did, but we had a deal."

I took another deep breath and gave his lawyer another glance. Then I breathed deeply again. I looked Pauly in the eye and put the index finger of my right hand right into his chest and calmly said, "You mark my words, and you mark the date on your calendar. I will make what I'm about to say to you my life's work: You will regret this fucking day. You hear me? You will regret—this—fucking—day."

14

stomped away from Pauly not knowing what to do or how to do it. I was in an unfamiliar place. I had to get out of the building before I did or said something I couldn't take back or recover from.

But the rage I had inside of my soul burned like fire. I was trembling with it. My hands were shaking like Pauly's probably were, but for different reasons.

My ire was all about my competitiveness and my acquired commitment to the protocols of the hallway. Unlike in a courtroom, battles like the one I was in with Pauly, and who knows who else, don't end with someone winning everything and someone losing everything. At least not very often. Political processes are generally give-and-take exercises, at least a little with things like this. So getting screwed by someone like Representative Chris Miller was not something I was going to take lightly.

To get swept like this could only happen to someone like me when the Speaker of the House, the president pro tem of the Senate, or the governor did it. Not when some nobody like Miller, who didn't know shit, reneged on a deal.

And what was Charlie Alderman's role? I couldn't imagine our friendship surviving this. If he didn't make a move to explain himself and give up plenty of the details about this colossal clusterfuck, he would be right there on my hit list with Pauly and Miller.

The sun would rise tomorrow, even in defeat, but that wasn't how my brain worked. I was hired to make things better for Bethany, and my expectation was that when this was over, she would tell everyone she knew in her DC world that I was the best contract lobbyist she ever hired. As things stood, that wouldn't be the report on me.

More importantly, for purposes of my next moves, whatever the hell those were, was that Miller broke protocol. He shattered it. And he didn't know that I was not going to just accept it. He also didn't know what kind of problem I could be.

Unlike Miller, Pauly knew that pissing me off was a mistake. He knew I meant what I said to him. He knew that I could be committed to a grudge as well as anyone and that I would never let this go. And he knew I was smart enough to mess this up for him.

Only the boys at the Winner's Circle the night before could say what had led to this stupid move by Miller. Pauly must have been hammered when he told Miller to go ahead and pull the plug on the conference committee. I actually did believe that Pauly was likely too drunk to remember what he had done. I also believed that he would have stopped it if he had been in the Statehouse a half hour earlier.

But it was too late. He had never gotten a dose of an angry Will before. I was betting he wouldn't enjoy it. I was committed to making sure he wouldn't enjoy it.

. . .

It would have been easy not to go to Grace that night, but I knew while I paced around in the living room of my townhouse that I needed to go. Even if I just listened. It was what I would recommend to someone else from the group if they didn't feel like going.

I rolled in right under the 7:30 wire, as usual. Instead of Greg Bryant giving me his customary "Oh thank God Will is here" welcome, I got a bit of a poke from Flip.

"I was starting to wonder if you cared about tonight," she said.

"You thought I forgot? That hurts," I replied.

The truth was I had forgotten that it was Flip's night to tell us how she got there. I had heard parts of her story over the years but in ten-minute segments.

I didn't know what chapter it was for her. I didn't care. I wanted to know everything about her, and hearing her talk about growing the grass in her yard for ten minutes would be like having my shoulders rubbed by a masseuse.

After forty-five minutes of the usual stuff, which was mainly torture for me waiting to hear Flip talk, Dot called on her.

"I was having a hard time seeing myself in love again when I came here," she began. She looked around the circle as she said it, making split-second eye contact with everyone there. She ended on me. The look she gave me either lasted thirty seconds or a blink of an eye. I lose time in her stares.

I immediately imagined she was talking only to me. At least I thought it was my imagination. It felt like we were the only two people in the room, and as far as I was concerned, we were.

"After my husband left, all I did was work and mother for three or four years. I'm glad I did. My girl needed that from me, and I needed to give her all of me. When she started school, and my shift at the hospital was cockeyed with her school schedule, I was in my house by myself from time to time during the day. I had lived there since she was born, but it was the first time I ever had the place to myself. Cool, right? It was initially, but pretty quickly I began to feel like a twenty-six-year-old empty nester. And I was all alone."

I'd never imagined her as sad or lonely. Or that she was struggling with anything. It's pretty stupid to think that about anyone, but what single mom anywhere hadn't struggled with something? I can't imagine my kids being raised by me alone, or by their mom alone. It took a lot from both of us.

Flip had hypnotized me again, like I knew she would.

"I realized that I missed being in love. And that even though I had loved someone, I had never been loved the way I thought I should be. Those little stretches of time alone in my own house helped me realize how much I wanted to experience that. Being here made me believe it was possible."

"When did we—this bunch—help you believe that?" I said. "I mean did I miss a week when that was covered? You and I started coming about the same time and neither of us miss much."

"I don't know when it happened, but I know this is where it happened." She and I locked eyes as she finished. "Maybe it's just that as my understanding of God and my connection to Her has grown, I feel like I'm easier to love. I don't know, but that's what I think it is."

· · ·

That night I sat down at my computer and searched for solutions to my problem. I needed to find a bill that could take amendment #2 regarding the cardboard in the clean room and amendment #3 regarding the scannable codes. There had to be a bill or two out there that I could slide these things into.

Getting those amendments in somewhere else would be the victory I wanted. I wouldn't be able to get the interstate inspection issue or the crazy security language fixed; those would be fights for another day. Those were the sections of the bill that ended up in federal court anyway.

At this stage in a legislative session, there are usually about a hundred bills that are lingering around, headed to a conference committee for one reason or another. These bills become available vehicles for last-minute crap like my stuff. In the old days, conference committees were truly free-for-alls, devoid of any discernable rules. With the internet and the extensive video coverage of committee hearings, legislators are less open to just dumping things into bills with no connection to the subject matter.

I found a few bills that I liked pretty quickly. One of them was a tobacco sales regulation bill. The other one was a pharmaceutical/prescription monitoring bill. Both were in the healthcare space. No one in the healthcare lobby would care about my stuff being thrown in there.

I'm sure Pauly and his puppets thought I was just going to stomp away mad. But they were wrong. I was going to load up my machine gun and open fire on all this first thing in the morning.

I called it the machine gun. Guys like me have those thirty "pals" who would do anything for us when we need them. And there was also a good list of others who knew that my firm and my clients spent plenty of money on campaigns. This bunch knew that if they could help me without screwing up any of their own stuff or having to work too hard, it would pay off for them.

My people were largely a different group than Pauly's. I could count on them to take my calls and at least entertain my ideas, no matter how crazy they might be. I don't always get my way, but this is really a stretch of every session that my value skyrockets. Little tweaks, little date changes, a change in a number or a rate—those little things really add up for clients at the end of a session. I didn't stop till the final gavel fell in any year, and it usually paid my roster dividends.

It's because I knew how to use a machine gun. The first step in spraying the legislature with bullets was getting to the Statehouse early. The more people I could pick off before the competition arrived the easier the whole thing would be.

And Pauly never came in early.

My first targets were the two leaders of the House Public Health Committee. From my research, I knew that the health chairman voted against Representative Miller's bill during the first half, and the ranking minority member had done me a favor at the end of every session for the last five.

I would get there early with my language in hand, on a flash drive, ready to email it, whatever it took. The legislative leaders on healthcare were my targets for my firing line. I was going to have everything packaged up nice and neat and made simple for them. They wouldn't be able to tell me it was too much work. The work was already done.

The Republican chairman lived on the Ohio River in the south. The Democrat ranking member lived on Lake Michigan in the north. One was African American, and the other one was definitely not. They couldn't have been more different in infinite ways. But they were deal makers. Big deals and small ones, and they made deals with each other.

With a text message here and a phone call there, I made it into the committee ranking member's office by 8:00.

By 8:15, I was walking out of the Statehouse altogether, heading to the Hilton a block away to meet with the committee chairman to get him to agree.

By 9:00, I was waiting outside the Senate Health chairperson's office waiting for her to arrive at the Statehouse. I wanted to see if she would let this great idea from the House go into a bill that was in a conference committee that she was in charge of. Lo and behold, these three legislators had trading to do anyway on some healthcare thing that I didn't care about. My involvement just moved it along and got the House guys to give in to the Senate chairperson. She got her way a lot.

By 10:00 the three of them had agreed to their deal, which included all the nonsecurity items that would have gone into the bill that Pauly and Representative Miller had screwed me on the day before.

Two hours. It took me two hours. That was fast, even for me.

And Pauly wasn't even in the building yet. I don't even know if Miller or Alderman were there yet either. It didn't matter. I had already gotten around all of them.

Miller was going to be pissed off. He probably thought that when he fucked me over yesterday that the protocol was for me to lie there and take it. I knew he was going to find out otherwise. I didn't know it would happen the next day.

Representative Miller broke the rules when he reneged on our deal. He was going to have a hard time finding sympathy because of that. And I didn't give a shit.

These kinds of conference committee deals needed to be approved by the caucuses in both chambers—Republican and Democrat, Senate and House—before they could be officially signed and put up on both floors for the final vote. Somebody would have to fight pretty hard in any of the caucuses to stop a negotiated deal by this group of players, but who knew what Miller or Charlie might try when they caught wind of it.

My machine gun deal steamrolled them. I didn't hear a peep from any of them other than confirmation that it was signed and done. All of twenty-four hours after Miller screwed me and I told Pauly I would make him regret flipping on me, most of what I wanted got done.

I hadn't talked to Pauly again since I poked him in his chest. And I still had not heard a word from my pal Charlie Alderman.

Sadly, I didn't think I would.

15

When a long session ends in Indiana at the end of April, it also marks the beginning of spring for us, albeit six weeks late. And springtime is a wonderful time to be in Indianapolis.

For those of us who spent the prior four months obsessing about every little thing that went on in the universe of Indiana politics, spring was the most glorious time of the year for the reason that the state legislators had returned home and were cleaning up all the personal and professional messes in their own lives that had been created in or by their absence. We didn't have to worry about them for a little while because not only were they not legislating, they were also not running for reelection. They also weren't raising campaign money, at least not very hard.

Long sessions, like the one we finished in 2015, were always in odd-numbered years. That meant no elections for state offices, and thank God for that.

That long stretch of time off work made everyone on the planet want to do what we did for a living. It was like summer vacation used to be for public school teachers. It was like the off-season for professional athletes, and it felt a lot like that because of the rehabilitative nature of it.

When the dust settled after the 2015 session, things seemed to return to the usual groove for me. My life was just as it had been for the previous several years. Oh, sure, Pauly and I wouldn't be friends anymore, but what difference did that make? We never spent much time together anyway. The same went for Senator Charlie Alderman. Representative Chris Miller and I never were friends, and now I wouldn't have to worry about the hassle a friendship with him might have been.

It was time to enjoy life.

The month of May meant one thing: the Indianapolis 500. For me, rebuilding my golf game for the actual Indiana golf season was the other thing, but the 500 was what defined Indy for much of the world. Years ago, the entire month of May in this town was dominated by the track and the race. In the peak of the 500's popularity, the track would open the Sunday after the Saturday running of the 500 Festival Mini-Marathon. The "Mini" is a 13.1 mile street run, which features one trip around the 2.5 mile Indianapolis Motor Speedway oval. Some of the best runners in the country compete in it. Those athletes blend with 30,000 others—a wild variety of runners, joggers, and walkers just trying to see if they can finish. They come from every state in the country and more than a dozen others, but the people around central Indiana make up the bulk of the herd. Soon after, the good people of the city would start conspiring which days of the month they could play sick from work so they could go out to the Speedway and watch cars test and prepare for the greatest spectacle in racing.

Tuesday through Sunday for the rest of the month, from morning to night, was beer-drinking season at the track. There were corporate tent parties in the infield where people in suits would show up for fried chicken, burgers, potato salad, and coleslaw, and then theoretically return to work. At these parties there would be guided tours of the garage area and Gasoline Alley, where the premium guests would get to walk through and meet the racing teams tinkering on their ground rockets. Maybe one would get lucky and run into one of the Andrettis, Unsers, or Foyts for a picture or an autograph.

Seniors in the high schools organized skip days to sneak out to the track for an afternoon in the sun with a cooler of beer. Sure, they got in trouble for it from time to time, but it was a rite of passage around here.

I am a race fan. That is not the same as a racing fan. I don't watch other races. I don't care about them. For me, the 500 is the *only* race.

Racing as a sport has gone through an abundance of change and popularity since I moved to town thirty years ago. But even in its worst years during that stretch, 250,000 people still showed up in Indy on race day.

The quality of the race is as good as it has ever been, but the changes that have taken place at the track and on race day are impossible to miss. Having been so many times, one might expect me to be nostalgic about the way things were. I'm not. The event is better now than it has ever been, in my opinion.

The lawless partying that took place in and around the track was once legendary. The drunkenness, drug use, and nudity were infinite. Kegs, biker gangs, amateur strippers, and fighting were the features of the Snake Pit, an area in Turn 1 of the infield where anarchy was the only rule. "Show me your tits!" was the standard rally cry yelled at any woman who braved the area. I can recall witnessing two grown people having sex in the back of a van with all its doors open and a small crowd watching and cheering.

You get the picture.

For a variety of reasons, and thank God for all of them, that has all slowly changed since the '90s. The event started to resemble a more normal sports attraction. Families wanted to go and watch the actual race.

Today there are noticeably more women, girls, children, and minorities coming to the race. It's possible that there are fewer people getting drunk, but I saw most of my first twenty races through the eyes of a drunk myself so how the hell would I know.

In any case, for a lobbyist, the biggest, most expensive, most exclusive event around is always the water that attracts us, the fish. No matter how it continues to evolve, the 500 will likely always be the biggest thing in Indianapolis.

Historically, the Motor Speedway gives tickets to every legislator. The seats are great for the pre-race festivities, but they aren't the best for watching the race. And race day is big on pageantry. If a legislator wants a great place to watch the entire race, they're better off calling one of us. Race-ticket dealing is a bit of a sport.

The pre-race festivities truly are something to see. The 500 runs on Sunday of Memorial Day weekend. It is the way Indianapolis celebrates that holiday, and we do it grander than any place else. The tributes to veterans, the military fly-overs, the dramatic playing of "Taps," and the release of the balloons are sentimental favorites of race day. They are celebrations of the holiday, but many of us from Indy only celebrate the holiday at the Speedway, so it's all we know. Throw in the homegrown standard, the singing of "Back Home Again in Indiana," and it is about a thirty-minute stretch of pre-race festivities that define our city.

While many do, I don't take legislators to the race. I arrange for seats, but I don't want those guys sitting with me. I love the race too much to entertain that day.

It's pretty important to go to the race with someone you like, since it's sort of an all-day affair. There are lots of race-day traditions on who goes with whom. I wish my boys gave a shit about it. I'm sure they will when they get older.

Greg would have been the perfect partner to go to the old Snake Pit with, but it didn't really exist anymore. He looked scary enough to be one of the hosts, and his oversize tattooed ass offset my country club look. We might as well go to the race together. I couldn't take his kind to the country club.

"I will say this for you: you get good seats," Greg said as we walked through the main gate near Turn 1 at the corner of 16th Street and Georgetown Road.

"You gotta be somebody to get tickets like this. You wouldn't know about that," I replied. "On the other hand, you could spend your way into this section."

"I haven't had a chance to ask, mainly because I don't care, but how did everything turn out in the Statehouse last month?" he said.

"It turned out well enough. No one got hurt too badly unless you count feelings."

"You feel better or worse about that shit job of yours?" he said. "I gotta tell you, I feel pretty good about your job today."

"I don't know, man. I got fucked with a little by a guy who has no business fucking with me, and it makes me wonder what that's all about. It's too complicated to explain, but I can't figure out the angle on it."

"Are you talking about that vaping thing?" he asked.

"Yeah. It's a scam or a scheme of some sort, and I seem to be the only one who cares about it. Not because I actually care, but because I hate not knowing what the play is from these assholes."

He looked at me with a little confusion. "Did those T-shirt people come out okay?"

"You mean your family?" I said with a laugh.

"Yes, smartass. My brethren. God's children," he said.

"They're screwed, or they will be next year. That is unless a federal lawsuit kills the whole thing. But hey, that's not my job or problem."

"You don't give a shit about them because it's not your problem?" he asked.

"That's why I hate this job, remember? Why don't you just shut
up and enjoy the seats before I tell security that you stole your ticket
to get into this section. That's a story they would believe."

I commenced greeting everyone I recognized in the Paddock
Penthouse, where our seats were. I knew about ten people from
the political world in our section. Of course Greg didn't know
a soul. Thank God none of them were sitting too close to us. I
had come to enjoy keeping my personal life a safe distance from
the swamp.

Thanks to Greg, I couldn't help thinking about the Statehouse
T-shirt people during the race. I wondered what they were going
to do. The vape shop model that they invested in wouldn't last past
next year, barring some unforeseen intervention.

Greg's comment about them was innocent, but it disturbed me.
Like I said, those people weren't my problem, but Greg was asking
me a bigger question.

Should I give a shit about people who aren't my problem? Put
that way, of course the answer is yes. With the session over and since
actively not caring about those people as a lobbyist didn't work out
well either, I was wondering why I should keep giving them the
shoulder.

Yes, I simply call it "the shoulder," and not "the cold shoulder."
The shoulder is an emotionless version of the classic descriptive.

I'd never spent much time trying to figure out why putting those
guys out of business was such a vital part of Pauly's plan. I still didn't
realize why it mattered or why it was time sensitive.

Now that I was thinking about it, I never knew much about
Pauly's client. He made me think his client and Bethany would want
the same things in the end. Bethany never communicated to me that

she wanted these mom-and-pop stores eliminated, though. She also never gave me any theory as to why Pauly should want that.

I knew Bethany's lawyers were prepping to sue the State of Indiana in federal court over many things specific to the law, but mostly on the grounds of discrimination and interstate commerce arguments.

For the life of me, I couldn't figure out why Pauly's company stood alone. I had the time to spend a little energy trying to figure it out, and I guessed I should.

Juan Pablo Montoya won his second Indianapolis 500 that year. He was a handsome Colombian driver who won the 500 his first time in 2000. He'd raced on every circuit, from F1 to NASCAR, but any two-time winner of the 500 was considered immortal. No one could get that lucky twice.

Another thing that the casual observer often overlooked about the race was that it had started as a showcase for the auto industry's latest and greatest technology a century ago. Indiana has always been a big part of the auto industry, and back then we were bigger than Detroit.

The car, the builders of the car, the team that preps the car, and so on are actually a bigger deal than the driver, at least for us purists. But we give the ceremonial milk to the driver to drink after he wins.

I never liked that part of it.

Walking out of the track that day, Greg said, "Thanks for bringing me with you to mingle with the royalty in the penthouse. You should have invited your girlfriend, Flip. I bet those seats would have impressed her."

"Shut the fuck up," I said with zero conviction.

"Whatever. I see how you two make eyes at each other. I don't know why you don't just go for it. If she looked at me like that it would be on."

"Are you serious? No one is ever going to look at your ugly ass like Flip looks at me—at least how I think she looks at me."

"You're such a pussy. Anyone can see what's going on there. I'm almost embarrassed to hang around with you it's so obvious."

"Like I said before, shut the fuck up."

I hated that he was right. For someone like me, who strives to appear fearless at all times, my cowardice with Flip was hard to hide. Yes, I was too chicken to make a move. What did I have to lose, except the dignity that I once had so long ago that I didn't even recall when or how I lost it?

No one downtown would believe that I was scared to make a move on a young woman of no particular importance. She was just a woman, like any other woman. I wished I could convince myself of that, just long enough for me to go for it like my big ugly friend said I should.

16

obbyists are great at getting to the bottom of gossip. And anecdotal evidence? We're all pretty damn good at that too. It's when we're on a search for actual facts that we find ourselves feeling around in the dark.

I got back to my penthouse office the Tuesday after Memorial Day and started daydreaming about the things I didn't know about Pauly's client, Indiana Tobacco and Liquid, LLC. I'm sure that when the lawyers or staff at my firm walked by my office and looked inside, they saw me in my trance.

In the Indiana Statehouse, there is almost never any reason to question whether the client or company someone is representing is legitimate or not. It is rare for a lobbyist to speak up in a meeting or testify in a committee on behalf of some entity of any kind and be asked questions like "Is your client incorporated?" or "How many employees does your client actually employ?"

This information is offered by guys like me all the time, especially when the information establishes credibility, but rarely does a legislator ask.

I logged into the Indiana Secretary of State's website and started searching for the basics, such as did the "Indiana" company even exist?

It did. I would have been shocked if it didn't. But there were a couple of things about it that seemed strange to me.

It filed for its business license on November 15, 2014. That meant that the business was founded right around the time that Pauly and God knows who else started prepping for the legislative initiative.

That wouldn't mean much to the legislators who advocated for the bill Pauly wanted passed. In fact, legislators would likely say that it made perfect sense for a brand-new company to want regulatory certainty before they made the really big investment—like building a plant.

I could see how a legislator could be convinced that it made sense. What was being overlooked, though, was that no one seemed to be asking about how Pauly and presumably his list of lawyers in the background were being paid. The company could not have generated a penny of revenue between the time that it formed and when Pauly began representing it.

Pauly made good money from his marquee clients. Otherwise, he was paid about the same as I was. But that asshole Bryce? He was one of the most expensive lobbyists in the hallway, since he was double-charging as a lobbyist and a lawyer. There were only a few people in the hallway who fit this bill, and it wouldn't surprise me if Pauly had a couple of them on his team. For the amount of time that I knew he invested in the project, Bryce would need $100K, minimum. Hell, I was being paid $50K. Who the hell was paying them?

From the corporate filing, there was only one officer of Indiana Tobacco and Liquid, LLC: Lance Meridian Jr.

For people in Indianapolis, Meridian is a familiar name. Not like Rockefeller or Vanderbilt, though. It's the name of one of the most prominent streets in the city. Meridian Street runs north and south and divides the city's east side from the west side. From 38th Street all the way to 86th, Meridian is lined with old-school mansions, and the governor's residence is on it.

I always assumed "Meridian" was some important family name. It turns out, for Indianapolis anyway, it actually is just a street. The original planner of the city, Alexander Ralston, named it. It seems to have been named appropriately, as the word is defined as "of or relating to midday or noon." On a map, that's what Meridian Street looks like: twelve o'clock.

But Lance Meridian's name rang a bell for me for different reasons. It was because I confused him with his dad, Lance Sr.

Lance Sr. had recently made a bunch of money selling off his start-up company for a little under $1 billion. The company sold and distributed accessories and things for wireless phones. I never really knew what they made or who they sold their products to, but when the company was bought a few years earlier it was big news around here.

I wouldn't know either one of them if I saw them. I only knew the name from stories I read in the *Indianapolis Business Journal*. In that regard, it was a big name that meant "recent influx of cash" to me. It would seem with a name like that, coming on the heels of a nine-figure corporate buyout, investing in a new market made sense.

But it was Jr., not Sr., who was the CEO of Indiana Tobacco. And he never showed his face, and his name was never mentioned during the session. In fact, when I found it on the Secretary of State website, it was the first time I had heard their family's name since the buyout four or five years before.

If I had been Pauly, I would have been trotting this guy all around the place. It would have made the whole venture seem more real, not less. But then again, I didn't know if Lance Jr. was sharp or just a trust-fund brat who didn't know shit and couldn't pretend that he did.

The other thing was that the address of the company was in a downtown residential neighborhood. It wasn't in a business district, and it wasn't a place where some fancy new manufacturing facility would ever be built. It looked to me from a Google Map search that it was probably where Lance lived.

Which led me to part two of my amateur private investigation exercise.

The Indiana Lobby Registration Commission requires that lobbyists like me, Pauly, and a few hundred others report every six months what we were compensated to do. The reporting period ended at the end of April and the reports were due at the end of May. I began looking for what this Indiana company paid their lobbyists and who all they had on their team.

This is where the bullshit part of this entire bullshit story became obvious to me.

In less than five minutes I could see that Indiana Tobacco only listed three lobbyists working for them: Pauly, Bryce, and a third guy from one of the law firms who saw me poke Pauly in the chest. That tab should have been in the ballpark of about $250K.

The company reported spending a little over $18,000. My rate to Bethany was $4,000 a month. That meant for six months, my tab would be $24,000. This company was apparently getting these three guys for about seventy-five percent of what I was being paid. Total!

In a word, that was bullshit. It was just not possible that these guys were giving away their services. The numbers were so unbelievably low, it was almost as if they weren't even lying very creatively.

I spent the rest of the day scanning through different searches trying to find something—anything—that would show if this company was planning a construction project somewhere in Indiana. I found nothing.

These guys needed the law passed so they could build. No one asked them where they planned to build, and they never volunteered the location or the schedule. It had only been a month, but I suspected they weren't planning on building anything.

While lawyers in DC were preparing their lawsuit against the State of Indiana in federal court, they had no idea that I was scratching around this stuff in Indianapolis. Through Bethany, I was able to track what was going on there. Occasionally, she even asked me to join the weekly conference call with the legal team and industry coalition, just to answer the odd, stray question about Statehouse junk.

The conference calls were brutal. Litigators seemed a breed apart when it came to running mouths. I was truly only there to answer the occasional question like "Which legislator said this?" or "Was there someone who testified or spoke publicly about that?"

But a funny thing happened while I was half-listening in on one of the weekly conference calls in early June. One of the lawyers made a seemingly passive statement about the security firm definition in the law. I couldn't tell which lawyer was talking, but in the middle of a long-winded legal rant, he said, "And this security firm definition was written for one, and only one, security company on the planet. I'm betting no matter how hard we search, we won't find a second firm in the world who can legally meet the security firm definition in this law." I literally jumped out of my chair when he said that. Of course! This was the entire scam. How could I be so stupid? There would only be one security firm. In the entire nation, there would only be one. It was brilliant.

No one would be able to get a license to be a manufacturer of e-liquid and sell their product in Indiana unless this one security firm said so. Pauly's real client was the security company.

But my problem still hadn't changed all that much. It had only shifted. I didn't know who this mystery security company was, and figuring that out might be harder than finding out where they planned to build a plant.

17

"Usefulness" was Danny's response to the opening question for the spirit group that week. What is your purpose? Life's purpose. That was the question.

Of course, Danny thought that way. Anyone could see that in him.

I decided to announce the obvious to him. "No shit, Danny," I said with a chuckle. "We all know you review your day based on how many boxes you've checked off on your to-do list. My Dad was just like that. He was a little older than you, but I assume this is just a boomer thing."

"I think it is a little bit. But my to-do list is pretty important, you know? It's not so much my obsession with trying to shrink it or complete every task on it, but by making it a useful list in the first place," he said.

"Useful." I love that word.

It's funny how we all spend so much time thinking we are accomplishing things big and small with our assorted tasks. More accurately, most of those tasks are only designed for one thing: to serve ourselves.

That's what Danny was talking about—making the list right matters more than just having some random, self-serving list.

"Keeping my own shit together is useful in that it means I need less from others. But I have more to offer than just keeping my own shit together. Most of us do," Danny continued. "We are all well aware of what a smartass Will is, for example—"

"Wait a minute there, boss!"

"—but I see all his attempts at wit one way: he is trying to brighten everyone's day. It doesn't always work, but it usually does."

"You don't get anything for sucking up to me, D," I said.

"He's right, Will," Dot said. "Maybe if you could identify the usefulness in what some must think is totally obnoxious of you, it might become less obnoxious and more useful."

"How the hell did this become about me?" I asked.

"It's not about you, smartass," Danny said. "I had the floor, remember?"

"Yes, sir. And I am happy to yield back to you, oh great one."

"See what I mean?" Dot added.

Flip sat there smiling at me with her easy smile, not displaying even the most remote temptation to chime in on any of it.

It's meetings like this that really made a difference for me. What would any God say to the question "What is life's purpose?" Usefulness to others would have to be in that answer somewhere. Regardless of the church, it would have to be in there.

. . .

Summertime for a lobbyist who is in the right frame of mind can be a glorious season. Those with kids have time to go on trips or coach sports teams. Many of us serve on nonprofit boards of some kind, and this is the time of year that those endeavors get the most attention we can give.

And it's golf outing season.

Outings are terrible for one's actual golf game. Every tee shot is an opportunity to swing the driver as absolutely hard and fast as anyone can in hopes of hitting it fifty yards farther than the player's capabilities. It's like gambling on the horses in the OTB—it actually works out ten percent of the time.

So golfers who care about their golf game, like me, have grown kind of tired of playing in them. But if someone is hoping to kill an afternoon in the sun, drink beer, and eat cookout food, the old golf outing routine can be fun.

The young folks really like them. And young lobbyists are the best at gossip. It's one of the many reasons I love the young people in the biz. Go figure.

Ironwood Golf Club hosts a lot of outings, too many really, but the routine is on autopilot. In mid-July, the House Republican outing is up first. The Republicans' majority of the 100-member House has ballooned to 71 and that makes for a crowded golf course. First, because that's a good ten or fifteen more members than they should have. Second, and more important, every lobbyist in the business better be there because their quorum proof majority means they have total control. Even the labor goons would be there.

I may not be much of a competitive player in the real world, but in the political golf outing world, I'm notorious.

"Good morning, kids! Have you all been working on your speeches for second place? I hope so, because my team is loaded again," I announced to my favorite group of young folks milling around on the practice green that serves as the front lawn of the clubhouse at Ironwood.

"Will, what do you do with all your trophies?" one of my young frat boy pals asks.

"I used to have a trophy room at my big house, but when I moved downtown, I had to purge them. Just not enough space. Now, I only keep trophies for one year and then I recycle them, unless I see that the plastic is not recyclable. Then I throw them in the trash right there at the golf course, immediately following the photo op."

"I'm sure the fundraiser loves to see that," he replied.

"Well, I do it with a great deal of charm," I responded. "Enough about me, what's the skinny?"

One of the young women piped up. "We were just talking about how ever since Governor Pence ended his political career on the Religious Freedom Restoration Act, none of our friends in his office want to work there anymore. Thoughts?"

"Who the hell would want to? The morning prayer he makes all the staff show up for is enough to run half the smart ones off. And after that, there would only be one smart one left, and that one can't be all that smart," I said.

But then the young man mentioned something important. "I hear Chris Miller is still pissed off at you for whatever it is you did on that vaping thing."

"Oh, really? Well, he better buckle up. It's going to get worse—for him," I said with a devilish sneer.

"Someone said the other day that the whole thing was about marijuana," the young lady added. "What's the story there, Will?"

"Marijuana? I haven't heard that one. I guess I have to chase that down now. Thanks a lot. Who told you that?" I asked with a hint of surprise.

"I can't remember where I heard it," she said in what appeared to be complete honesty.

"Jesus. Now I won't be able to focus on beating your asses on the golf course while I track down the marijuana rumor. Pot used to be so much more fun when I was your age. Thanks a lot for ruining it," I said with a flash of my middle finger to the small group of twenty-somethings as we headed to our golf carts and got ready to scatter out on the course.

I played it as cool as I could, but I didn't need a new rumor on this shit. It was going to be a long afternoon anyway, but now I'd probably look like I was back in my trance.

I had no idea who to ask about marijuana. That is a strange place for a good lobbyist to reside. We often don't know the answer to a question, but we almost always know who does. Not knowing either is a fail—a big one.

As the proposed construction of an e-liquid manufacturing facility was the big whopper that Pauly and his boys sold, I am also certain that no one in the Statehouse voted for the bill last session because of any connection to marijuana. Indiana was one of only a few states that didn't have anything legal in the pot world—medical, recreational, or any derivative. Leaving this out of the discussion, if there is any connection to it at all, would be an unmanageable scandal. Even for Pauly.

I played like shit at Ironwood that day.

. . .

The next legislative session was six months away. The effective date of the law that was just passed was about a year away. There was a giant lawsuit being filed on it in federal court. The FDA was working on issuing rules on the whole thing, and they could preempt Indiana's new law all on their own. And almost no one in Indiana government—politics or media—gave a damn about any of it.

I worried that marijuana was something commonly connected to vaping, though, and I had a duty to report to Bethany what I'd heard, so I called her.

"I heard a hot rumor today at the House R outing," I said to her on the speaker in my Jeep.

"Oh yeah?" she said in a half-interested tone.

"One of my young gossip buddies from the hallway said she

heard this whole thing was supposed to be about marijuana. Now, I have no idea what that could possibly mean. Do you?"

"THC oil is available in states where marijuana is legal, and it can be vaped just like our juice is. But Tobacco America doesn't want anything to do with THC, marijuana, or any derivative. I don't get how this is about pot. Did you get anything more than that?" Bethany asked.

"No. This young lady wouldn't know anyway. She probably overheard someone talking and didn't get the whole context. But this would be complicating in any number of ways, no matter what the play is," I answered.

"Just keep your ears open. Our focus for the rest of the year is on the lawsuit, so anything you hear on the ground could help that. I'll let these guys know what you heard. Thanks."

I didn't know who the one and only security firm was. I also didn't know what the connection was to marijuana. Bethany wasn't asking me to do anything on any of that. Good for me. I could focus on my off-season like a normal lobbyist should.

It was summer after all.

18

August 13, 2015 was a memorable day for me. Greg, Dot, Danny, and I went out to eat before our theology group. Greg told me that Dot had invited Flip to join us, but I guessed he was just messing with me. He thinks she has a crush on me, which would be incredible if there were a single ounce of truth to it.

City Barbecue is not an Indianapolis-based joint, but I pretend that it is. I eat at two of them mainly, the one downtown and the one on Rockville Road on the west side, not far from Grace. The folks know me downtown. They know Greg out west.

Not much on earth smells better to me than barbecue. Even barbecue that doesn't actually taste good almost always smells good. Until it burns.

I walked in the door about five minutes late and spotted my gang in a booth in the corner. Flip *was* there, looking like she didn't belong. I smiled at the thought because none of us seem to belong with each other.

As I arrived at the booth, Dot asked Greg, "So all these local vapor shops are going to be out of business soon?"

"Hi, everyone. Jesus, Greg, you couldn't let me tell her the story, could you?" I asked.

"Hey, if you want to dominate the conversation, don't be late," he said.

By now, Greg had heard most of everything I knew about this whole vape saga but had reserved judgment and advice. I wasn't really looking for any. He thought Dot, Danny, and Flip would enjoy knowing a little more about what I did professionally.

I couldn't believe he was telling Flip everything. Like I wanted her to hear about the sleazy world I worked in.

"Well?" Dot asked.

"Yes, Dot. It looks like all the vapor shops are going to have to shut down after July 1. I would tell you the whole story, but I don't know what Sasquatch here covered and what he didn't."

"Sasquatch? That's a good one," Greg said. "I mean, coming from an angry elf—"

"We prefer little people, Kong," I snapped.

"Will you two knock it off?" Dot said. "I actually think this is interesting. What are you going to do about it?"

Over the past few years, any time there was some sort of problem with the government, I was the guy in the group who knew a little bit about who to call or when to call them or what to ask. It created the appearance that I was some sort of fixer for my friends. Secretly, it was a role I loved. Clearly, my friends thought I could fix this one any way I saw fit. I didn't see it that way this time.

"Dot, I don't know that I can help these people. Even if I could, I don't know that my client would want me to help them. This is what I get paid to do. Sometimes I don't get to just freelance in the Statehouse when I am on the job."

Greg decided it was the time to judge me. And out loud. "Oh, come on, Will. You know this whole thing is bullshit. You know these guys are getting screwed because they're the little guy, and you know that your client will survive either way. I've heard you say it, sort of, a half-dozen times."

"Here it comes. I knew you would snap eventually. So you think I ought to throw everything I have at helping these poor helpless souls just because I know shit that they don't. Right?"

"You're goddamned right I do! What the hell do you have to lose? You bitch about the shit everyone does in that place, but you're just like them. You know these guys are getting fucked, and you know they shouldn't be."

I looked at him, frozen, not knowing what to say. I knew he was right.

"Well?" Dot asked.

"I don't know that I can do anything about it," I said to her with a defeated tone.

"Let's change the subject. It's really none of our business," Danny added, throwing me a lifeline.

"I'm gonna go order some food," I said as I got up from the table and headed to the cashier.

Greg was right, and it sucked. It especially sucked to have to face it in front of my only friends—one of whom I was secretly hoping might actually be interested in me.

I was filling up my cup with Diet Pepsi—which was my only complaint about the place as a loyal Diet Coke drinker—when a well-dressed African American woman came up to me.

"Mr. O'Courtney?" she asked.

"Yes?"

"You probably don't remember me, but you helped my nephew get his life back on track a long time ago. Do you remember Kenyatta Robinson?"

He was one of my old students from my stint with the Department of Corrections.

"Yes, ma'am! Of course, I remember you, and I will always remember Kenyatta," I politely said.

"I saw you and wanted you to know that he is back in Chicago and doing well, thanks to you," she said with an appreciative smile.

"That's wonderful to hear. I knew there was a good man inside that child," I said with a touch of pride.

"You might have been the only one who thought that back then, but we are so glad you did. You probably didn't know it at the time, but if he hadn't met you, he'd be dead now. Meeting you saved his life, and when I saw you come in here, I just couldn't pass up the chance to say thank you."

"You are so welcome. Tell him I said hello and that I'm still here to straighten him out if he ever needs a little more help from Mr. O'Courtney." I giggled, putting air quotes around my name.

"I certainly will, and bless you," she said with a handshake as she returned to her table.

I turned to see Flip standing at the soda fountain behind me, looking at me with a most curious look in her eyes, and a slight little grin to go with it. She didn't speak, and I have no idea what she might have overheard.

Every once in a while, I came across some old acquaintances from those days. It had been a while since my last one. They always cheered me up—even though I was always a bit worried that someone might be mad at me for being hard on them or their families. It was a worry about something that had never happened one time.

Running into Kenyatta's aunt was an odd chance encounter that could not have come at a better time. Back at the table I found that the conversation had moved on. Thank God.

As I would expect, I had not heard Flip say a thing about the vape drama. She was always listening, but it was no surprise that she hadn't said a thing to me.

I knew this day would come. Did I really not consider what Greg and the rest of my people, my real friends, would say about my involvement with TA? He was only looking out for me. He knew that I knew that these people were getting screwed, as defenseless and unsuspecting folks do all the time. He knew that if I wanted to, I could find a way to help them. And he knew that at some point, I would have wished that I had.

I honestly didn't know what I could do. An opportunity to undo this mess hadn't presented itself to me in the representation of my client either. Even though I didn't know it very well, the T-shirters' story was different than my client's story. It was more compelling. At least it was if legislators cared about actual people.

Anyway, the shit Greg said to me got butterflies stirred up in my stomach for the first time. I was madder than hell when I got screwed last session, and that adrenaline came from pure rage. This was different.

It was as if I had subconsciously told Greg the confusing details of the story in the hopes that he'd spit them back at me with plain words. I guess that's a little like what we did in our group every week. Speak freely. Let others listen and hear with an objective ear and then give it back. That wasn't in any rule book or instruction guide that I knew of, but that was the flow.

At the meeting, the night's topic was about maintaining constant contact with God. We talked about this subject every four to six weeks, even though we could talk about it every week.

I was still a little rocked by what we'd talked about at dinner. It was clear that my friends thought I should throw myself and my livelihood in front of the train at the Statehouse. Fear was my only excuse for not doing exactly that. Contact with God should have helped me overcome that, right?

I opened the discussion after we got past the introductions: "Sometimes when I do something I am proud of or ashamed of, I have to ask myself if anyone else would be proud or ashamed of me, or it, too. Whether the people who matter most to me, or even God, would look at what I had done and say to me: 'I'm proud of you for that.' Or 'Yes, I agree you should be ashamed of that.' Good days are the ones when I am absolutely sure what God would say to me, or how He would judge me. Bad days are the ones when I'm not."

The dinner group knew what I was talking about. The other half-dozen folks in the room didn't have a clue. I was sitting between two guys who hadn't been at the restaurant, and I hoped one of them would take the bait and the discussion from there.

But Flip decided to speak up from across the circle, which was kind of out of order and *way* out of character for her. "I sometimes look at people who seem to be beaming and wonder, What is that about? What is causing their light? Why are they so . . . happy? Wondering about them and the details ends up making me happy too. And then I feel connected to them. The same goes for the dark. It's how I stay connected to God, by following the signs I see in other souls."

That sounded like a come-on to me. Of the three times in my life that I have been hit on, this was the best one yet. I didn't even care if I was just imagining it. No matter whether it was real or imagined, she was definitely saying that she was paying attention to me. Close attention.

After the meeting, while we were straightening up the room, she came over to me and asked, "Can I talk to you when we're done here?"

Oh, God! I thought. "Of course," was the only response I had in me.

Flip left the room and headed out before I did, and I started hustling to finish up straightening the room and get all my own shit together to rush outside.

Dot stopped me on the way out. "Slow down there," she said.

"Dot, I gotta get going," I said in an impatient huff. "What?"

"Take it easy, and just be yourself. That's all. Go!" she said as she waved me on like she knew what was happening with vivid clarity.

I got out to the parking lot, and I was scared to death of what Flip might say to me. I tried really hard not to look as scared as I was.

"Did the conversation at dinner upset you as much as it looked like it did?" Flip asked, confirming that she actually had been paying attention.

"It wasn't the conversation; it was the situation. Greg is right, and he knows it. He's been fighting the urge to say it out loud, probably hoping I would rise to the challenge without his intervention. I guess I need you guys to help me see clearly."

She gave me that damn hypnotic look without speaking for a second, or two, or three. I couldn't take it.

"What? Do you even realize what you're doing when you stare me down like that?"

"What am I doing?" she asked without an ounce of sarcasm.

"You're hypnotizing me, goddamnit."

"Oh, that. Maybe it's you doing that to me. Did you ever consider that?"

I took a deep breath. It was a loud, obvious release of tension, one that provoked that fucking easy smile of hers. "No, Renee. I don't have any secret Yoda Jedi powers."

"Renee? Interesting. I forgot you even knew my real name."

A second, slightly quieter deep breath spilled out of me.

"Before you completely deflate over there," she said, "I wanted to suggest a change of scenery for you."

"Huh?"

"My daughter and I go to brunch on Sundays. Sometimes we invite people to join us. Not always, but sometimes. What are you doing next Sunday around eleven?"

I had to get it together. "You want to change my scenery with brunch?"

"No. I mean yes. Well, you have to come over and meet her first, that's why I am asking you to come next Sunday. She won't agree to some stranger coming. You have to make a good impression first, before I ask her if we can invite you. It's sort of a process."

"How many people have made it through this . . . process?"

"Don't you listen in the meetings? No strange man has ever been invited, asshole."

She was right about that one. I knew that. "You know I was joking."

"Well, stop joking for a minute. This is important."

If she only knew. "Yes ma'am. I am in. All in. Just tell me how to proceed."

"That's exactly what I'm doing here. I couldn't wait for *you* to do it any longer. I need you to come by and see us after dinner on Monday or Tuesday night, just to say hi. She'll be doing her home-work or the dishes, but I want to give her a chance to check you out. You think you can handle that?"

"Hmmm. It will be tough. What should I wear? Or do? Or say?" I asked with a touch of excited sarcasm.

"Damn, Will. Just be yourself. She will either love you or she won't. But if you want to act, why don't you try acting like you are very happy just to see *me*. Yeah, right," she said as she walked toward her car.

"I can do that!" I called after her.

She turned to me as she walked backwards and gave me a one-handed wave that looked more like she was clenching and unclenching her fist, while flashing one last shot of her damn easy smile.

Did she just ask me on a date? And if so, did that mean I didn't have to feel like a creep anymore? The man-code on that was a resounding "hell yes." But it wasn't what a date used to feel like. It seemed more like an interview.

Either way, I had the distinct feeling that my life had just changed forever.

19

While back in the penthouse office that next Friday, in an enjoyable daydream about Flip, I got a strange phone call from a strange fellow. Matt Cobb was a lawyer who guys like me knew from the Statehouse, but the legislature was not really his specialty. He used to be one of the top staffers at the Alcohol and Tobacco Commission. I couldn't recall if he was the chief judge or general counsel or executive director. But that was his brand: he was an expert on anything that happened at the ATC.

The alcohol lobbyists knew him well. He represented the craft brewers in the state, which was what brought him to the Statehouse more than anything else. I had never dealt with him, so I could call him strange mainly out of ignorance of how he operated.

"I have a few clients who hired me to help them get their e-liquid manufacturers' licenses by the time all this stuff goes into effect next summer," he said. "There seems to be some concern that there might be an attempt to change the law this year, or lawsuits, or FDA rules, that might change the game between now and then."

"Yep. I would say the specifics of the licensing are still a little in flux because of all those things."

"Would you be willing to get together with me and walk me through what the story is? My guys are telling me about their view of the drama, but they are also telling me that you probably know the drama better than anyone."

"No problem, Matt. Shoot me some dates, and I will try to accommodate."

"On their way. Thanks, Will."

I had no idea who hired him. That was so often the game in the lobby. We all knew each other, but in a new arena, we always had to spend some time figuring out each other's interests.

Either way, I was gathering info from anyone who had it. I wouldn't be turning down any meetings at this point. Matt fired off a breakfast slot for Monday, and I was free so I took it. And as a bonus, we were meeting at Café Patachou. I would eat at Patachou with the Devil himself, look him in the eye and order the Overachiever Omelet because of the fresh horseradish that's in it. I wondered what the waiter would say if I asked for extra horseradish. Someday soon, I'd find out.

. . .

I walked into Patachou on Monday morning a little later than our 8:30 appointment. I saw Matt in the surprisingly empty restaurant at a table along Washington Street. Three other guys were sitting with him. That was a protocol problem, and Matt Cobb was about to get a scolding right in front of his clients, if that's who those three were.

As I approached, I saw that the table was covered with now-empty dishes. The four had all already had breakfast.

"Good morning, Matt. Am I interrupting something?" I asked.

"No, of course not," he said. "I want you to meet three of my clients—"

"Matt, you didn't tell me you were bringing clients. I thought I was meeting with you alone."

"I'm sorry, Will. Is that a problem?"

"It's an ambush, that's all. Was breakfast good? I thought that's what I was here to do. Eat. I wasn't prepared to speak with anyone who wasn't a lobbyist. We'll just have to see if I can be helpful."

"Again, sorry about that. I'm sure we can be productive. This is John Watson, his brother, Jeff, and Aarav Patel."

"Aarav, have we met?" I asked.

"You might remember me from one of the hearings last session," he said.

"Oh yeah, you testified in the House hearing before I was on the job. I remember you from the archive video," I said. "Well, guys. What can I do for you?"

"Bluntly, we want to know if the framework that was set up by the new law is going to survive or not," Matt said. "These guys want to prepare to get licensed next summer, but we are curious to know if the law is safe."

I laughed at him. Rudely.

"Is that funny?" Aarav asked.

"Honestly, yes. It is," I replied.

"Why is that?" he responded.

"Because I don't know anyone, other than the proponents of this shitty law, that would be merely *curious* about it. Everyone in the business should be against it, and that should include all of you too, unless you do something in the industry that I just don't get. So, being *curious* about it makes me *curious* about all of you," I said.

Then I followed up with, "Tell me what it is you guys do, if you don't mind."

John Watson didn't seem to appreciate my tone. "We distribute e-liquid and vaping components all over the Midwest, and Aarav manufactures the liquid and sells it retail. Is that good enough?"

I laughed again, sarcastically. "Uh, it's good enough for me. But it makes no sense to me why you wouldn't be *against* the law. In any case, Matt, your question is . . . what do I think is going to happen? Is that right?"

Matt responded nervously: "Yeah, that's what we wanted to talk to you about."

The waitress came over and asked if I needed a menu and what she could get me to drink. I was so pissed off at these guys already that I canceled my own breakfast.

"Nothing for me. I won't be here long," I said to her, announcing my agitation publicly.

I turned back to them. "Well, guys, I don't know what you know. But I will tell you what I know and what I'm doing. I assume you know about the federal lawsuit. Depositions are starting in that case now, but the trial won't be over before the effective date of the law on July 1. The FDA's rulemaking will be fully briefed and ready for a decision on their rule before July 1, but who knows when they will issue it. Someone will be filing a bill on my behalf repealing all the language with regard to the security firm. I'm sure other people have ideas of their own, but that's what I know."

John Watson continued combat mode with me. "Do you think your bill is going to pass?"

"I don't have any way of gauging those odds. There are a lot of moving parts on this one."

"Well, we can work with the law as it is," Watson said, "so why should we support your bill?"

This guy was just asking for my wrath, and I was happy to give it to him. "I don't give a fuck if you support my bill or not. You guys asked for this meeting, not me. Cobb, is there anything else I can do for you this morning?"

Matt Cobb shifted into damage control. "Take it easy, everybody. I think we got off on the wrong foot here."

"You're goddamn right we did," I said. "What the hell are you even offering me? In other words, why the hell am I even still sitting here? You didn't even wait to eat breakfast, which was the invite, dumbass. Jesus Christ, is this your first day?"

Cobb knew I would talk shit about him behind his back in the hallway if he didn't get the meeting back on track.

"Will, these guys are trying to figure out if they should join your side of the fight. We can agree it's a bad law, but they think they can comply with this shitty law, as you call it."

"I wasn't really shopping for people to join my team, and I don't think I want guys on it who think they don't need the law changed. Again, why am I here?"

Watson took over again, because he clearly thought very highly of himself. "The law isn't perfect, but we can get a deal done with the security company. If we try to make the law perfect, we might make it worse. And it might piss off the security company and hurt our ability to make a deal with them. That's our dilemma."

"Well, that is certainly a dilemma. *For you.* You might want to give a moment's thought to what this means to *me*! My client isn't even going to talk to the security firm that you think you can make a deal with. We are going to walk away from Indiana until this law is repealed or stricken down by the court. And what I do for my client in the Statehouse will not make *their* situation worse. I have never made a client's situation worse. Ever. If you think you can live with this law in some fantasy of yours, I don't need you with me. One more thing. I don't see how you joining me would help me at all anyway. Is there anything else we need to discuss?"

The four looked at each other confused and a little stunned. I have no idea why. They didn't offer me anything. They were only there to see if I could help them. Fascinating strategy.

I stood up, buttoned my jacket, looked at the three newbies, and say: "Gentlemen, it's been a pleasure." Then I turned to Cobb and said, "Matt, thanks for breakfast." I turned around and walked out.

After I shook off those relatively minor parts of the morning while walking to the office, I realized what they told me was actually valuable.

They thought they could cut a deal with the security firm. Why did they think that? Because the mystery firm was no mystery to them. They also thought their support of my agenda should mean something to me. Why did they think that? That one might just be a result of bad advice from Matt Cobb, or they might just think they had some political juice that I didn't see.

In any case, I didn't think I would be getting a Christmas card from them, and I didn't think we would be partners on this thing. That meant they would be with Pauly, for whatever that was worth. Pauly probably thought they were already with him anyway, since they believed they could cut a deal with the security firm.

I needed to solve the security mystery. Either these guys figured it out or they got recruited. Probably the latter. I probably should have tried to pry that out of them before I gave them the "fuck you" treatment. If Pauly's guys weren't going to manufacture or build a plant to manufacture, they couldn't control a market with no manufacturers. That's why they were recruiting guys like Cobb's clients.

And Pauly and Cobb spent time together representing alcohol folks at the ATC.

After I calmed down following the lovely breakfast I didn't actually have, my mind drifted to Flip, and I couldn't shake out of it. I was supposed to go see her and her daughter that night or the next night.

Everything about her was easy. Cool. Calm. I had no idea why the thought of her made me so anxious. She made me feel like a teenager.

152

Fuck it. I decided to text her, determined not to fuck it up.

Flip—are you busy?

Fifteen minutes passed. She was slow-walking me on purpose.

I was. Not anymore. RU?

> I was taking a nap while I waited for you
> to respond, but I'm awake again now.

LOL—smartass. What's up?

> Maybe I just wanted to know when I
> can see you.

Maybe? Took you four days to text/not
call to say "maybe?"

> Definitely. That's what I meant to write.
> Can I come over and meet your girl
> tonight or should we do it tomorrow
> night?

You remember where I live?

I'd dropped her off after a Thursday night meeting about a year ago, maybe two. She had walked to Grace that night, but it was pouring rain when we were done. She lived in the little cookie-cutter neighborhood just south of the church. I drove her home out of pure humanity. Yes, I remembered exactly where she lived.

I remember the street, but not the
number.

7364. I gotta go get my girl. Text me
when you are on the way. 7 or 8 OK?

Jesus Christ—that was three hours away. What the hell would I do for three hours? Flip acting like it was no big deal that I was coming over to see her at her house only made it worse—almost torturous. For some reason, I suspected she knew that.

I went home, changed into my gym clothes, and went to the Y. I had time to kill, and the treadmill was my only friend. I had already worked out that morning and didn't need the exercise, but I needed a distraction. The after-work crowd didn't recognize me, and I didn't recognize them. The staff probably thought I was having a crisis or something.

Maybe I was.

Mission accomplished on killing time, and then came the real pressure: a twenty-minute drive across town for what felt like the first date of my life.

I'm on my way. Be there in 20.

We are doing the dishes. Be done
before you get here.

That was good news. Dirty dishes could ruin the mood.

The west-side drives were harder than they used to be. I was having trouble staying inside the lines, as if the lanes had shrunk.

As I pulled up to her house, I realized that I hadn't brushed my teeth since right before I left to meet Cobb for the nonbreakfast. I parked and frantically chewed a piece of gum that I was luckier than shit to have in the Jeep. I fumbled around trying to use my phone camera to see if food was stuck in my unbrushed teeth, and I discovered that I suck at using my phone for that and then became paranoid that she might be looking out the window and bust me.

I walked up the little Midwestern slice of suburbia's sidewalk to 7364 Westwood Drive, constantly scanning the area to see if anyone had spotted the old creep calling on the young princess. I saw no one.

Doorbell.

With a flash, the big door opened leaving just a storm door between me and a little girl. She didn't say a word. She was checking me out like she would a Martian who had landed on her porch. Two seconds of that was all I could take.

"Hi! I'm Will. What's your name?" She turned and ran away from the door before I could get all of that out, yelling, "Mom! He's here!"

From the back of the house Flip strolled to the door with an easy smile on her face and bare feet—she seemed to be oddly shoe-averse. "Come on in. Please excuse my butler there. She is still in training."

"Good help is hard to find. But don't worry, she'll be mowing your grass soon enough," I joked.

"Is that what your boys do for you?" she asked.

"That's the minimum. My boys are slaves to me. At least they were before they became adults and went off to college and adulthood. Now I have to lure them over with food or tickets or some other kind of bribe. You can ask them—they won't deny it."

"I will ask them," she confidently replied. "Come on back here so I can introduce you to my assistant."

We walked toward the kitchen in the back where the little girl had resumed whatever homework-looking project she was laboring over at the kitchen table.

"Mallory? I don't think you said hi to Will, did you?" Flip asked.

She looked me right in the eye and with her mom's easy smile politely said, "Hi, Will."

"Hi again, Mallory. It's good to finally meet you."

She continued smiling as she returned to her homework.

Flip grabbed my hand and led me toward the front room. "Don't let us keep you, Mal," she said. "We'll be in the other room."

It *was* a date. I remembered going over to girls' houses as a high schooler when their parents were in the other room. That was exactly what this felt like.

I sat down on the end of the couch, and she plopped down right in the middle of it next to me. She turned to me in a sort of a cross-legged posture, looked deep into my eyes, which seemed to be a genetic thing in the house, and said, "So . . . what did you want to see me about?"

I froze for a second. I actually forgot the original reason for my visit for just a moment. Oh, I got it. I got it. "I came here to meet Mallory, of course, but she appears to be busy."

"I know that," she said.

"Damn. Did I say that's what I wanted? I thought I said I wanted to talk to you."

"Whatever. Now that we have all of that out of the way, how are you?" she said in a slow and deliberate way that was a little on the excessive side of flirtatious. It was more like . . . seductive.

"Busy, I guess. It's getting to be that time of year in my biz."

"I hope you are busy. You have important stuff to do," she said.

"You think so?" I asked.

"I told you that I have been listening to you. I know what's happening in the Statehouse."

"Yeah, what I do is pretty important to whoever is paying me. That's for sure," I flippantly replied.

"I think these vape shop owners will appreciate your work

someday soon." She then flipped the conversation abruptly. "When was the last time you went on a date? A real date, that wasn't some business dinner with someone who happened to be a woman. I mean, with an actual woman?"

I had no defenses. She'd been listening to me talk in that damn group every week, so she already knew that I hadn't been dating. The only thing I could be with her was honest because I felt she already knew the truthful answer to any question she might ask. That might have been an exaggeration, but it was too late for me to try and remember everything I'd said over the last three years when I didn't know she was actually listening.

"I can't remember when that last date was. But it was the best . . . in a hot kind of way. I'm sure you've heard about dates like it. If I could just remember anything about it. I guess it's been a few years now. It's pretty sad to say out loud—so thanks for making me do that."

"I imagine you as a pretty good date," she said. "Like someone who likes to go to concerts and plays, or games, or I don't know, ice skating."

"Ice skating? I hate ice skating. I suck at ice skating. I don't suck at many things, but ice skating is definitely one of them. But I guess I only know that because I have been a few times. Tomas, my younger son, used to like to skate. Glad I don't have to do that shit anymore. The rest is accurate enough. I would much rather go to a concert than fall on my ass on some ice in front of someone I'm trying to score with."

"Score? Really? I don't see you as someone who actually tries to score. Especially since you don't even notice when someone is trying to score on you." She could see that I was nervous, and she was toying with me.

"What about you?" I asked. "I mean, getting back to the whole 'When was your last date?' line of questioning."

"Not quite as long as you, but at least a year, maybe two. I have Mal to keep my social calendar full. Brownies and soccer and dance classes are demanding. Plus, I've had my eye on someone in particular."

Mallory was like all the parents of my teenage girlfriends— she could sense when something good was about to happen and thought it was the perfect time to chime in.

"Mom! When are you coming to help me?" she yelled from the kitchen table.

Flip didn't take her eyes out of mine for a couple of seconds, which seemed like a whole lot more. Then that easy smile returned to her face and she said, "Two minutes, Mal. I haven't even invited him yet."

I had no idea what that meant. "You haven't invited me to what?" I asked, loud enough for Mal to hear me.

"We like to have Sunday brunch, and she and I discussed it, and we would like for you to join us this week." Again, loud enough for Mal to hear her.

I knew all of that, but I'd forgotten about these kinds of games parents play with younger kids. Flip made it seem like a bigger deal than it would have otherwise sounded, even if I hadn't been warned.

"Am I the first one you two ever invited to brunch? I want to know where I rate, because I promise you it's the first time I've ever been invited, except for tailgates."

"No, you're not the first. We know people besides you. *We* have friends. Real friends."

"Fair enough," I conceded. "I'm in. Should I pick you up or meet you at your spot?"

"You better pick us up. We also like to spend Sunday morning before brunch debating where we want to go."

"Mal? I'm in for Sunday brunch," I yelled into the kitchen. "Thanks for inviting me!"

"You're welcome, Will!" she yelled back with an almost odd level of polite maturity.

"I better get back to our homework," Flip said as she stood up. "You'll be here at 11:00? Oh and don't wear anything fancy. We could be going to McDonald's, Bob Evans, or Patachou, if you can handle that range. Dress appropriately for all of them."

"Handle it? I can recite all the menus," I said as I started to get up.

As I stood she ambushed me by grabbing my chin, steadying my head, and then softly kissing me on the lips. This woman was killing me.

Afterward, she said, "Good, then we will both see you then. Goodnight."

"Goodnight, Mallory. I'll see you Sunday," my voice quivered into the kitchen.

"Bye, Will."

I was out the door and into the Jeep, amazed I didn't do anything to embarrass myself. At least as far as I knew. I think.

"Brunch? Jesus Christ, I hate going to brunch," I said to myself. I'm a big eater, and when I pig out late morning the rest of my day is wrecked. That's right, I hate brunch.

At least I used to.

20

After running my mouth at those guys at Patachou, it struck me that I probably shouldn't waste any time finding someone to get my bill filed. I'd already told those guys I was having it done, so I guessed I better put up since it was too late to shut up.

Bethany wasn't even asking me to get a bill filed, although she knew I thought it was important, so she was letting me do it. She thought the FDA and the court was where this situation would be fixed. I thought things would go our way there, but I worried that the State of Indiana would try to defend itself if we couldn't get the legislature to see how they were being manipulated. The court and the federal government tell states bad news all the time. Only some of the time does the state just accept it; other times, states try to find a way to fight back.

Whenever I needed placeholder bills filed, I started with my buddy Representative Ben Rizzo. Riz was one of those guys on the Democrat side who passed a lot of bills. He was a guy who got along with everyone in the building and because of that, he handled a lot of the tough issues for the Ds.

He was about my age. He was a golfer. He was from a big family. At least two of his brothers played golf—I knew this because I'd played with them in one outing or another. He was a lot like me in those ways. He was cooler than me, and taller than me, but he had this weird attraction to Boston sports teams, which forced us to snipe at each other fairly regularly. It really wasn't all that weird; his dad was originally from Boston. As a result, while Riz grew up in Fort Wayne, Indiana, he spent his childhood rooting for the Celtics (acceptable), Red Sox (tolerable), and even the fucking Patriots (which is like rooting for the plague in Indianapolis).

Most importantly, though, he was a good legislator. He knew how to manage the place. And if he had room on his list of five bills, he would do this. No sweat.

He wouldn't communicate in any meaningful way via text or email, so everything had to be verbal. In person was preferred, but over the phone usually worked.

"Riz, I need an easy favor out of you," I said on the phone.

"What is it this time? Let me guess—you need a bill filed that doesn't mean anything to anyone but you. We're on a streak, it seems, and yes, I'm keeping track."

"You are a genius! I do need a bill filed. It's on this e-liquid thing, and you can file it and just let it die on the shelf, unless you know, something crazy happens."

"Yeah, right. I've got a spot left so send it to me. We can talk about it later," he said.

"You got it. Thanks man. Oh, and one more thing."

"What?" Riz asked as if he was in a hurry.

"Fuck Tom Brady."

I got nothing in response but a hang up. Go figure.

As much as this was a big favor to me, Rizzo would like being able to tell everyone else in the hallway that he couldn't file a bill for them. In that way, there was something in it for him too. Each House member is only allowed to file five bills during an even-numbered year, and when that limit is reached, it makes it easier to tell everyone else asking no. At least, that's how I tried to convince him to do this stuff. He went along with it, acting like he didn't know he was being played. But what both of us knew is that both of us knew better.

That was all the prep work I needed to do for the 2016 legislative session. The bill would be filed in early January.

. . .

Sunday morning came and I was ready. Flip wasn't at church on Thursday. She'd texted me that she had a school function so I wouldn't worry. If she only knew how much I would have. I was ready. I was cool.

I had to stop at the gas station around the corner from Flip's house and kill a few minutes acting like I was shopping so I wouldn't show up early. I slow-walked up and down the aisles, noticing that there wasn't anything on the shelves that I eat anymore—and I was amazed at what I once did. Then I realized how hungry I was and how pro-brunch I had become at that very moment.

There was a McDonald's next door to the convenience store. I could happily do that for brunch with the right company, which is what I'd have.

When I arrived at Flip's right on the number, Mal was looking for me out of the front window. It looked like she had her long blonde hair all done up with a pink ribbon. She disappeared as I got out of my Jeep and then reappeared as I was halfway up the sidewalk. I didn't think she saw the bunch of daisies I had behind my back, and I realized that this date was more about her than it was about Flip or me.

She opened the door and said, "Hi, Will. Whatcha got behind your back?"

"A little boring something for you," I teased and then disappointed her when I proudly showed her the flowers.

Her mom came trotting up the hallway to the door and saved us both by saying, "Oh, how nice that he brought us flowers!"

I corrected Flip by telling her, "The flowers are really for Mal."

Flowers were cool if Mom said they were cool.

"Where are we off to for my first, special, world-famous Sunday brunch this morning?" I asked with fake enthusiasm that seemed to adequately disguise my actual enthusiasm.

They both said in unison and with great pride, "Bob Evans!"

I wasn't sure Flip remembered my comment about knowing all the menus, so I quickly shot back at them, "They have the best gravy in town, and I looove gravy."

Mal corrected me. "We are going for waffles and sausage."

"I see." And in a somber deal-making tone I asked, "Would you consider sharing some of that if I am willing to share some of my biscuits and gravy?"

She smiled that easy smile while she thought about it.

I needed that brunch. Passing all the tests a nine-year-old girl threw at someone like me who was under intense pressure to pass each one of them could be exhausting. I impressed her with how much I could eat and that I had two sons who were older than she was, who loved me, and whom she would get to meet soon.

We had a ball.

"Tell me Mal, what is your favorite thing to do?" I asked her.

"I like going for hikes in the park, and I like to get dirty there."

"What? I'm the best at getting dirty! Me and my boys like to stomp in mud puddles."

"Really?" she said in complete awe at the thought of it. "Mom doesn't ever do that, do you, Mom?"

Flip shook her head. "I'll leave that to you two."

"Next time you guys think about inviting me somewhere, that's where I want to go."

Mallory blushed and smiled at her mom at the thought.

I took them home after we ate and gave Mal a parting knuckle bump. For Flip's goodbye, I just stood and looked at her and took her hand—I thought a kiss might be too much for the moment. Besides, she was in charge of that.

I must have been right about that.

Afterward, I went home and crashed on my couch, exhausted like I had been in a Vegas casino for a day and a half.

That pretty little girl had worn me out. I thought her mom enjoyed watching her daughter do it. I enjoyed watching her mom watch.

As I was going to bed that evening, I got a text.

She loves you. I knew she would. Goodnight.

Yes, life had changed forever.

21

The months leading up to winter and the next session were like a disgusting romantic comedy. Everything Flip, Mal, and I did together was nothing but laughs and smiles. The adults tried to take it slow, and the biggest chore we had was exactly that. I kept them away from the Statehouse, which was easy because I was only occasionally there anyway.

My boys, Liam and Tomas, came to brunch with us at least every other Sunday, and we had eggs all over town. Mal loved Liam too. We all began calling him Leem—one syllable—because she said his name so much and so fast. Luckily he was going to school in town. Tomas had gone out of town to college about an hour away, so we saw him less, but there was always a little bit of disappointment every time one or both of my boys couldn't come on Sunday.

I discovered during that stretch that Mal had never had any men in her life. After brunch on the Sunday before Christmas, I had the talk with my boys.

"You two need to be sensitive to Mallory. We are the only men she knows."

"Jesus, Dad. How do you think we would let her down?" Liam asked. "You're the one who needs to watch his ass."

"Yeah, Dad. She's not gonna have any complaints about us. This is all on you," Tomas added.

All I could do was look at them and nod, letting them know that I knew—and ending the family meeting faster than any talk we'd ever had.

"Good talk guys. I feel better." That's all I had to say as they laughed at me in a rush of pity.

. . .

The first day of the legislative session was Wednesday, January 6, 2016. They probably could have started on Monday, January 4, but I'm sure someone in leadership was on a cruise somewhere so they made the state wait a couple of days to get going.

It was a big election year. When tensions are high in electoral politics, progress in policymaking usually comes to a grinding halt. That's what most of us expected this session.

Representative Ben Rizzo was going to file my bill, but probably not until the end of the week. Protocol dictated to me an unpleasant task: I needed to tell Representative Chris Miller that I was having a bill filed to repeal a big chunk of the law he passed last session. That was going to piss him off, but I couldn't break that protocol, especially if I was going to throw fits when others did. And I was sure that others were going to break lots of rules on this one. Maybe even Miller would, again.

I'm not sure he realized the state of affairs in court either. Our federal case was in the midst of depositions with trial dates set for April. But a surprise occurred the week before in Marion County Court, and I didn't know if Miller even knew about it.

The T-shirt crowd filed a lawsuit in Indianapolis, specifically targeting the unreasonable and discriminatory nature of the security requirements. The legal strategy they had invested in seemed a stretch. Ethan Murphy, their spokesman, put out a press release listing several nationally prominent security companies that couldn't meet the lofty and specific definition. Murphy claimed that there was no company that met the definition. Not one.

That was a problem for Pauly. A big one. And whether the court gave a shit about that or not, the new law could not be implemented without a qualified security firm. That couldn't be the outcome Pauly wanted. There was absolutely no money in that.

Even though they wrote it specifically for someone, all the vape companies across the country who cared about the Indiana market would argue the law needed rewriting because there was no qualified security firm. And that really couldn't be the outcome Pauly wanted. As I said, there was absolutely no money in that.

Pauly and his goons—I mean team—probably thought they could win in state court, so they may not have even been worried about it. No matter. I still needed to tell Representative Miller that his law had two lawsuits filed on it in two different jurisdictions and that I had a bill filed to repeal the worst part of his original stupid law. After I thought about it for a minute, I decided the chat could be fun.

After the first session day adjourned, I went straight to the doorman on the R side of the House Chamber and asked to see Representative Miller. The doorman left a message. Having no idea whether I would get in or not, I sat down at the bench next to his desk.

About two minutes passed and the doorman's phone rang. "You can go on up," he said. Interesting. I hadn't expected the quick green light.

I climbed the two flights of stairs to Miller's office on the inside of the Chamber complex. He was sitting inside at his conference table, facing the door. Before I could knock, he said, "Come on in Will."

"Mr. Chairman, thanks for taking a minute with me," I responded.

"What can I do for you today?" he asked politely, as if he had not tried to annihilate my character behind closed doors eight months ago.

"Let me get right to the point. I just needed to give you a heads-up that Representative Rizzo will be filing a bill, on my request, that deletes all the security language from HB 1432 from last session. I didn't want you to find out about it and be surprised or curious about where it came from or why he filed it. He is doing it for me."

"Thanks for letting me know. I don't think there will be much happening on that issue this session, though," he said.

That was an important sentence.

What he meant by that was that he wouldn't let Riz's bill move. I, of course, already knew that. But he likely took a little pleasure in telling me that himself. I'm not sure if he had a good grip on where this whole thing stood, though, since I assumed he only received progress reports from Pauly's team.

"Yeah, I expected that. Riz is filing the bill as a placeholder just in case something needs to be done. You know, there are two lawsuits in two different jurisdictions challenging most of it. The industry is pretty confident in the outcome of the federal case. I can't speak to the case the T-shirt folks filed last week here in Indy. It's a fascinating claim they're making, that there is no security firm on earth that can meet the definition in your bill. That seems like a problem."

"I heard about that. There are plenty of companies that qualify, so I don't know where they get their information," Miller said.

"Really?" I said. "Our guys can't find one either, but admittedly, we haven't been looking very hard."

"That's a dead end, Will. All of that stuff is in good shape."

"None of that matters much to my client either way. I just wanted to let you know that the Rizzo bill is mine, and that we are watching the lawsuits more than the legislature this winter. If you guys aren't entertaining anything new, we can all spend the session in wait-and-see mode. I'm good at that."

"Sounds like it. Anything else, Will? I appreciate the heads-up."

"That's it, Mr. Chairman. I'll get out of your hair."

We shook hands politely, and I was out of there.

It was entirely possible that I'd just had the most uncomfortable meeting of the session, and I did it on the first day. I predicted this session would be done by March 10, so it would only be a little over two months of dicking around, waiting for action in the courts, and then seeing how the ATC implemented the law—if it survived.

. . .

I hadn't been on one of those painful conference calls with the lawyers since before the holidays, so I didn't know what was going on other than depositions. I didn't know who they were deposing or what sort of information they even needed for their constitutional arguments.

But two weeks after the session started, I got a call from Bethany that changed everything. I was sitting on a bench on the north catwalk between the House and Senate when her number popped up. I headed up the hallway while I answered it, hoping a phone booth was open for me to duck into.

"What's up?" I asked.

"Something incredible happened today in a deposition of the general counsel of the Indiana ATC," she reported. The words seemed very excited for her, but they were spoken in her typical deadpan.

"Lay it on me," I insisted.

"One of our guys asked her if she knew of any entity in existence today that met the definition of 'security firm' in the new law. She said no. He pressed her and asked her how the ATC could implement the new law if there was no security firm that met the definition. She replied, 'We can't.'"

"What! What the hell does that mean?" I was almost yelling into the phone.

"It means that if nothing happens to the law, and there is no action by the court, no one will be able to operate in Indiana on July 1. No security firm means no licenses can be obtained!"

I was blown away by this. "The T-shirt guys were right?" I half-yelled again.

"Looks like it. At least in the eyes of the ATC," she replied.

"Pauly and the boys will try to fix this in the Statehouse," I warned.

"I assume so," she said. "But there's more."

"Oh God. Here comes the bad news. Like I said before—lay it on me."

"I don't know if this is bad, but opposing counsel asked the ATC lawyer about a company named Schulte's. It's based in Wabash. They seemed to believe they met the definition, but the ATC lawyer said she disagreed. Ever heard of this company?"

"Nope. But I can guarantee it's connected to someone here in the Statehouse. I'm on it . . . unless you mind—" I sort of asked for permission there.

"Keep it cool, but yes, I want to know who these guys are," she said.

"You got it."

She hung up without saying goodbye.

I was a little shaken. My mind was spinning trying to figure out what these guys had planned. Obviously, the original bill was written for this Wabash company but somehow they fucked it up. If I were on Pauly's team, I would have tried to make it fit at least two companies just so the monopoly argument would be dead. Now it didn't even fit one.

These guys were going to have to fix this with an amendment somewhere. The session was two weeks away from the halfway point, and I would be fighting an amendment that hadn't been written. There was no bill that immediately came to mind as the vehicle, and as far as I could tell, no members of the body even knew this problem existed. I couldn't explain to legislators why they should be against an idea that wasn't even being presented by anyone.

If I were on the scheme team, I wouldn't make a move until after halftime. But now I'd have to monitor all the possible committees and read every word of every amendment that was filed until I found their magic clarifying amendment. I am supposed to be doing that anyway, so, yawn, all right.

The State Chamber was having their big dinner that night, and I was joining one of my other clients at their table. I asked my State Chamber pal, Grant Easterly, to introduce me to the Wabash Chamber exec so that I could ask him what he knew about the company. On the internet, the company looked more like a hardware store than a security company.

The event was at the Indiana Roof Ballroom, like it is every year. The Roof is a grand room that sits on the top floor of the Indiana Repertory Theater, across the street from the Statehouse. It has room for a hundred and fifty tables of ten on its floor, and the Chamber takes great pride in filling them every year. The main floor is surrounded by a second tier above it that looks like storefronts from an old Italian village, and the ceiling is painted dark blue with stars stenciled into it. At most events I go to there, I find myself staring up at those stars while being lulled to sleep by an awards ceremony, or trying not to feel embarrassed for the act on the stage that is so unfunny it hurts.

At the Chamber dinner all the attendees have name tags, but there are ribbons attached to the VIP people who serve on committees, contribute certain amounts, take out the trash—you name it, there's a Chamber ribbon for it. My pal Grant has about five of them on his name tag. Hooray for him.

"Meet Weston Jeffers, Will," my ribbon-toting buddy from the State Chamber said. "He's the boss of the Chamber in Wabash."

"Yes, Weston!" I said loudly in the crowded room at the Indiana Roof Ballroom. "There's a business in your city I want to ask you about."

"Sorry, we don't have much time to chat, but which company? Maybe I know it off the top of my head," he yell-talked back to me.

"Schulte's Hardware or Security. Ever heard of it?" I asked.

"Sure—the county chairman owns it now, I think. Mike Gilliatte is his name. Have you guys not met?" he asked with a bit of disbelief. Weston clearly didn't know that I'm not a Republican, and even if I were, I would never be enough of one to know all the county chairmen.

"No, we haven't. At least not yet. But that helps me a lot. I'll look him up. Don't let me keep you, Weston. I know you don't want to miss Charlie Cook's talk, so I guess we better get to our tables. It was a pleasure meeting you!"

He gave me a wave while dribbling the bourbon he was drinking over the back of his hand without noticing. He didn't realize that he'd saved me a bunch of time. He also didn't notice the "Holy shit!" fireworks that were going on in my chest.

In this room "county chairman" meant the county chairman of the Republican party. And the county chairman of the Republican party might have had something to do with the election of someone who mattered in this whole mess. Actually, it might close a loop I wasn't really looking for.

My former pal, Senator Charlie Alderman, was from Wabash. Mike Gilliatte, who was the GOP chairman of Wabash County, had probably been trading favors with Charlie for a long time. And Charlie passed a law last year that was designed to make Gilliatte rich by giving him monopoly control of the e-liquid market in Indiana.

This was starting to seem like a scheme unlike any other scheme. In a brutally obvious way. And it was starting to become clear why my ex-friend Charlie Alderman didn't want me working on this issue in the first place.

22

The first half of the 2016 legislative session ended with-out Pauly's team making any moves. As I expected, they wouldn't be trying to fix their problem that came out of the depositions in the federal case until the last possible minute. With the first half of the session over, the list of potential bills that these guys could use shrunk considerably.

As soon as the second half of the session began, I started to see Pauly and his lawyers hanging around together in the hallway. I hadn't seen them together in the hallway once during the first five weeks. I saw them talking to the legislators who were the managers of the last couple of options to insert something to fix their prob-lem. They were doing it in the hallway. Right in front of me. It was as if they either didn't care that I knew they were working it again, or they were too stupid to know that I knew exactly what was hap-pening. This is also something only a few of us can do: recognize what is happening in the huddles without being in them. Putting their old team together, displaying anxiousness on their faces, and talking to legislators that were on the target committees completely showed their hand. It was the same with players at the World Series of Poker. They knew what the player across the table was holding long before the amateurs did.

I spent the first few days of the second half watching them scurry around the hallway and kiss ass. I kept Bethany up to speed each day, so she would know they were back on the job and that a new play was coming, even though I hadn't seen anything in writing yet.

The second Monday of the second half rolled around. I was sitting on a bench outside of the session watching the schemers talk to Senator Charlie Alderman, and Ethan Murphy, the leader of the T-shirters, just happened to be walking by. I don't know what came over me.

"Hey Ethan," I said. "Are you watching what's going on over there?"

"Over where?" he said.

"Right there. The guys who are trying to screw you guys and my client are trying to fix their security definition right there with Senator Alderman."

"Oh yeah? Is that what's going on?" he asked.

"You better believe it. They're working on changing that definition that will address your lawsuit and fix at least one of their problems that came up in the federal case."

"What difference does it make how they *fix* it?" he asked.

"Excellent question," I conceded. "We probably ought to compare notes while we're waiting for them to drop their bomb. Do you want to step into my office?" I invited him to my bench.

He seemed caught a little off-guard by the invitation. I assumed that he'd never been invited to anything by anyone in the Statehouse. The sixty or seventy faithful T-shirters that flanked him last year had dwindled down to just the occasional pair here and there. Ethan was as much an outsider in the Statehouse as he'd been a year ago. The hallway doesn't often welcome new faces without a reason. And as his own interest group had predictably lost hope, I expect he felt very alone.

"How are things going with your lawsuit here in the county?" I asked.

"I'm not optimistic that the court even cares about it yet, since the effective date isn't even here. My lawyer isn't either. It's as if people think that the harm all of us are about to feel doesn't count until we have to close our doors for real."

"How many vape shops are there in Indiana?" I asked. "I guess I never really got a good handle on the retail scope, since that's not what my client does."

"My last count was 224," he said.

"Oh shit! I had no idea there were that many. Are all of them members of yours?"

"No, no. There are only about fifty members of my group. And I use the word 'member' loosely. These guys are not real big into organizational discipline, you know?"

"Do they even understand what's happening? I mean the guys that are a part of your group. I assume the other guys don't have a clue."

"They understand more about the bill than legislators do. The excise cops and the ATC folks do too. But this place . . . it's like the people who got elected to come here don't *want* to know what they're doing."

I laughed a little at that. "Yeah, ignorance is bliss with this bunch, no question. Whatever happened to Matt Cobb and his clients? Were they members or associates or friends of your bunch?"

"They were for a little bit, but they quit returning my calls right after I filed the lawsuit. I don't know what they're doing. For all I know they may be focusing on other states or they might be moving."

That didn't make sense to me.

"They told me late last year that they thought they could cut a deal with a security firm and get a license here. That's pretty hard to do since there is no such thing as a security firm. What do you make of that?"

"Pauly James and the guys from Schulte's are going to have to bring in someone that actually manufactures and distributes the product, since I think we all know they aren't going to be doing it themselves. I think the only people who still believe that Pauly's client is an actual manufacturer are these idiot legislators."

I sort of drifted into one of my trances, thinking how crazy the situation was.

Ethan looked at me with a bit of concern. "Are you okay?" he asked.

"Sorry. I drift off into la-la land sometimes when I get to thinking. These guys don't actually think they can run over 200 shops out of business and then cut a deal with a couple of them and make people think it's not a monopoly, do they?"

"Why not? And who cares what people believe? My guys are already trying to figure out what to do when they're out of this business. They just don't think anyone cares, so most of them don't think any of this makes a difference. Here *or* in court."

"That's what Pauly and his goons are counting on. They're betting that you guys will just walk away without bitching. And they're betting that even if you keep after it, which you're having a hard time doing, that none of these politicians will listen to you anyway. That last part was clearly part of the original plan," I said with disgust.

"It's a pretty good plan, right? I can't get anyone to care, that's for sure. My own colleagues are already writing it off. Do you realize that if 200 of these vapor shops had to invest $20,000 apiece to get up and running, they collectively lost $4 million? It's probably double that. These assholes from Wabash are screwing citizens out of millions, and the legislature doesn't care one bit."

He actually said "Wabash." I was surprised he knew anything

about the rather simple geographic connection between Schulte's and Senator Alderman. Maybe he didn't. He might have just been talking about Schulte's, all by themselves.

"So, you got to tell me what the problem is with the definition for Schulte's or how they fixed it so that it includes Schulte's and *only* Schulte's. At least in your opinion, please."

He paused for a minute. "There's a problem with the certifications that they thought they had from those two obscure associations. I don't know who works there, but I am almost positive that there was confusion on who had the Door and Hardware Institute or the International Door Association certifications. Maybe it's not a matter of who had them, but when they had them."

"That sounds about right to me. It's been good talking to you, Ethan," I said as I stood up and extended a hand to shake, knowing that I might have been talking with him too long already. I wouldn't want people to erroneously think he was a client or a partner on something—and that's how the hallway works. I wasn't ready to vouch for him.

He stayed on the bench and shook my hand and asked, "What can we or anyone do about all of this?"

"I don't know yet, man. I get the feeling we don't know the whole story, and that it may be after the first of July before we do. We just need to keep paying attention to everything we see and hear. I'll see you later."

I walked away without slipping up and committing something that I shouldn't. In my heart, I wanted to tell him that I wasn't going to let these bastards get away with this. I didn't want to be his partner, at least not yet.

These guys were going to bankrupt 224 independent businesses not by making it difficult to be regulated, but by making it impossible. As a bonus, nowhere else in America was this happening. Nowhere.

Were the T-shirters so used to getting screwed in every facet of their lives that they didn't know when to fight? Did they think it was better to walk away and lose twenty, thirty, or fifty thousand dollars than to try and fight and potentially make the loss worse?

One of the things I always did when I found myself in a spot where it felt like I was outmatched was to start looking for friends. My brain started working.

When I smoked, I occasionally bought a carton, but for the most part, I bought cigarettes a pack or two at a time. I usually bought them at the gas station. When I was in college, I bought them at the 7-Eleven. I would get a Big Gulp fountain Coke and a pack of smokes and go back to the house and have a picnic. Good times.

Why weren't the gas stations or the convenience stores worried about this law? Didn't they sell vape liquid? Shouldn't they be pissed if they were forced to stop? Even if they were not required to stop because none of their vendors had a manufacturer's license, a monopoly meant the price would go up. Way up.

And the liquor stores. What about them? Smokers drink. Vapers probably do, too. Liquor stores had sold me a fortune's worth of Marlboro Lights when I was younger. I assume guys like I used to be still wanted to buy a cold six-pack of beer and their vaping supplies on their way home after a hard day's work. Shouldn't these retailers give a shit about this?

Neither of these businesses would put up with this sort of scheme on cigarettes. If this were the future of nicotine, these retailers wouldn't want to be beholden to Pauly and his group of criminals.

If I'd owned a convenience store or a liquor store, I would have been raising hell about this. I was determined to find out why the hell they weren't, at least not yet.

23

Tuesday morning: the second day of the second week of the second half of the session. I had two priorities racing through my mind while I plowed away on the Stairmaster at the Athenaeum YMCA: convenience stores and liquor stores.

I knew the guys who represented the associations of both groups. These lobbyists were friends of mine and had been around for as long as I had in one role or another. They knew how this kind of thing worked, so the conversations should get straight to the point.

It was entirely possible that they didn't know any better, at least I hoped so. Hell, it had taken me a journey to figure out what I knew so far, so it would be hard for me to be too judgmental.

With these groups there were also member companies, which had their own lobbyists as well. Not all liquor stores were mom-and-pop shops. There were a couple of chains in the state that owned dozens of stores. The same went for convenience stores. Chains could complicate things the way Bethany did; interstate companies see things through a broader lens.

I reviewed everything from last year's hearings. No one from either industry testified at any of them. No member of either association, or the associations themselves, participated in either lawsuit. By all indications, they were sleeping at the switch.

. . .

That morning, I got to the hallway around 9:30. Morning committee hearings were going on, and people were scattered all over the place. I wanted to talk to the leaders of these two groups, and even though I had their cell phone numbers and every other contact point for six or eight lobbyists who worked in either trench, I wanted to ask these guys about this stuff face-to-face.

Lying is so much more difficult in person. Multiply that by ten when the face-to-face discussion is a surprise. That's what I planned to do: ambush.

I was trolling around the building for probably a half an hour before I spotted the association lobbyist for the convenience stores.

Shane Thomas was a curly-haired lifer, kind of like me, but five or ten years younger. He spent time working on staff in the legislature for a few people for a few years and then at a couple of agencies before he got hired by the convenience stores. He wasn't the top guy in the group, but he knew the weeds in the building.

"Hey Shane—where the hell have you been?" I half-yelled as I approached him.

"Jesus, Will," he said, startled. "What are you yelling about? I've been here every day just like you, smartass," he replied.

"Hold that thought. I have an issue I need to talk to you about. I just can't believe you guys have been paying attention to it at all. If you have been, I'm even more confused."

"This is why I don't like talking to you. You never come up to me and say, 'Shane, I have great news for you!' It's always 'Shane, I'm about to wreck your day.'"

I piled on a bit. "Well, today it's more like 'I'm going to save your ass.' Is that better?"

"Doubtful, but give it a shot," he said.

I cleared my throat. "Have you been paying attention to the e-liquid law from last year and the lawsuits that have come from it?"

He took a deep breath and rolled his eyes at me like he knew something bad was about to happen to him. "We looked at it last year and decided that we didn't manufacture, and that it didn't do anything to the retail tobacco permit, so it didn't really matter to us. Why do I predict you are about to tell me that we were wrong?"

"I think you were wrong," I said with a giggle. "You guys sell the liquid and the components for people to vape, right?"

"Of course we do. It's a new product line that's growing, but we don't know where it's headed yet. We see smokers migrating, which is obviously a big deal. So what?"

"What if I told you that the new law was going to limit the number of potential suppliers from hundreds down to five or ten or even two or three?"

"I would tell you that prices are going up, and probably some other bad shit," he said.

"Well then, it sounds like you and I just became partners. There are 224 vape shops that we know of in Indiana that are prepping to go out of business on July 1 for a couple of reasons. First, many of them manufacture their own liquid at their stores, which won't be allowed any more without a license. None of these guys will be able to get a license. And second, there won't be anyone else able to supply them with product they can sell at retail. That last part applies to your members exactly the same way. Now, I know this won't put you out of business like it will them, but imagine a market with no price controls and no market pressure either on the one product in your stores that is growing—"

"Hang on there. This is not the only thing that's growing—"

"Fair enough, but if in five years half the cigarette smokers everywhere else in the country are vaping and this is the one state where it costs double or triple to do it—"

"Okay, I hear you. But how do you know that's what's happening?"

"Because my national vaping client, which is the largest vaping manufacturer in the country, is planning on walking away from Indiana. That alone will send prices up here. But I would guess that all the national manufacturers are going to walk away with us. If that happens, and as things stand right now, it absolutely will, your situation will change drastically."

"I'm going to have to talk to the boss about this. Jesus Christ, Will—"

"Would you have rather found out later?"

"I would rather you kill this shit for us all," he piped back.

"Me too—I love being a hero, you know?" I said as he walked away while simultaneously making a phone call, clearly back to his mother ship.

Mission accomplished there. Next up, the liquor store association. I predicted this one would be a little more complicated. This was Pauly's world. I was friends with all of them socially, but Pauly represented the wine and spirits distributors in the state. In that regard, these guys kind of lived with each other. I was betting that they would agree with me in principle, if there weren't, oh, other considerations. Who knew, maybe I was wrong.

It took the rest of the morning of me trolling around, trying to act like I was just killing time before I spotted the person I needed to speak to. Jason Farmer was the guy. He was almost my age, and looked like me, but he came up in the ranks through Republican campaign work. He did some contract lobbying and worked for the hospitality industry for a time before he went out of the Statehouse for a few years and had a job in the real world. When the leader of his former group in the hospitality world prepared to retire, he came back into the fold and bought him out.

He was a good guy, but representing liquor stores, which was a big client in Jason's group, could be nasty just like Pauly would have it. They were pigs in slop to some extent. Although I never thought of Jason as a pig, it was hard to stay out of the slop in that world.

I loved the guy's name too: Farmer. I usually call him "Framer" instead, because I thought it was funny. No one else did. And then there were the constant almanac jokes and questions about the harvest that we enjoyed. But those were only funny because he was such a city guy. I doubt he'd ever actually been on a farm in his entire life.

He was fast-walking on the third floor headed for the south stairway, when I cut him off from the opposite catwalk. He gave me the "Don't fuck with me, I'm in a hurry" wave, and I said, "Wait one damn minute, Framer. I need to talk to you about booze!"

"Goddamnit Will, I'm running late!" he said with some sincere frustration.

"Well excuse me, I thought you just had to piss or something the way you were scurrying across the floor."

"Can it wait?" he asked.

"That depends. Are you coming back after lunch?"

"Yes, right after," he begged for a release.

"Then I'll see you at 1:30."

"Great, great." He scurried off while mumbling under his breath.

"Bring a fucking weather update with you!" I yelled after him.

I parked on a bench on the catwalk between the Senate and the House on the south side of 3, where I would be sure to see him when he returned. Between about 1:15 and 1:40 PM on a day when both chambers are due in at 1:30 could be a crowded stretch in the hallway. Lobbyists filled the hallway as if being present when the gavel fell had some sort of value. I couldn't remember when I figured out how stupid that was, but as long as most people kept doing it, it was a good way to take attendance for guys like me.

Today, though, I was only looking for the one guy. Everyone else was just in my way.

At 1:35 I spotted him. He wasn't walking fast anymore. I waited to see if he would come to me, or if I would have to chase after him again. He walked right by. Hmmm. I got up and followed him around the corner to the north catwalk where he normally put down his briefcase.

"What the hell, Framer, you don't want to talk to me about booze?" I said.

"I'm not ducking you," he replied. "I just forgot. What's on your mind?"

"I want to know if your members sell e-liquid and vape components in their stores. That's all."

"You know they do, Will," he answered. "So what?"

"Do you care about a monopoly being formed in Indiana on those products? Are you okay with most of your suppliers leaving the state and one company controlling the pricing, supply, and everything else?"

He looked at me like he knew what I was talking about but didn't want me to know that he knew. So I poked him again.

"Hello? Are you in there, Framer? Are we about to have a thunderstorm or a hurricane or something? You seem distracted."

"Shut the hell up, Will. I know what's going on in the courts on the e-liquid bill," he said.

"Oh, really? Then you know that there is no company that meets the definition of a security firm at present?" I asked.

"I know that's what the ATC thinks."

"And you don't?" I fired back.

"I've been told that is all going to be worked out," he said, as if he didn't know that he'd been busted.

"That's all I needed to hear from you. See ya," I said as I started to walk away. He objected, because he knew what I really just said to him was "Fuck you!"

"What the hell, Will? What the hell is that supposed to mean?" he asked.

"It means I know that you're on the team. The wrong team. Like I said, see ya."

He wasn't done talking to me, and while he knew he'd just shown me his hand, it was clear he didn't know why it mattered. If I were a betting man, I would have bet everything in my pocket that he would be giving Pauly an update about our talk within the hour, maybe even immediately.

What I'd learned was that there were a few people who weren't participating in the e-liquid saga because they didn't know why it mattered. The convenience stores proved that.

But as Bethany and I both suspected, there were some folks on the sidelines for reasons that would not be obvious to someone on the outside. When the liquor stores had been given assurances that they would be taken care of, and when there was no reason for them to believe that on their own, it was clear that some side deals had been made.

I could also assume that the individual liquor store lobbyists were following Jason Farmer on this. They had been promised something. That's why they weren't taking business offers from Bethany's competitors to fight Pauly on it. It was also likely the reason why they were overtly staying away from the issue in the hallway too.

I realized I was fighting more people than I originally thought. But none of them were registered to lobby for anyone involved.

I checked with lobby registration like I told Bethany I would. Of course, however, that was still a self-reporting system.

The more I learned about this whole thing, the more I realized that it wasn't just any screw job. This one was different.

I needed to see Flip. We didn't have plans, but I felt I needed a few minutes. Mal would be sitting at the kitchen table doing her homework around 7:30. I decided to drop by unannounced.

"What a nice surprise," Flip said when she answered the door. "Come on in—maybe you can have a turn helping with homework."

"I'm on it, until I get fired."

"Is that Will?" Mal yelled from the kitchen.

"It is Will the Expert Homework Genius, if you must know," I said as Flip and I headed to the kitchen. "Do you need any help yet? Because I just found out I get to help tonight if you do."

"Nope. I'm just reading tonight. I don't think I'll need any help."

"Well, I'm here for you with my secret answer machine if anything comes up," I said with a flash of my phone as I kissed her on top of her head.

"We'll be in the front room, Mal," Flip told her as she led me back to the couch.

"What's up?" she said. "I didn't expect to see you tonight."

"I'm getting a funny feeling again at work, and I wanted to tell you about it. Okay?"

"You know it is. What?"

I told her about my day and about how, as I suspected, there were more people on the other side of me than I originally knew. I needed her objective input. The whole thing felt even dirtier than it already had—and I sensed it would be getting worse.

"What do you want me to say?" she asked with an easy, expressionless look on her face.

"You know the story. You listen to me, and you see me struggling with all of it. I want to know what you think I should do."

"Okay, baby. Here it goes."

With a start like that, I was suddenly unsure that I wanted to hear what she had to say.

"I think you should do the right thing," she said, and stopped.

I waited for her to continue, but she didn't. I looked down at the floor and started fading into a trance, but then she softly grabbed my chin and turned my head so we were looking eye to eye.

"Whatever the right thing is, and however it is that you do it in the world of the Statehouse, that's my advice. That's what I want *for* you. Not *from* you, but *for* you." She let go of my chin. "I want you to be able to look back at this and be able to hold your head up and answer anyone who asks with an answer describing exactly what you did. Even if no one ever asks, I want you to know in your heart that you did the right thing. That the goodness I see in you is what guided you through a difficult time. And even if you don't get what you thought was justice, you will be able to be at peace because you did the right thing. That's what I think you should do."

An instinctual question immediately popped into my head and then fired out of my mouth. "And damn everything else that might happen to me for doing it?"

"There isn't anything else, baby," she said with a dismissive shake of her head. "Not there. Not for you." She put her hand on my cheek as she now often did.

I smiled back at her, stood up from the couch, and bent over and kissed her.

"Bye Mal! Text me if you get stuck!" I yelled back toward the kitchen as I headed for the door.

"Yeah, right!" she said, sounding just like her mom for a flash.

Flip got the door for me and gave me a hug without saying another word.

24

The Wednesday meeting of the Senate Public Policy Committee meeting was scheduled for 1:30, but it was only a procedural meeting to set up for next week's main event.

I was not delusional about my prospects of stopping Pauly's expected fix the following week or even during that session. The lawsuits wouldn't be done by March 14, and neither would the FDA rule. Bethany wasn't asking me to throw myself in front of this train—and that was what it was, a runaway train.

Even though Bethany didn't ask me to prep the media, and might not even approve of me doing it, I needed at least one good reporter to understand my version of the whole story. None of the Statehouse reporters were paying attention.

Engaging the media wouldn't be easy. But because I was at the beginning of doing the right thing, as Flip would have described it, I needed to focus on a paper and a reporter who might *consider* covering a long, complicated story. That paper was the *Indianapolis Business Journal*. The reporter was someone I didn't know very well, at least at the time.

Her name was Hanna Chastain. She was a reporter for some sort of education trade publication before she went over to the *IBJ* about six months ago. For guys like me, that was a huge promotion, but mainly because I never would have read her stuff at the other place.

The locally owned *IBJ* is an interesting part of the Indiana media market. One might think it's like a heartland version of the *Wall Street Journal*, in that only the rich folks with fat portfolios are reading it. I'm sure that was the case originally. They only publish their actual paper once a week, but they distribute a large amount of "breaking news" type stuff through email alerts and specific newsletter and email blasts.

I hoped Hanna was up for covering the story. I hoped her paper would see the big picture as worthy of their time. The T-shirters likely didn't read the *IBJ* and likely neither did their customers. My goal was to create generic outrage at a story of insider trading. Who knew? Maybe it would work.

. . .

Thursday morning, the House was going in at 10:00 so I got there around 9:30, hoping Hanna was as eager as a new young reporter should be. And there she was, sitting on the floor of the House, in the media section all by herself. I could see her through the hallway glass.

I went to the Democrat side of the chamber and lied to the doorman. I told him I had a 9:30 meeting in the minority leader's office, and he waved me in. I walked right by the leader's door and headed straight to the front of the chamber.

She was a young pretty brunette. With her glasses, she looked like a brainiac. I had found in twenty years of dealing with reporters that most of them were smarter than the average fellow. That tended to happen with people who read.

She was not all made up with hip clothes and too much makeup, so she seemed like someone who was very serious about her job. I hoped she was one of those types who let her work do the talking. Then again, most reporters who weren't TV usually did.

"Hanna?" I asked.

She looked up from her laptop through her glasses with a slight bit of surprise and said: "Uh, yes?"

"My name is Will O'Courtney. Here's my card. I want to talk to you about a story that I think you and your paper will find interesting. No one is covering it, not because they understand it and choose to take a pass on it. They aren't covering it because they absolutely don't understand it."

"I'm sorry, I'm right in the middle of something," she started to explain.

"Don't let me keep you. Ask your colleagues about me. I won't waste your time. But I probably need to talk to you sometime today. Call or text my mobile number when you're done with your project there. I gotta get off the floor—I lied my way in here, and I don't want to get into trouble. Talk to you later." I turned toward the door.

"Wait a minute, I don't understand," she called after me.

"Ask around," I said over my shoulder. "I'll be here when you have time to talk."

My reporter friends would vouch for me if she asked them. They'd tell her that I loved reporters. And I loved being off the record. And I was a huge gossip. And that I would track down whatever research I could that would make writing a story easy.

These are a few of the things that overworked reporters love in a source.

The House was not on the floor for long—I think there was a consensus to get out of town as soon as possible, since the next three weeks would be a grind. The gavel fell at about 11:30 to adjourn for the week, and at 11:35, my phone started buzzing with a text.

191

Will—Hanna here. You have quite the
reputation!

> I don't know about that . . .

When can we meet up?

> Do you have to cover the Senate this
> afternoon?

Yes.

> Well then let's meet over at Pearl Street
> about an hour after they're done, OK?

The Senate found a way to stretch ten minutes of business that afternoon into more than two hours of session time. They didn't adjourn until just after 4:00. I'd not eaten all day, so I scarfed down that salad I'd been thinking about since that morning before Hanna had a chance to get there.

At 5:00, in she came.

I stood to shake her hand and introduce myself properly this time. "Hanna, thank you for coming. Let me reintroduce myself. Hi, I'm Will."

"Yes, yes, I know. It's good to meet you," she said as she sat down.

"Is your first session at the *IBJ* overwhelming, or do you have it under control?" I asked.

She smiled at the question, since it was a little like asking a man if he had quit beating his wife—neither yes nor no worked as an answer.

"I think I got lucky on my transitional year. It's been a bit of a snoozer, until I met you of course!" she said with a bit of manufactured enthusiasm.

192

"I hope meeting me is a good thing for you. I think it will be, if I manage to tell the story well."

"All of my colleagues tell me you can tell a great story."

"Coming from some of them, that is definitely not a compliment, but let's pretend it is since you and I just met, okay?"

She snickered and nodded.

"What I'm about to tell you is a story filled with things I know. But there are still plenty of things that I don't know. The things I don't know, I will learn . . . eventually . . . one way or another. That much is certain."

"Sounds dramatic," she said.

"It is dramatic. Let me start with how I got involved. Last year, the legislature passed HB 1432. It created a regulatory framework for the manufacturing of e-liquid in Indiana. Are you familiar with it?"

"A little. I did a story on the lawsuit that the vape shop owners filed here in the county late last year. Is that what this is about?"

"That is the issue, or the scheme, that I want to tell you about. That local lawsuit is just a tiny part of the picture, though. But just to make this easy, let me start there. In the lawsuit, the plaintiffs claim that the new law requires that manufacturers who want a license in Indiana must contract with a security firm to certify compliance with all the new standards. Fundamental to their suit, they claim no company meets the statutory definition of 'security firm' and therefore the law cannot be implemented. You remember?"

She nodded.

"We agree with them. My client is involved with a federal lawsuit challenging the same law for a whole list of different problems, but this one came up in depositions. The ATC's own general counsel agreed, under oath, that they are unaware of any entity that meets the definition."

Hanna started scribbling and whispered to herself, "I didn't know that." Then she spoke up. "Who is your client?"

"I represent Tobacco America, and they do not know I am talking to you." I still couldn't believe I was representing a tobacco company. Adding insult to injury, I was telling a reporter about it like I was that tobacco company's secret weapon. Nauseating. "Just so you know, this entire conversation is off the record. Good thing for me to make clear before I start telling you the juice."

"Oh, good! There's juice," she said.

"You probably don't remember that the proponents of this shitty law from last year sold the legislature this idea that they were going to build a new, safer, cleaner, state-of-the-art manufacturing facility that would create jobs and end unsafe vape liquid."

"I was covering education last year, so no, I don't know anything about last session."

"It's all in testimony on the video archives. And it was all part of an elaborate lie. Of course, it's easy to lie to people who don't want to know the truth in the first place, but that's a discussion for another time."

"Why do I get the feeling that you're about to make me feel terrible about the Statehouse?" she asked.

"Because you're no dummy," I said as I started a ten-minute description of the details. She scribbled notes frantically until I said, "Hanna, put down the notes. I'm not going anywhere. I'll tell you this story over and over and over if need be. This is a project, not a one-time leak."

An hour and a half later, she had heard the bulk of everything I knew and a few of my theories about the Wabash connection to Senator Alderman, the mentions about marijuana, which I had not investigated, and other mini-dramas.

"Do you believe there are corrupt legislators in on this?" she asked.

"When I hear the word 'corrupt,' I equate that with the breaking of a law. I don't know of any laws being broken, except the lobby registration laws, which of course are just infractions."

"But there could be financial motivation behind this for Alderman or others, right?"

"Of course. I would be at least a little surprised if there weren't, but I don't know of anything. For the life of me, I can't figure out why these guys would risk their political lives, if not their own personal freedoms, over something like this just because Pauly James buys them a lot of steak dinners."

"Why are you telling me this now?"

That was an excellent question from such a young reporter who was new to the beat.

"Because next week, in the Senate Public Policy Committee, Senator Alderman is going to fix this problem for Pauly and the rest of these assholes. I wanted to talk to you now so that when that happens you will recognize it for what it is."

"And is that the story you expect me to write about?"

"No. It is not. It would be great if you did write about it, but the story is obviously bigger than next week's crap. I just want you to know the story as well as I do, and I want you to trust what I am telling you. If those things happen, you will write plenty of stories about all of this. Important stories. Ones you will remember for the rest of your career."

"You think so, huh?"

"If the media can get past the fact that the people who are getting screwed by all of this are just regular people who have no political clout or any real sophistication of any kind, then this story is a jaw-dropper. If we were talking about monopolizing milk or gasoline or smartphones, the Statehouse would be surrounded by people with pitchforks and torches. But because no one gives a shit about these people or this product, the legislature is about to make Pauly and his goons rich beyond their wildest dreams."

"I agree with you. I just don't know how to handle this one," she said.

"That's why I am giving you plenty of advance. You have to figure out how to handle it your own way, and when you do, it will be awesome."

"You think so, huh?"

"Is that your trademark catchphrase? Here's mine: I gotta run—I have to be somewhere at 7:30." I stood up. "Call me, text me, email me any time of day, any day of the week. I will help any way I can. Again, ask around on that one. Sorry I missed the pizza that I hope you get to eat."

She gave me a half-hearted wave and grunted, "See ya." She then dug back into her feverish note-taking mode even before I had completely turned around to leave.

Hopefully, she was as smart as she seemed.

I was going to have to hustle to make it to Grace on time. I felt like I'd just taken a giant step toward doing the right thing.

I wondered what step two would be.

I wondered what my friends would think of my start toward doing the right thing. I wondered what they would think of me.

25

It had been an eventful week, and it was only Thursday night. But it would be a Thursday night unlike any other Thursday night. Even if what made the difference was only in my head.

I hit the lights perfectly on the way out to the west side from downtown, so I actually made it with a couple of minutes to spare. I got to the door just in time to walk in with Flip. She could see I was beaming. She amazed me how she recognized it when she saw it but seemed above caring about the reasons why.

In the room, the first person I saw was Greg. He was so damn big it was hard to see around him sometimes. I looked him dead in the eye and said, "Hey big man, you would have been proud of me today."

"I'm proud of you every day, sweetie," he fired back.

"Oh, yeah. I forgot. I'm your number one," I responded with a flash of my middle finger.

"Boys, we have guests this week," Danny intervened. "Please keep it together."

"Sorry, D. And sorry for him too. We'll behave," I said. "Welcome to Grace!" I exclaimed with a whole new attitude to the new faces in the group.

I was so self-absorbed with my big move with Hanna and the *IBJ* that I wanted to tell everyone. But by the time it was my turn, I'd already calmed down and had half forgotten. I had to rally a little.

"I don't have much to say tonight. Just that I had a really good day, and I'm happy I can spend the end of it with all of you. Well, *most* of you."

Dot was mildly shocked at the circumspect nature of my comment, but she happily followed me with, "See everybody next Thursday. I hope everyone can have a week like Will's day."

We got up to straighten the room and Greg came over to help, or pretend to help.

"What the hell are you so proud of, smartass?" he inquired.

"I told a reporter the entire story. Even the stuff I suspect but can't really or even remotely prove. She's at least a little enthused by it, and I think I'll get some media attention on it now. That's all. It was all off the record, so no big deal."

"You want a medal for that?"

"No, monster mash, just your undying love and devotion."

"I'll think about it, pip-squeak."

Flip was standing there listening without comment, smiling at me like she might have heard but didn't care. She probably didn't care about the details. She didn't care enough to react or pry for them.

We worked our way out of the room and walked down the hall toward the exit together. I slithered my way to the back of the pack of six or seven of us, where Flip was dragging.

"Did you hear what I was telling G?"

"I did," she said with her easy smile that might have been a touch brighter than usual.

"What do you think?"

She stopped me and took both my hands and did her hypno-stare and said, "How would you like to share some leftover pizza with a couple of younger women right now?"

"Do I have to tell my girlfriends about it if I do?" I asked.

"That's between you and them," she whispered.

"I think you should know that one of them has these beautiful green eyes, kind of like yours."

"I hate to interrupt you lovebirds," Greg said, "but are we having lunch tomorrow? Or are we having lunch Monday?"

"What the hell are you talking about? I'm pretty sure you aren't on my calendar. Let me check." I looked him in the eye for a couple of seconds. "Nope, no Greg, no Bryant, no random giant ugly ass. No lunches on this calendar anywhere."

"I just thought of it a second ago, so now you need to clear a spot for me. You can choose tomorrow or Monday," he said, like it was some sort of flexible offer.

"Okay, smartass. I'll take tomorrow, but we have to meet at Coat Check Coffee at 11:30. That's not just my final offer, that's my only offer. Now if you don't mind, I have leftover pizza to eat."

"Done. You two are so cute, in that disgusting, I-can't-look-away-from-the-ten-car-pile-up-freeway-crash-with-horrific-fatalities kind of way."

The three of us headed for our cars as I give him a good-night wave that looked a little like another flash of my middle finger.

. . .

I spent hours at Coat Check doing my typical Friday morning client maintenance crap while waiting for lunch. Greg rolled in a little before 11:30, surprised to see that I was already there.

"What the fuck is up with you today? You haven't beat me anywhere since . . . well, never."

"I'm hiding from my office so I can get some shit done. I've been working here all morning. Don't confuse my promptness with excitement to see you, Megatron. Well, let's hear it. Why are we here?"

"I have a friend that might want to hear your story, probably the same story you told the reporter yesterday," he said.

"What kind of friend might that be?"

"A friend that might be an FBI agent," he said.

I froze for a moment. Why would the FBI care about this? Why was I immediately scared of that too? Why was he being weird about this?

"Uh, why the interest from your so-called friend?" I asked.

"Dunno. Maybe I know a little. I asked him some hypotheticals about your predicament a while back. He investigates public corruption—that's his beat. One thing led to another—"

"You what? You told a fucking FBI agent the story? Jesus, Greg!"

"Take it easy. He doesn't know who you are or any names. It's not that big a deal. But he told me if my hypothetical wanted to tell him the real story, that he would listen."

My instinct was to be furious at him. That's where I started. But I froze into a trance and my mind started racing through the what-ifs.

He interrupted my paralysis.

"If you really want to do the right thing, you should think about taking him up on his offer." He paused again. "I talked to the guy weeks ago, but I didn't want to say anything to you until you had decided to start making a move. Isn't that what you decided when you leaked your shit to the reporter? Or am I wrong?"

"He said he would listen?" I asked. "Is he interested in it, or is he just saying that if someone wanted to tell him a story like mine he would suffer through it?"

"He wants to hear this. Stop looking for a way out of doing this, pussy. Are you in or not? Maybe I should see what Renee wants you to do—"

"Oh, fuck you. This isn't about her," I said in a weak attempt at lying.

"Hell yes it is, and you know it. All of us, especially her, know what's right. Hell, the reporter and my buddy might think you're crazy in the end. They might not even care about your bullshit— and you're acting like this is a no-brainer."

"It's a no-brainer to me," I said.

Then he made another confession. "I know Ethan Murphy."

Holy shit. I sat back in my chair by the window overlooking New Jersey Street and took a deep breath.

"I don't know him well, but I have friends who do," he said. "You've been making fun of the T-shirters since you met them, and I get it, they aren't your people. We've been laughing together about how they *are* my people. The truth is, they actually are. I know about ten of them. Three or four of them have put some money into a vape shop. They don't know I know you, but I wanted you to know that I know them."

"I don't even know what to say to that, man. Why would you keep this from me? Why wouldn't you just say that you wanted me to help out some friends of yours? I wouldn't have been sweating this for the last six months."

"I knew you would come around. Well, I hoped. I wanted you to do this because you thought it was what you should do. Not because I asked you to."

"Do what? How does the FBI even help me or your friends?"

"Dude, I don't know if they do or not. But if my guy starts sniffing around, it will rock that place. Won't it?"

"And that will get us . . . what, exactly?"

"I don't know. Jesus, Will. You gonna talk to him or what?"

"Tell me about these friends of yours for a minute. What are they planning on doing, or do they even know that they're about to be screwed?" I asked.

"They're used to being screwed more than guys like you are. But no, I don't think it has sunk in yet. It was a big deal for them to scrape together the money they needed to open up their shop. And they're still just scraping by, but they're convinced this is the future, so they still have hope."

"When you say they think this is the future, and they have hope, do they think they're going to get rich in this business?" I asked.

"There you go again," he said with a shake of his head. "Getting rich to them means something so much different than what getting rich to you means."

"Enough with that shit. Do they think they're going to get rich or not?" I asked.

"They think if it is successful that they will have freedom. Freedom from having a boss. Freedom from punching a clock and taking orders all day. Some small version of the kind of freedom that you have. I don't think they have even done the math on the money because that's not what they want. It's not about a pile of money for them, it's about being able to live life the way they want to live it. That's what getting rich means to them. So, on those terms, yes, they think they can get rich."

"Wow," I deadpanned.

"What?" he asked. "I know it's small potatoes to you."

That one pissed me off a little.

"You must think I'm the biggest snob on the planet. I don't know, maybe I am. Or maybe I used to be. I know I don't want to be. Not anymore." I paused for a second and took a quick glance out the window. "I guess freedom is priceless. For anyone."

Life is made up of a few key days or even moments. Or choices. This seemed like one.

Ten years ago, the mere mention of the feds would have freaked me out. It still did. It was as if my own lack of self-respect led to an intuitive sense that I was doing something the feds would find problematic. Or even illegal.

The longer I thought about it, the sillier it sounded. I don't break laws. Not anymore. I used to round corners, and I even quit doing that. My clients don't break laws. Why shouldn't I talk to someone who would likely find the offensiveness of this situation corrupt? I knew that Pauly, and his clients for that matter, were not the Boy Scouts. I also assumed that they had legitimate reasons why interest from the feds would scare the hell out of them, maybe even paralyze them.

I was having trouble coming up with reasons not to take Greg's lead and meet with his FBI friend. The only reasons I could come up with seemed to be based entirely on tradition.

If my friends in the legislature and in the hallway knew I brought the feds into the circle, my name would effectively be mud. The only important question was whether or not I should care.

I decided I'd better let this one sit for a day or two. The weekend couldn't have come at a better time.

. . .

I was back in the Statehouse on Monday. Pauly and his lawyer goons were back at it on the Senate side, talking to members of the committee. I was keeping track of every conversation I saw them have with a legislator, and I decided that it was time to make sure the members knew there were people who would disagree with Pauly's bunch.

I focused on the ten Public Policy Committee members and decided to text each an individual warning.

A typical text went like this:

> Senator, I just wanted to let you know that if there is anything happening on the e-liquid front, please let me know so I can brief you on what's happening in federal and state court. Thanks, Will.

And this was a typical response:

> Thanks, Will. I will let you know if I hear anything.

By the end of the day on Monday, no one was talking. It was a little disingenuous that they weren't even telling me that Pauly had been working them. It was even stranger that Pauly had not seemed to make a hard ask of them. My assumption was that Alderman would just bury some tweak in a large amendment on Wednesday. It would be a whisper of legislative language, buried like a needle in a haystack of an amendment, being amended into an already over-weight Christmas tree, what we call a bill that contains a variety of unrelated issues, hung on it like ornaments.

Pauly's ornament would be hard to find unless someone was already looking for it, like me.

As the day crept on, it became obvious that the committee was not doing anything as a group. The rank-and-file members were only listening to the hallway. There were plenty of other things in the bill about which the alcohol boys exclusively cared.

All members of the committee had gotten a text from me, except Charlie. I didn't expect to hear any more from them until the next day at the earliest. And on Tuesday, I should shake each member's hand and follow up on my texts.

Tuesday was a repeat of Monday. I was so anxious for something to happen, I decided to check back in with Hanna.

Hanna—it's Will. How's it going? Do you
need anything from me?

> There's a lot of stuff here. I am still
> wading through it. What's going to
> happen in the hearing tomorrow?

I'm not sure, but I am betting that
Alderman will try to bury the fix in a
bigger amendment to disguise it a little.
That's what I would do. As of right now,
none of the other committee members
seem to be working on it for him.

> Anyone else covering this?

Not that I know of. I still don't think
anyone else cares (yet).

> I will be there tomorrow—see you then.

That was a great sign. She was doing the work of confirming what I told her, and probably finding out some stuff I didn't know. That's what she should be doing—if she was interested in the story.

Wednesday morning came fast. I got to the Statehouse early, walked around, made flybys of every Senate committee I could just so as many senators as possible could see that I was there and available. By mid-morning, I'd made sure most of them had seen me.

And then the phone call came. It was a Statehouse number, but I didn't know whose.

"Will, this is Marianne Billings. Do you have a minute to talk about this e-liquid thing?"

Marianne Billings was a senator from the southwest corner of the state and had been in the legislature forever. She'd been in the House for more than twenty years and had been in the Senate for about ten. She was a Republican, but was the most moderate member of the Senate Republican caucus. She was reasonable. I'd never known her to be susceptible to the kind of influence that came from entertainment or even campaign contributions like Pauly and I would both try to use on anyone. I was fascinated to hear what she had to say.

"Yes, Senator. Of course, I have a minute. I have lots of them."

"Chairman Alderman asked me to carry an amendment in committee this afternoon that changes a definition from last year's law. He's telling me that the law defined the security firm so tightly that very few companies could qualify and, with his change, more companies could get into the business."

It was almost exactly what I had expected. "Senator, to be honest, I can't believe that is an accurate description of what he's trying to do. But I don't have the language in front of me, so I would have to read it to be sure."

"I have a constituent who owns a vape company, and she says we need more security firms or they are going to be run out of business."

Alderman and Pauly had gone pretty low this time. They had convinced someone with a Girl Scout reputation to do their dirty work for them. They probably found this constituent, too. Nice work on their part.

"That is technically correct, but I need you to hear this. Right now, there is no company on the planet that meets the definition, so the number of firms is exactly zero. I don't know what is in the amendment the chairman has asked you to file, but I bet it moves that zero number to exactly one. And that one company is in his district."

"Really? What will that do to my constituent?"

"It means that your constituent will have to agree to whatever terms this Wabash company names if your constituent wants to get a license. Without multiple companies, Alderman's constituent will have a monopoly—a monopoly that will be able to virtually extort whatever they want out of your constituent."

"Will, that's hard to believe."

"I know it is, Senator, because I know you well enough to know that it is not what you intended to pass last year. There are two court cases going on right now debating this issue. Again, I don't know how the words on Alderman's paper read, but I would be shocked if it did anything other than what I'm predicting. Hell, I've been waiting for them to pull this stunt for weeks."

"Okay. Let me talk to my person from home."

"Make sure you ask them if they have a deal with the Wabash security firm. Because if they don't, they should be thinking about how that will actually happen."

"Okay. Thanks, Will."

And there it was. It was almost exactly as I predicted, with the dramatic twist of Charlie Alderman and Pauly finding someone else to do it for them. That might seem like a small thing, but it wasn't. Especially if I looked at this whole mess through a lens of public corruption, in search of abnormal behavior.

26

Chairman Alderman was presiding at the hearing, and there was only one bill on the calendar. Of course, the bill represented the entire legislative session in the arena of alcohol and tobacco regulation. In Congress, Christmas tree bills like this were on the agenda every day.

In the Indiana Statehouse, it was a little more unusual.

It was even more unusual when there were a hundred pages of legislative language that was mostly uncontroversial, and half a page that might be criminal. The room was packed with the usual suspects, all of whom cared about the usual stuff. And me. And Ethan Murphy.

I had hoped the convenience store association would be ready to cry foul and provide new testimony from a new angle. They would want to speak up eventually, but their governing board was still catching up. Shane Thomas was in the room but wouldn't say a word today. Hopefully he would get the green light before Monday.

There were seventy people jammed into a seating area set up for fifty. I didn't know who in the crowd knew what was really happening and who didn't. I knew it was more than just the few of us who were talking about it in public, but that was about all.

Bethany wanted me to play nice, which to her, meant not to testify. But since the room was full beyond capacity, the situation allowed me to stand off to the side. It was an awkward place to be when one was trying to blend into the crowd. Of course, I wasn't trying to blend in. I was standing there for the express purpose of fidgeting, demonstrably rolling my eyes, shaking my head, snickering, and sarcastically giggling just enough to be noticed but not enough to get thrown out. It was a delicate balance sometimes, or so it would seem. I made sure to lay it on thick.

Alderman called the hearing to order and immediately called the only item on the agenda, HB 1686. If the members of the committee had a clue that they had been duped by Alderman into believing this was no big deal, consent would never have been given. Had they returned my texts and calls this morning, I could have spooked them into at least a little bit of anxiety. But they had been living the lie of this whole episode for a year now, so waking them up was not going to be that easy.

"Senator Billings," Alderman said, "would you like to discuss your amendment?"

Nice. He was playing this charade like it was legitimately *her* amendment.

"Mr. Chairman, I present to the committee amendment number one. It is a technical change to the definition of a security firm within the e-liquid manufacturers licensure law that was passed last session. It appears that the definition was made too tightly, and we need to modify it so more potential firms can meet the definition. I would like to defer to representatives of Indiana Tobacco to explain the details and have committee discussion on the matter. I believe there might be some differences of opinion of what the amendment does, so I would like all those perspectives aired here today. Thank you."

Alderman invited Pauly to the table. "Mr. James, step right up."

Pauly headed to the table and in full aw-shucks mode sat down to explain in the most innocent way possible the screw job he was in the midst of putting on the State of Indiana.

"Amendment number one tweaks the definition in last year's law which Senator Billings refers to in a very specific way. Last year, the General Assembly passed a law that created a licensing framework for e-liquid manufacturers. Fundamental to that new process was the creation of guidelines for the private sector to help the state implement the law. The ATC is simply too burdened to go out and inspect every one of the companies that manufacture e-liquid that will be sold in Indiana. The law established the definition of which type of companies can contractually do these inspections. It statutorily detailed the required qualifications of any entity wanting to be a security firm."

The depth of his lying was phenomenal.

"For a firm to meet the definition in the bill, they need to have certifications from two national organizations. The current law requires that two employees of this private entity have these two separate certifications. What I think the committee was trying to articulate last year was that both these certifications are held within any qualifying company. There are firms where the certifications, and expertise that come with them, are held by the same person. That's what the amendment before you today clarifies: that the employee or employees who hold these certifications can be one person *or* two people. That's all."

I loved how *he* told the committee what *they* meant last year almost as much as I loved watching the committee let him do it.

"Thank you, Mr. James. Are there any questions from the committee?" was Alderman's move.

Senator Billings chimed in, with obvious nervousness. "Mr.

Chairman, I believe there are other people here who want to speak specifically to this issue."

"I have one person signed up to testify," Alderman replied. "Ethan Murphy? Is this the issue your testimony is related to?"

Ethan stood up and calmly said, "Yes, sir."

It was funny that Pauly didn't have to sign up. The chairman invited him up. It was as if he was on the committee and not just some member of the public like everyone else on the planet. It was another subtle sign of who was actually in charge.

Ethan walked up and sat down at the table. He was a little more polished than he was a year ago, and his suit seemed to fit better.

"I appear today on behalf of the Hoosier Vapor Association. I testified in opposition to the bill last year that created the law that this amendment attempts to fix. There is a long list of things wrong with that law—"

"Mr. Murphy, does this language change or expand the number of qualifying security firms or not?" Senator Billings asked.

"Senator, it might. But no reputable security company, like the ones we use as examples in our lawsuit, will qualify."

"How was it discovered that the language needed changing? Do you know?" Senator Billings asked.

"It became apparent during the deposition process of a second lawsuit that my association is not a party to. It's in federal court in Louisville. The ATC's general counsel gave testimony that she was not aware of any firm that qualified."

Chairman Alderman couldn't let that kind of discussion continue so he put a stop to it. "Thank you, Mr. Murphy. Are there any other questions from the committee?" He paused for a second, maybe two. "Hearing none, can we take the amendment by consent?"

With my arms crossed, I put a big smile on my face and shook my head at any member I could make eye contact with.

It was a bold move on Alderman's part. The committee's nervousness was visible. And while there was a low-key murmur of "consent" spoken by about half of the committee, Senator Billings could not help herself.

"Mr. Chairman, I think that this matter needs further discussion. I realize that time is now running short due to our session deadlines, but I am not comfortable with what this means for a constituent of mine who contacted me earlier this week."

Alderman continued to act like it was no big deal, even though you could see the members of the committee squirming. "You have my commitment that we can discuss it further in caucus and on Second Reading, Senator."

And then he moved on before anyone else could actually say their reservation out loud.

"If there are no other motions, what is the will of the committee . . ."

It sounded like his vice chairman uttered the important words: "I move the bill do pass."

Our friend, the ranking Democrat Senator Anderson, quickly followed with "Second."

Chairman Alderman, almost in synchronized rhythm said, "Call the roll."

Hanna was waiting for me in the hallway. There were a couple of other Statehouse reporters in the room, but they didn't seem to care about the insider debate that had taken all of five minutes. I gave her the directional-side-head shake, symbolic of "come walk with me," as I walked toward the north end of the fourth floor where no one was congregating. No one ever congregated there unless there was a hearing going on in the Court of Appeals.

"Do you think anyone else cares about this now?" she asked.

"They don't seem to. Does it look like anyone does to you?"

"I've been looking into all this and following up on all of your . . . stuff, for lack of a better word," she said.

"And?"

"Oh my God! Everything I confirmed or discovered was worse than I thought it would be. I haven't interviewed anyone yet, but that will be unbelievable. Literally. I don't feel like I have been lied to yet in my three years in this building. This time, I know these guys won't tell the truth. I just know it."

"Yeah, this is dirty, like I said it was. There is no question about it. And you're right. We haven't heard the worst of it yet. I'm certain about that too."

"I can't believe the way the committee just sat there. It's obvious that something slimy is going on, and you can see that they know it. What is Billings thinking?" she asked.

"I think she got duped into thinking it was no big deal, but she started to get it while it was happening. Now, I bet she's going to be on fire."

"What would happen if they didn't put this amendment in and nothing changed in the law?"

"I think selling e-liquid in Indiana would effectively become illegal on July 1. Wouldn't that be fun?"

"Jesus!"

My phone started buzzing with a Statehouse number again. "Hang on, Hanna, I need to see who this is."

"Will, it's Marianne Billings. Can you meet me this evening around 6:00? I want to show you something that I predict will make sense to you. I would send it to you, but it's confidential."

"Of course, Senator. Will you still be here in the building, or should I meet you somewhere else?"

"We need to meet somewhere else. This thing has me so upset. I need to leave the building, and I don't feel like whispering later when I show you this."

"How about Iaria's?" I offered. "None of the Statehouse folks will be there at 6:00."

"See you then, Will. Thank you."

Iaria's is on the southeast side of downtown on the edge of Fletcher Place. It's my favorite Italian joint in town. Actually, it's my favorite joint of any kind . . . in any town. The place and its food might be more of an addiction than a preference, but I digress.

Hanna was still lingering in the north end of the fourth floor when I got off the phone.

"Who was that?" Hanna asked.

"Are we partners now, Hanna?" I asked with a stern and deep tone. "I need to know that I am off the record with you indefinitely, so we can talk freely. I don't want to read my name in your story or stories without knowing what comment you are using. I need to know that you are protecting me as a source."

"You are my first and only actual source, so yeah, I will protect you. And so yeah, we are partners."

"That was Senator Billings. She has some confidential document to show me that is upsetting her. I think these guys fucked up by trying to manipulate her."

"What document? What the hell can it be?"

"No idea. I told her to make sure that her constituent had a deal with Schulte's before she did the amendment. Maybe it has something to do with that. I hope it does."

Hanna was spinning. "And you'll call me later?"

"If I'm your only source, then all either one of us has is each other, right?" I said as I headed for the stairs.

27

aria's is one of my happy places. Most people I take there end up admitting that it's a great joint, but in the foodie world we live in today, a vintage Italian restaurant, circa 1913, doesn't inspire the way it once did. Dom runs the bar and that's where I always sit. I don't know if he's in charge of the place, and I'm not asking. He's the boss to me. When it's crowded, I sometimes have to go sit in the family room, which is still cool, but it's not the same. The food is the same, but I know where I want to sit and that's in the bar that Dom runs. I doubted Senator Billings had been there lately, but if we had to get out of the fray, this was as good as it gets. At least for me.

She walked in right on the number, and there was almost no one in the place so she had no trouble spotting me in the corner.

"Thanks for meeting me," she said. "I think you'll want to see this."

"I don't have a clue what you're handing me, but if you *think* I'll care, I guarantee I will."

"It's a contract. It's for security services, from that Wabash company you expected would be in the mix," she said with a tone like she expected I already knew the information. "I need to clear that up."

"Senator, I assume this was why your constituent originally thought your amendment was helpful. But I have just been predicting this shit, you know? I have no way of knowing what the story behind the curtain really is. I'm on the other side. But if you don't mind—"

"Read it!" she yelled before realizing she was yelling. She then followed with, "By all means, read it!" with her agitation turned down to a yell-whisper.

I read it quickly, flipping to page two of the five-pager, where I saw the first alarm.

"They want your constituent to report sales and revenue data to them on a monthly . . . and quarterly basis? What the fuck for?"

Senator Billings kept her scowl steady and simply said, "Keep reading."

I got to the fourth page and saw the big one. The contract required the licensee to pay the security firm, Schulte's, five percent of the licensee's revenue. All revenue! It was to be paid quarterly during the life of the contract, which was five years.

I didn't even know what to say to that. I glanced up with what must have been a look of total astonishment.

"Uh . . . this reads like . . . a contract to pay the local mob boss for the privilege of doing business on his block, for crying out loud!"

"Yes. That is exactly what it is. It doesn't just read like it, or seem to be like it, or smell like it. That is exactly what it is!" She took a deep breath and tried to gather herself. "And those bastards are not negotiating these contracts. This is their only offer, take it or leave it."

I didn't know how the bastards, as she described them, were going to structure their elaborate scam. I knew the scheme would be offensive, so that part was no surprise, but the "how" certainly was. I'd tried to explain to anyone who would listen how this monopoly would work—that Schulte's would *control* the market.

"Schulte's is supposed to be a security company, right? Why would they get a cut of revenue? That would be like paying the painter or the landscaper a cut. Am I missing why they think people will just sign up for this shit without talking about it?"

She silently glared at me while steadily shaking her head.

"Senator, this was not exactly what I predicted. But I know about monopolies. And this will be a monopoly, just like any other monopoly when all the dust settles."

"What if they want to change the terms later, or disagree? Without them, my guys are out of business! What if my guys strike it rich? This security company gets rich with them?

"Will, I can't tell you how sick to my stomach I am. I guess I always knew something was odd about this whole thing, but so many things we do are odd, this didn't seem all that special. I can't believe we let it happen." She paused. "That's not even accurate. We didn't just let it happen—we are the ones who did it."

"I know, and I am sorry for you," I said, without an ounce of honesty. "What you put into that bill today, if it passes, enables this extortion. It makes the bill you passed last year work, but it only works for the bastards. And no one will believe me when I predict it. They have to hear it from you."

She sighed again. "I don't have confidence they will listen to me either. Not now. I'll look like an idiot bringing it up now."

We looked at each other for a couple of seconds.

I turned to Dom behind the bar and yelled: "Do you guys sell food here? Or were we supposed to bring our own?"

He looked at me with zero emotion and grunted, "I didn't want to interrupt the big damn meeting you were having." Out from behind the bar he strolled. "Here's a couple of menus. Ma'am, let

217

me know if you have any questions. Or you can ask him—he eats here more than I do."

"Thank you, sir," I replied to him with full-throated sarcasm.

A fast dinner helped the senator get a firm grasp on everything I knew and most of the things I suspected. Of course, the manner of the cash flow was something the contract helped clarify. She asked me what I thought she should do, and I told her to file an amendment that stripped all the security firm language from the law, just like Representative Ben Rizzo's bill would have done. That would cause a fight that probably wouldn't end well inside the Senate Republican Caucus.

She could also file an amendment for the floor that simply removed the amendment she filed for Alderman. If she pulled out her own amendment, and the bill became law, the Indiana market would shut down. Bethany and TA were going to walk away from Indiana anyway, so that shouldn't matter to them. I cared about that more than my client did. But more importantly, it would force Alderman and Pauly back to the table.

If no one could get a license because there was no security firm, but the rest of the law stayed in place, no one would make money, including Pauly and his team, whoever the hell that was.

I walked into Pearl Street to a crowd of people who look wildly unfamiliar to me. They were young and mostly watching a game that might as well have been cricket. I was in a tunnel and immune to everything around me. No one seemed to notice my suit and tie or how badly out of place I must have looked.

Hanna was sitting in the back near the bathrooms where no one else wanted to be because of the bad view of the TV. It was the same table we had last time.

Before I reached the table she started in: "Well? What the hell did Billings have for you?"

"Take a deep breath, Hanna."

"Why? You get me all jacked up on this and now you want me to calm down?"

"I don't actually want you to calm down—it's just that you're the only one more fired up than I am, so—"

"What the hell did she have?"

"Okay. This is confidential. She wouldn't let me have the papers she showed me anyway and you won't be able to get your hands on them either. At least not yet, or at least not from her."

"Quit stalling already."

"All right! Jesus. So, here is how this whole thing is going to work." I relayed the whole story from Senator Billings. Hanna frantically wrote her notes with a strange, adrenaline-driven look on her face like she was playing linebacker in the Super Bowl. She didn't ask any questions while I told her the main points.

"Basically, it's legalized extortion," I said. "Everyone with a license in Indiana will have to pay Schulte's five percent of their revenue just for certifying that they comply with the rest of the law. There will be no ongoing services of value, and even if there were, it would have nothing to do with driving sales or profits. It's like the old neighborhood mob bosses, like the Robert De Niro version of Vito Corleone from *Godfather 2*."

She put down her pen and sat back in her chair. She finally took that deep breath I'd told her to take earlier. And then the questions began. "This is all in the contract? There are documents floating around with this structured relationship that can be cited, on paper?"

"It is in at least one version. Based on what Marianne said, and this matches all my suspicions, anyone that will get a license has this same offer in front of them. I expect this is the deal across the board. I would have thought they would try to grease Marianne's constituent. Since there is no sweetheart deal for them, I can't imagine there being one for someone else."

"Oh—my—God," Hanna said. "How much money are we talking about?"

"Right now, it might not amount to all that much. But I assume the Schulte's folks expect a migration from cigarettes to vaping. My client is counting on that nationally, so why shouldn't everyone else? Imagine all the smokers of today being vapers tomorrow. And these guys getting a five percent cut of all *revenue* in the Indiana market. It's a big number. I was on a call a couple of months ago when one of the TA execs expected Indiana to generate $200 million a year. That's every year. So, yeah, it's real money."

After another deep breath from her, she said, "I'm writing my first story about it this weekend. I'm nervous."

"Why?"

"The legislators are going to be mad about it. Really mad, I bet."

"I don't know about that. We'll see. They might shrug it off and hope it goes away. Empires usually don't crumble over one bad story. Just don't make any errors, because like I said when we first met, there will be more stories to write on this before it's over."

I needed the first story to be a good, clean setting of the table. If for no other reason, I needed it to be something that interested people who hadn't been paying attention from the start. Mainly, the FBI.

Just before bed, I send Greg the text.

I'm ready to meet your friend.

28

I woke up on Thursday morning to three text messages. It was a setup exchange between Greg and his FBI pal, Ted, who everyone apparently called TK. By the time I chimed in, all that was left to do was agree to a Friday coffee at Coat Check. That's one way to start the day—a friend no one in the Statehouse knows sets me up to meet with the feds.

I arrived at the Statehouse around 10:00 and found a seat on a bench outside of the Senate again. I wanted to stir up the committee members and encourage them to engage in conversation with Senator Billings. She was going to need their help in caucus, and the discussion of the bill likely wouldn't come up until next week.

I had decided to start taking the "I told you so" approach. Nothing makes a legislator more nervous than telling them that what they have done, are doing, or thinking about doing will be a complete disaster. And not arguing with them about it but *promising* them the disaster.

The Senate didn't come in until 1:30, and there were only a couple of committees going on, so the hallway was pretty bare outside the chamber. I sent the usual texts to a handful of committee members who'd looked particularly nauseated by yesterday's events. The text went like this:

> Just let me know if you want me to walk you through the e-liquid security firm nonsense you guys amended in yesterday.

So far, no one was jumping at my offer. But eventually at least some of them would.

While I was sitting there on the bench, Hanna Chastain came around the corner. I spotted her first, but I didn't have anything pressing to tell her, so I didn't jump to get her attention. Then she saw me. And she jumped, sort of. She came charging at me like she didn't have my mobile number or something and had been searching the world over for her newest friend.

"Will O'Courtney, just the man I wanted to see," she announced as she approached my bench.

"Oh God. Tell me you aren't pissed off at me over something. That's all I need today."

"Why would I be pissed? I am jacked up about this story! I'm on a deadline—my bosses are excited about it now after I told them everything this morning. And all I am doing today is getting comments from legislators. The timing has worked out perfectly for me. Thank you, thank you, thank you!"

"You came firing over here to thank me?" I asked in disbelief. "Will I be thanking *you* when I read your story on Sunday?"

"It might sound like you wrote it—without the quotes. I mean . . . I assume you know everything about it," she said.

"Oh, I think you should be ready to learn new stuff every few days on this one, Hanna. I know I am," I told her, even though I was glad she at least thought I knew everything about this shit. "Stay

focused, young lady. Don't worry. I'm not taking on any new partners. It's just you and me. I'm not going to leave you for the *Star*."

"Okay, okay. I'll keep chasing these guys for their comments and
talk to you on Monday. Unless one of these guys wants to openly lie
to me today, then I'll text you immediately." She laughed.

"Deal. You know I'm open twenty-four hours a day. Now go
get 'em!"

We needed to avoid spending too much time with each other in
the building. If her story was a good one, in my eyes, there could
be some pissed off legislators. I didn't want them thinking I planted
the story. At least not yet.

The *Indianapolis Star* is the biggest paper in the state, the one
that stands out in size and subscribers. All the reporters in the
building from papers based in Fort Wayne, Evansville, Northwest
Indiana, and the metro area of Louisville compete with each other,
but they all know they are at a disadvantage against the *Star*, which
has more resources than everyone else. The *Star* is like the New
York Yankees of the Statehouse.

I was a little pissed they hadn't given this any attention so far, so
fuck them. It was me and Hanna on this one.

None of the eight members of the Senate I texted that morning
responded until right after lunch, when they all suddenly wanted to
see me. One by one, they either called or came out into the hallway
looking for me. No text responses, which meant they didn't want
anyone to know they were asking around about it. I could tell that
each of them thought they were the only one who thought it was
time to try and get a handle on exactly what they were doing. Each
acted like our conversations were secret, though they never asked
me to actually keep them secret.

Pretty normal behavior, really, with the tension rising.

Then one of them made an incredibly self-aware suggestion.
Senator John Middleton from Indianapolis didn't even want to hear

my spiel. He came out from the Senate chamber, called me over to the door, and said: "You need to talk to our chief of staff. He needs to hear the story and understand it before we get together for our Monday caucus meeting. He's expecting your call."

These senators were starting to realize that they'd worked themselves into a corner, and they didn't know how to find their way out of it. I knew the chief. He was about my age but had been around even longer than I had. Plus, he was a lawyer and a good one. It wouldn't take me long to explain the situation to him. On the other hand, it might take him a while to explain to me why he hadn't done something to stop it yet.

Andy Bauman, my hipster pal at the Senate front desk, set it up, and fifteen minutes later I was upstairs in the private conference room with Peter Jansen. I don't think I'd ever had an actual meeting with him before.

"Peter? I'm not sure if you wanted this meeting or if I did," I said as I entered the room.

Peter was notoriously void of emotional expression. "Why don't we wait till later to decide that. Tell me what's going on in 1686 and what happened in the committee yesterday."

"Do you know what happened last year?" I asked.

"Maybe," he said.

"Well then, I'll make this quick." I sat down and caught him up on the broad strokes of the bill. If anyone was likely to actually know this stuff on the inside, just from standard diligence, it was him. After I finished the standard description, I asked, "You with me so far?"

"Uh-huh."

"So what happened in committee yesterday is those assholes convinced Marianne Billings to put an amendment into 1686 that would fix the definition so only their guys in Wabash will fit it. Read it, Peter! And don't overlook the part where after July 1, no new licenses will be granted. Not for anyone."

"I got it, Will," he said.

"Well, I'm glad we could have this talk," I stood up.

"What do you suggest we do about it?" he asked.

"I suggest you throw yourselves in front of this train, because I'm in a mood to just let it roll over you now."

"Seriously. I want to know. How do we fix it?" he asked, knowing the answer but wanting someone else to tell him.

"Peter, you'll have to strike all of the security language from the law. You tell Charlie Alderman that it's over. And then we all agree to not speak of this filthy little scheme ever again." I knew there was no chance in hell Pauly and Alderman would just walk away.

Peter stuck to his expressionless approach and said, "Thanks."

I gave him a sarcastic huff of a chuckle, tinged with a hint of pity. On my way out the door I said, "See ya."

That meeting happened because of Hanna. She was asking senators for comments on the whole mess, and none of them were prepared to give one. The senators who didn't understand any of it were pissed off for looking stupid. The ones who did get it didn't want to look like they were in on it. I'm sure the media office was at a loss on how to advise them. And those folks worked for Peter. And Peter was the one who knew what most of the factual answers were. He didn't like the answers, but he knew what they were.

He also knew that he was going to have a hard time convincing the caucus that what I told him and what the words on the paper actually said didn't match whatever bullshit story Alderman would feed them on Monday.

Most importantly, Peter knew the Senate should be scared of me now. He knew that I was armed with the most powerful weapon: knowledge.

What he didn't know was that I was about to tell the FBI the whole damn story.

I left the building that day feeling pretty good about things. I had a reception I needed to attend that evening, so I wasn't going to be able to go to church. I always hated missing my friends, but especially that night.

I would see Flip and Mal on Sunday at brunch as a consolation, but three days seemed a long time.

Friday morning came faster than I thought it would. I finished my workout and answering emails by 9:00. Coat Check had become my home court, and I doubted I would have any Statehouse types to try to evade anytime soon.

I walked in at about 9:20, found a corner table, and ordered an Ethiopian coffee, which was a first.

I was about to text Greg's friend when I heard, "Will? Ted King. Good to meet you."

I stood up, happy he'd solved the name mystery. "Ted King? I won't lie. I was worried your last name was Kaczynski."

"Yeah, yeah, I've heard it before."

TK was about my age. A little taller, with a goatee. We could almost pass for family. And he was dressed similarly to me, except his V-neck was a Colts sweatshirt.

"I hear you have quite the story about the Indiana Statehouse," he said.

"I do. And there will be a story in the *IBJ* about it this weekend. So that will help confirm the high points of what I'm about to tell you. But first, how do you and Greg Bryant know each other?"

"My wife knows his ex-wife from school. They go to yoga classes together, and my daughter babysits his kids every now and then. You know, the usual. You two know each other from church?" he asked.

"Sort of. It's a church group we're both in. Kind of a Bible study group. So how does this work?" I asked.

"Why don't you tell me what you think I need to know, and I'll interrupt from time to time with questions. Public corruption is the department I work in and have for more than ten years. I'm going to recognize some of the people you talk about. Don't let that freak you out. It usually does when people find out that guys like me have been watching them."

I guessed that would turn out to be an understatement.

"Should I assume, for purposes of telling the story, that you don't know anything about the whole e-liquid saga?" I asked.

"For purposes of storytelling, yes. But I'll tell you that I know about Pauly James and his clients. I know about Lance Meridian—both Senior and Junior. And I know about Karl Satterfield. And now you know why I'm interested in your story."

He was going to love what I had to tell him. "It all started for me a little over a year ago . . ."

. . .

The digital version of the *IBJ* comes out on Sunday mornings. It's scheduled then so the good businesspeople of the city have their paper copies in hand on Monday morning. You know the type—the people who read it and the *WSJ* to make people think they are somehow on the show-me-the-money team.

But the people who were firing out of bed on Sunday to read that week's edition could likely be counted on my hands. They included those having their business profile published with their glamour shot photo in their best suit and tie; the owners of businesses who expected to be on top of this week's list of fastest-growing businesses, or most profitable, or largest employers; and me.

Front page—what would definitely be above the fold in the actual paper version—the headline read, "E-liquid law raises questions about industry's future in Indiana." There was a studio-grade photo of some vape accessories and a bottle of juice. There was a highlighted quote from Ethan Murphy: "This is all a scheme to monopolize an emerging market by the legislature."

The next thing I did before actually reading the story was to scan it for my name, then 'unnamed sources,' and if I found nothing, it would be perfect. Perfect it was!

Mission accomplished. It appeared that at least the first mission had landed. I could tell by the actual size of the story that there was plenty of gas left in Hanna's tank for the next one. But this should adequately rattle some cages for Senator Billings during Monday's caucus meeting.

It would be a battle between righteousness and Charlie Alderman behind closed doors. I wished it were on pay-per-view.

Brunch was going to be particularly good.

29

The Statehouse was busier than it usually was on most Mondays. All amendments in the Senate would be discussed in the Republican caucus meeting at noon. I knew Senator Billings would be filing at least one amendment on HB 1686, probably two. And there would likely be others. Hanna's story might be at least a little concerning to some of the members who were not on the committee. It would raise questions about what should be expected if the bill were changed at all.

Charlie Alderman would be on the defensive. I'd have loved to be a fly on the wall in that meeting. The only way for him and whoever his supporters were to convince the group that nothing shady was going on was to blatantly lie to them. Or, should I say, *continue* to blatantly lie to them.

Senator Billings called me at 9:30 and asked me to come upstairs and see her.

I was correct. She had two amendments ready. The first one simply took out the amendment that Charlie Alderman had manipulated her into filing for the committee hearing. The second one basically took Representative Ben Rizzo's bill, striking all the language that created the security firm and related references to it.

I liked the second one—a lot.

She wanted me to read them and make sure they did what she intended them to do. They were perfect.

After we finished with the tedious stuff, she asked me, "Did you see the *IBJ* story?"

"I did. I wonder if anyone else around here will see it before noon," I said.

"Oh, they'll see it. I emailed it to all of them and had my assistant deliver paper copies to every senator's desk in our caucus."

Holy shit. Well, there's no place for them to hide then. "Thanks, Marianne. You are one of a kind," I said as I got up.

Right as I got back down to the third-floor exit from the Republican side of the Senate chamber, I received a text from Peter Jansen, the chief of staff.

> On 1686, there's a provision in the bill
> that says no applications for licenses
> can be filed or approved by the ATC
> after July 1. None at all. Did you
> overlook that?

> No. I know it's in there—thought I
> mentioned it to you. If I were you, I
> would strike the paragraph. But like
> the rest of this shit, it's no accident it's
> in there. That provision will close the
> market forever.

Someone else was going to file that one. I didn't know who, probably Senator Middleton. He was the one who sent me to Peter Jansen in the first place. Each of the three amendments would lead to three tough conversations for Alderman in the caucus. I wouldn't want to be him at noon.

Caucus meetings always take longer on deadline days. It was the last day of the 2016 session for bills to be amended on the floor. Often these debates and votes were more significant than the final up or down ones. The members didn't start rolling out of that meeting until around 2:30. I only had the one issue being debated, so for me, it felt a little like a jury deliberating whether or not to convict or acquit.

Everyone came out looked tired.

The call to come to order by the lieutenant governor came at 2:45, and most of the senators went from the caucus room on the fourth floor to the floor of the Senate without coming out into the hallway. They proceeded straight to the calendar without any resolutions or pomp and circumstance. They were all business today.

After they motored through a few bills without any bumps in the road, Senator Billings came out into the hallway and had the doorman get my attention to come over to the door to chat with her. I assumed she would tell me what the caucus had decided on the amendments and let me know if there was something I could do to help.

Before last year, Alderman would have been one of the guys who leaked to me *exactly* what went on in the private meeting.

"Will, I have no idea how this thing is going to play out this afternoon. Do you?" she asked.

"Of course I don't, Senator. I thought you guys were working that out upstairs," I said sarcastically.

"We didn't vote on it. We discussed the amendments, and there was plenty of nervousness and disagreement about what was real and what wasn't. But in the end, I think each member would have their own reason for voting whichever way they voted."

"You didn't decide upstairs? Why not?" I asked with surprise.

"No one called for a vote, and I wasn't going to. I didn't want someone to tell me not to make either of my motions to amend, so I didn't ask permission. If they wanted to vote no on them, that was their business."

"Is there anything I can do?"

"I think you need to be here in case someone needs to talk between now and when the bill gets called."

With that she turned and went back into the chamber.

I was planning on doing that anyway. It could be two hours or more before they called this thing for second reading.

Ethan Murphy was milling around with a couple of T-shirters. The three of them were clearly anxious. Pauly had two or three lawyers with him doing the same thing. It was hard not to show my surprise on seeing Karl Satterfield make an appearance. He was making a fly-by through the hallway. It was something I might do if I wanted people to know I was around and paying attention but not really responsible for anything in particular. Karl stopped by Pauly's huddle only for a moment. It looked like he gave them a ten-second *rah rah* and then proceeded to prance out of the scene. The rest stayed put and kept nervously talking to each other, which likely amounted to a whole lot of nothing. It was like watching a bunch of 1950s fathers-to-be pacing around in the maternity waiting area while their wives were going through childbirth alone.

I opted to sit on the bench as slouched and relaxed or apathetic as I could be. Other lobbyists, mainly young folks, took turns occupying the other half of my bench, engaging in catty discussions about anyone within eyesight.

Then a strange thing happened. Charlie Alderman came out into the hallway and searched the place from wall to wall like he wanted to find someone specific. I was still on my bench, and he and I locked eyes for a second, and for a moment, I actually thought he was coming out to see me. Then he spotted Pauly's huddle and made a beeline for them. No surprise.

I didn't take my eyes off them, which was easy since they made no effort to take a walk at all. But after about a minute of animated conversation, Charlie left his two sponsors and came walking right at me. Surely he wasn't going to try to talk to me now. It had been almost a year since we'd spoken a word to one another. He wouldn't like anything I had to say. I was pretty sure I wouldn't like anything from him either.

"You got a minute, Will?"

"You know I do, Charlie. I'm just waiting on the big show, and it can't start as long as you're out here," I said with a know-it-all attitude.

"Walk with me."

We rounded the corner, and he kept strolling toward the Supreme Court Chamber at the far north end of the third floor as he started talking.

"Will, none of these shitty amendments of yours can pass today. You know that, don't you?"

"I don't have any amendments, Charlie," I said, keeping a steady, shit-eating grin on my face.

"Whatever," he said. "Listen to me, it would be better for everyone if the amendments weren't called. If Billings and Middleton call their amendments, they're going to be defeated anyway. If we have to go to the microphone and argue over them, the implementation of this law this summer will get even tougher than it was already gonna be."

"Bullshit, Charlie." I kept my calm, I-know-more-than-you-do façade.

"Oh really? Well, I assume your client wants a license here, doesn't she?"

"Not enough to negotiate a contract with your pimps over there in the corner she doesn't."

"What?" he asked in amazement.

"That's right, Charlie. TA is walking away from Indiana over this until we blow this thing up. There is no way in hell we're going to let your fucking buddies extort money or market share out of us." I lowered my voice to just above a whisper and said, "You can take your fucking little scam and stick it right in your ass."

"You're out of your mind!" he half-yelled with pure amazement.

"No, I'm not. You assholes have miscalculated how this was going to work. I want to see you go to that microphone and lie your ass off this afternoon about how many security companies can meet your definition. I want it saved in the video archive. And later I'm going to hang it around your neck. Trust me, Charlie. You guys pissed off the wrong guy this time. I told Pauly he would regret the day he fucked me over last year, and trust me, so will you."

He stood there looking at me like he truly couldn't believe the shit that was coming out of my mouth. Speechless. Red in the face. But still speechless.

So I broke the silence. "Anything else?"

He took a deep breath, put that senatorial smile back on his face, and said, "See ya later, Will."

Then we both headed back toward the chamber. When we walked by Pauly and his legal goons, I couldn't see Charlie's expression because I was walking behind him, though I could see him shaking his head. And I could see Pauly frowning at Charlie first, then me second.

I couldn't resist. While I had their attention, I gave them my middle finger right in front of a pretty good-sized crowd of people who probably don't care for that kind of vulgarity. Fuck them. If there ever was a time to fly my bird, that was it.

I went back to my bench, and ten minutes later the bill was called.

There were only three amendments filed, and they were all amendments that Charlie was going to have to fight.

"Senator Alderman has called House Bill 1686 for the second time. Are there any motions?" the lieutenant governor called.

Senator Billings stood and said, "Madam President, I would like to call amendment #1."

She went to the microphone. "Madam President, and members of the Senate: Amendment #1 makes changes to the e-liquid law, which was passed last year."

After describing the amendment and closing with "I ask for your support," she stepped away from the microphone, but she did not go back to her seat. She seemed to expect there to be questions, but no one had any. They were scared to go to the microphone and talk on the record.

"Further discussion?" the lieutenant governor asked. Nothing.

Senator Billings then requested a roll call vote. I didn't know why she did that. When legislators are scared, they tend to vote no more often than yes. She needed people to vote yes.

The voting machine was opened, and the board lit up with red votes; 18–29 was the tally. Only 18 of them were willing to vote yes. Most of the ten Democrats voted no also. Three members were missing, but three votes wouldn't have mattered. The amendment was defeated.

The lieutenant governor asked for other motions. Before Senator Billings could call her next one, Senator Middleton stood up and said, "Madam President, I call amendment #3."

He went to the microphone and explained how the market would not allow any new entrants after July 1. He explained how he didn't understand that last year and doesn't believe the Senate did either. "We don't do this in any other market, and I don't know why we would do it in this one. I ask for your support."

"Further discussion?" the lieutenant governor asked. No one. "Hearing none, all those in favor vote aye," and what sounded like a pretty average-size and unenthusiastic group said, "Aye."

She followed with, "All those opposed?" and an abundance of folks in loud voices yelled, "Nay!"

The lieutenant governor calmly said, "The motion has been defeated."

This was significant for the body. They had now had a chance to correct an obvious problem that any Republican would instinctively oppose: a statutory deadline to enter what should be a competitive market. That deadline made it clear that the General Assembly was purposely locking people out of the market. It was like they were too stupid to see what they were doing to themselves. It really wasn't that complicated.

"Are there further amendments?"

That was where it was really going to get good.

Senator Billings rose again. "Madam President, I call amendment #2."

She returned to the microphone.

"Madam President, members of the Senate. Amendment #2 corrects a mistake I made in committee. All it does is take out of HB 1686 the amendment that I authored for committee. That is all it does, and I ask you for your support."

Now, this was a real jam. She was asking for the body to help her retract her own committee motion. I had never seen someone do that. It also would make the entire e-liquid law impossible to implement and would effectively make selling e-liquid illegal in Indiana if it ultimately became law in the form Billings proposed.

The lieutenant governor again asked, "Further discussion?"

Alderman couldn't let this one go without commenting. He raised his hand and rose from his seat.

The lieutenant governor said, "The chair recognizes Senator Alderman."

He put on his nicey-nice voice. "Madam President and ladies and gentlemen of the Senate, I ask that you defeat this amendment.

I understand Senator Billings's frustration, but I asked her to assist me with this in committee just as a way to manage the workload of the committee. Had I known there was any confusion or hesitancy on her part, I would have handled it some other way."

He did not want to have to say that in public. Now he won't be able to claim he had nothing to do with it later.

"The language in the bill is vital," he said. "This law and this bill are not perfect. But the law was passed to protect our young people from this dangerous stuff, and we can't take any steps backward in protecting our kids. I'm sure we will have the opportunity to fix anything that doesn't work with the law later."

The lieutenant governor asked again, "Further discussion?" No one else rose. "The author has the right to close."

Senator Billings was steaming. She went back to the microphone.

"Madam President and members of the Senate, I have been a member of the General Assembly for twenty-eight years. I have never seen or even heard of either the House or the Senate not allowing the author of legislative language to withdraw it. If Senator Alderman has a fix for the problem in the law and this bill, it is my opinion that he should have suggested it here today or should prepare to do it in conference committee. The language in question right now was my language, and I want it withdrawn. I ask for your support. Oh, and I request a roll call vote again."

It would be unheard of for this motion to be defeated. I agreed with her. I bet no one could give an example of when a request like this, in any appropriate procedural manner, had been defeated.

The voting machine opened. It looked red again. Not quite as red as the last time, but it was going down.

The motion was defeated 21–26.

The lieutenant governor proceeded, without any apparent understanding of what had just happened. "The bill is ordered to engrossment. Continue the roll."

This was one of those times when people like Pauly and Karl and all their cohorts should be giggling a little. They'd won the battle after all. But I looked dead at them, and there wasn't an ounce of joy on any of their faces.

They knew. They knew I wasn't done with them.

I hadn't looked at my phone for almost an hour. I'd left it on the bench when the bill got called. When I finally checked my messages, I saw I had one from Ted: "We need to talk." He was goddamned right we did.

30

I n my world, any 8:30 AM meeting that was scheduled at 6:30 the night before translated to "emergency." I hoped that was true, because I was ready to light this whole thing up.

Sleeping seemed like an impossibility. It was too soon to bother Flip, no matter how badly I wanted to. I lifted weights that morning, as I did every Monday morning, but maybe some treadmill time in the evening would help. I gave it a try.

I often wondered what gym zombies thought about when I found myself being one. I was pretty sure no one else in the gym was thinking about what I was that night.

I left the gym at 8:30 PM and headed home, knowing I would be back in just over nine hours. Maybe the physical exhaustion from two workouts in twelve hours would help me keep everything a little more relaxed on Tuesday.

I was in the lobby of my penthouse offices waiting for TK a little early. The receptionist didn't know what to make of it. I was wearing a suit and tie and acting less cool than usual. She must have thought some bigwig was coming.

At 8:30, the elevator door opened and out walked TK, in jeans and a sweatshirt. Apparently, that was his uniform. If I'd tried to convince the receptionist he was a special agent, I would have failed.

"Good morning, sir," I said. "To what do I owe the pleasure of an 8:30 meeting with a man of your stature?"

"I have a question or two about our project before I go any further, and I predict that you have the answers," he replied as we walked toward the first conference room down the marble walkway.

It was a typical high-rise conference room with a giant board-room table and a panoramic view of the south side of downtown. Lucas Oil Stadium, Bankers Life Fieldhouse, and the corporate headquarters for Eli Lilly and Anthem were visible from the window.

"Nice view," TK said with the tiniest hint that he might be impressed.

"Nice waste of money, if you ask me. When I was younger, though, maybe it would have impressed a date . . . I don't know. I'm too old for that shit now. So what's up?"

"Have you ever heard of Madison Properties, LLC?"

"Nope. But I hope I'm about to."

"Pauly James created this company about five years ago. It has about a hundred shareholders, and so far, it looks like at least ten of the shareholders are lobbyists. Maybe more. But I can't figure out what the company does or why he formed it. Do you think you could help me with that?"

"A hundred shareholders? Jesus! What does that make the company worth?" I asked in amazement.

"We haven't nailed that down yet. It looks like some kind of pyramid scheme, but not really. It's like these people are pooling their money for something that hasn't happened yet. My question to you is, can you recall any talk of people in your business putting money into a pot to develop some kind of business—that would only exist if some law passed?"

Oh. My. God. The iPad gaming scheme. That bullshit little idea that was floating around with these guys awhile back. It didn't seem like five years ago, though.

"Wow. TK, I do. But it wasn't anything to do with this. Pauly and some of those guys from the Winner's Circle had this idea to roll out gaming on iPads, you know, mobile gaming on tablets. The business was going to allow for gamblers to gamble remotely, but through a designated casino property here. I don't know the details, but it was going to need to be licensed, which was the hook. They were trying to get people to buy into the venture, and then they'd share the profits if they got the law passed, the licenses locked down, and so on. A handful of friends threw in a thousand bucks, or maybe two thousand, to be part of the ownership of the company. I never got officially invited, but I didn't have a couple of thousand dollars to burn at the time, so I would have probably said no anyway."

"That's how this whole thing got started," TK said with total confidence.

"Wait a minute," I said as I faded off into one of my trances for a couple of seconds.

"What?" TK asked.

I snapped back into focus. "That's why no one was working this thing? These dirty motherfuckers!"

"What? I don't understand," TK asked again.

"Don't you get it? The reason no one was available to hire to fight this e-liquid thing in the Statehouse is that they all own a piece of Pauly's company! The company that's about to have the market cornered!"

"I'm still not following why that's such a big deal. Help me understand."

I took a deep breath.

"The reason why so many members of the Senate, and the House for that matter, are willing to do the wrong thing on this is that they're being lobbied by a bunch of people. It isn't just Pauly and Karl Satterfield. It's the whole damn hallway! Well, at least the contractors. I have been fighting an army of people who actually *do* have a financial interest in the outcome. A huge one! And they aren't disclosing what they are doing because they aren't being paid, like TA pays me. They only get paid, and in profits, if the law passes and the company takes off. Which of course it will when they have the market cornered." I paused for a couple of seconds and then reminded him, "And what I just described to you is illegal as hell."

"What's illegal about it? Remember, I enforce federal law."

"Lobbyists in Indiana can't be compensated based on legislative outcomes. It is specifically prohibited in state law. This kind of shit is the reason why. This right fucking here. It makes people want to do corrupt things. It's the same as our law that prevents casino companies from making campaign contributions in Indiana. The legislature didn't trust those guys twenty years ago when they legalized casinos. Holy shit! This is unbelievable! You got names?"

"I have some of the names of the shareholders. We will probably get most of them pretty quickly. But I have something important I need to know from you, which is why I asked to meet with you on such short notice."

I felt some sort of build-up growing in the room, as if just talking to him at all wasn't already a big deal for me.

Bluntly, he asked, "I need to know how far you are willing to go with this."

It was a good question. It was the only question really—at least to me.

The answer was that in my heart I had decided that what had happened and was happening just wouldn't do. I couldn't let it go on.

"I'm willing to do whatever you think I can do to help blow this thing up. I'm ashamed of it. I'm ashamed of them. And it makes me ashamed of me."

"I guess we should go over this list of shareholders then," he said as he pulled a folded piece of paper out of his back pocket. It had about forty names on it. He slid it across the table at me, obviously confident that I was going to be familiar with much of it.

I scoured it, stopping every few seconds to look up at him with a slight bit of surprise and even occasional disappointment. After I'd looked it over, I half slapped the paper back toward him and pushed my chair back away from the table in nauseated disgust. I spun my chair around toward the big window and sunk into another trance for a minute.

"Well?" TK asked. "How many are on there?"

I turned back around and snatched the list back. This time I took a pen from the middle of the table and started checking the names I knew. First, I checked the registered lobbyists on the list. "Seventeen," I said to him. Then I went back through the list and checked another six names of politicos who I didn't think technically lobbied, but who were involved in political campaigns. "Unless you just want to know players in general, then the number is twenty-three."

I shoved it back at him.

"Piss you off?" he asked.

I stood up and started to pace the window wall.

"Some of those guys are—or were—friends of mine."

"Is that a problem for us? I mean, does that change how committed you are to this?" he asked.

I turned back to him from the window, put my hands on the gigantic table, leaned over, and said, "Not one fucking bit."

"So, the first set of check marks are lobbyists that I can find registered? The others I can find on campaign finance reports?" he asked.

"Yep. But the lobbyists will show up in both places."

"Can I call you later today?" TK asked.

"You can call me whenever you want. Nothing is more important to me than helping you—and you helping me."

I wasted the rest of the day in the Statehouse. There wasn't anything for me to do, and what I learned from TK had paralyzed me anyway. I found myself looking at every conversation taking place with people who were on the list, wondering if they were talking about this scam in their huddles. It began to make me start running through all the conversations I'd had with these people over the last year.

Had I told them things I shouldn't have before I knew they were involved? Had they been watching me and eavesdropping on me? Had they said things that should have tipped me off and I was just too obtuse to notice?

The longer I sat there in the hallway, the more I began to see that my willingness to help the FBI was not that big of a deal. I wasn't part of the crowd I once was. I didn't know when or how it happened to me, but I had left the Circle. And I knew it happened before today, and I realized I would never go back.

Later that day in the Statehouse was the third reading deadline in both chambers. HB 1686 needed to be voted up or down or die on the calendar. There was no reason to believe that Tuesday would be any different than Monday, and it wasn't. Senator Alderman presented the bill, Senator Billings objected to the way it was handled, Senator Middleton complained that it was anti-free market, and it passed 31–18.

I was sitting ultra-reclined on a bench outside of the Senate when Hanna Chastain came out into the hallway right after the vote to ask me if I had any comment. Bethany had already told me that I was able to give statements to the media that went something like "We continue to feel strongly in the unconstitutional problem that the original law presents, and we look forward to a favorable ruling in federal court. After that, we will work with the General Assembly to rewrite this unmanageable and unconstitutional law."

After I gave her the spin doctor comment, Hanna asked, "Will there be any more drama on this thing?"

I laughed for a second, before I realized she wasn't joking. "Hanna, I can promise you more drama. My advice would be to take good care of your notes, pay attention to everything that goes on at the ATC for the next couple of months, and be prepared for me to drop a bomb or two on this."

"Don't leave me hanging," she said as she walked away.

She shouldn't have worried about that.

31

After I rang the bell, I could hear Mal running down the hall to answer the door.

"Hi Will!" she said, apparently happy to see me as she let me in.

"Well hi there, young lady. What are you doing?"

"Dishes," she said as if it was the thing she hated most in all of creation. "We are doing the dishes," she clarified with a touch of curiosity about whether my arrival would get her out of it or not.

"I love doing the dishes! Can I help?"

By then, the boss had strolled down the hall. "We're almost done, so maybe you can help next time. Come on back here while we finish," she said. No kiss or hug for me, but she put her hand on my cheek and gave me that hypnotic look for a moment. I wondered where she learned how to do that.

"Sit down," Flip said as they continued the drying and putting away part. "What have you been doing? It seems like brunch was a week ago."

"No kidding. Except that I haven't eaten a thing since then, and I'm getting hungry again," I joked.

Mallory piped up. "Nuh-uh. You can't go two days without eating."

"Well, maybe I snacked a little," I lied again.

"Mal, get your homework going," Flip said. "I'll finish this, and Will and I will let you have the table."

"Is your homework too hard for me?" I asked.

"Probably—it's too hard for Mom most of the time," she proudly replied.

"Well I'm going to sit on the couch then, where I'm safe from your books," I said as I got up and headed to the front room.

When Flip came in to join me, she bent down to kiss me on the cheek and then sat down.

"I heard that!" Mal yelled from the kitchen.

"I didn't hear anything!" I said. "You must be imagining—"

Flip took my hand and got my attention. "What have you been doing? I know you're up to something—my phone has been too quiet since Sunday."

"You're curious about the details of my drama?" I asked. "Now? That's so out of character. You think spilling all I know to the FBI is interesting?"

"Only if it might hurt you," she said with a quiet resolve, as if unimpressed by a detail I thought should have shocked her.

"I guess I'm a little hurt, to be honest with you," I said. "But I just have to get over it—you can help me get over it."

She looked at me like she had no clue what I meant but was worried I got stabbed or shot or something.

"Relax, it's just that I found out this morning that some guys I considered friends are in on this shit. I'm not gonna lie, it shook me up a little bit."

"What are you going to do?"

"That's what TK—he's the FBI agent working it—was asking me this morning. He wanted to know how far I was willing to go with him on this."

"And?"

I tried to give her a dose of her own medicine with a deep and deliberate look back at her. That seemed like trying to stare down the ocean, but at least I tried.

"I'm going all the way, wherever that is. I may have to change careers when this is over, but I've decided I don't want to stay in this one unless I can do it on my terms."

"Good," she said.

That sounded a little judgmental.

"Good? I thought you might agree with me taking your advice, verbatim."

"What if you choose to walk away on your own over this? I sense that there are plenty of other reasons for you to choose that anyway."

"What should I do then?" I asked.

"I'm sure you'll think of something. You weren't going to die in that Statehouse. You just might find out that it turns out to be the best part of your life."

She didn't care where I landed or what I did. She really didn't care. The apathy she had for it made her seem so strong to me. Stronger than I was. Maybe it wasn't apathy at all. Maybe it was faith. Faith in me.

Flip knew what the right thing was to her, and what I was doing was that right thing. I couldn't be anything but good if I wanted to be in her life.

The real fighting over HB 1686—not that it was real fighting—was over. Representative Ben Rizzo stopped me in the hall on Wednesday to ask what was going on with it all. He'd heard, but he wanted my version. I caught him up to speed but wanted to make sure he knew that there would only be one security firm, and anyone who said otherwise should be required to name another firm.

"When I go to the microphone and complain about all of this, will Chris Miller just lie about it?" Riz asked.

"What he will say will not be true, but as I have been saying for a while"—I transitioned to my best hillbilly accent—"that boy don't know no better." Back to my anonymous-sounding Midwestern tone, I said, "Pauly and the boys seem to have brainwashed him. I doubt anyone else will stand up and argue the point in the House. Even Charlie Alderman stood alone on this in the Senate."

"We will put up some votes against it, but when it passes, how is this all going to pan out between now and July 1?" Ben asked.

"If I were Pauly and company, I would make sure there are between 10 and 20 licenses granted, and I would scatter them all over the state. That will make the monopoly argument sound stupid. Except, of course, for the fact that all of them will be paying the one security company a five percent cut of everything."

"You're right. Let's see if they think it through or if they get greedy," Riz said as he headed back to the House chamber.

Of course, the greed part of this was also over. Their cut would come out of everyone, no matter how many players they let into the game.

That final vote wouldn't happen for a week, and the act wouldn't be signed by the governor until at least the week after. In practical terms, that would put a time crunch on any company trying to work out a contract with Schulte's and get all their filings done with the ATC so they could get their license approved before July 1.

Later in the afternoon, the concurrence motion was called for debate and vote. It was presented as an alcohol bill, as it was, of course. But Ben Rizzo was going to give a little speech, just for the record.

"Mr. Speaker, and ladies and gentlemen of the House. There is one part of the bill that is before you today that is a mistake. A big one. Section 24 of the bill modifies the definition of security firm for the e-liquid manufacturer's licenses, that was established last session. The purpose of the definitional change this year is the same reason it was created last year: to create a monopoly. There is one company in the entire country that meets the definition in this bill. Again, just like last year's bill intended. This new language was inserted in the Senate committee. This complaint was raised by parties in committee, and by a significant number of senators on the floor. Even with all the agreement contained in this bill, I urge you to vote no. We will be back here next year to fix this if you don't. Thank you."

This speech was a call to Democrats to vote no. There were 71 Republicans and only 29 Democrats in the House, so the vote would be symbolic in every possible way. Rizzo was the Democratic leader on these issues, so I expected most of them to follow him.

Of course, Representative Chris Miller couldn't just stay in his seat and keep his mouth shut. He had to go to the microphone and deliver one last lie to the body.

"Mr. Speaker, members of the House. I have heard this mantra about the monopoly that this law was designed to create, so I checked into it. I found out this morning that there is at least one other company who has shown interest in providing services here and this company meets the definition. The company is based in Virginia, but I have been told that they plan to enter the market here as well. You know I respect you, Representative Rizzo, but I just wanted to make sure the body was aware of the latest information. Thank you."

These were the last comments. The Speaker opened the machine for voting and the bill passed easily, 63–30. Most of the 30 no votes were Democrats, but a few Republicans joined them. Likewise, a few Democrats voted yes. This was the kind of vote that was driven by the majority party, but when asked, they would say it was bipartisan.

The truth was it was nonpartisan. There wasn't much ideology involved since neither party advocated for corruption—at least not openly.

32

The 2016 session ended Thursday, March 10. By the time the gavel fell in the Senate that evening, I was already at Grace with my friends. I guess I should have had some level of anxiety about what the weeks and months ahead would mean for me, but I didn't.

I sat there in the church that night and sort of listened while fading in and out of my trance. The decision-making process for me on what I wanted to do on this thing was over. My client's confidence in the court proceeding was growing. I was in love, which was the biggest of all surprises. And I was about to help expose a bunch of scumbags for what they really were. It was hard to be anything but entirely happy.

Moving into post-session life would be odd. I would have time to spend with Flip and Mal and to help TK and Hanna do their thing. Hopefully it would be void of pressure. I was sure that would end up being a bad prediction.

After that first long weekend, I came out of the Athenaeum YMCA on a Monday morning to two text messages. The first one was from TK, wanting to know if I was free for lunch. I suggested meeting at Coat Check.

The other was from Ethan Murphy.

Will, it's Ethan. Have you heard about the contracts?

> I guess not. I have no idea what
> you're talking about.

Schulte's isn't even offering contracts to any of my members.

> What do you mean?

They're telling my people they can't keep up with demand and they won't have time for any of us.

> Geez. None of your members are
> going to get a deal with them?

It doesn't look like it.

This was only a little bit of a surprise. Not taking care of any of those guys appeared to be punitive. Strategically, it made no sense to me that they weren't even talking about a deal with any of Ethan's members. They should at least be playing the game a little. Every move these assholes made seemed to be at least a little bit wrong. I wondered if TK had a way to monitor any of this.

In any case, I expected lunch would almost certainly be a good one.

. . .

We met on the sidewalk and headed inside.

Standing in line to order at the counter, he asked, "You know anything new?"

"I heard this morning that they weren't offering contracts to Ethan Murphy's members. I find that odd. You might say it's suspicious."

"I would say that is suspicious, but it's just like everything else they do," he replied.

We ordered our lunch and headed to a table in the corner by the New Jersey St. window that had become our routine.

"It's been more than a week since we met last. I told you my news, what do you know?" I asked.

"Let's talk about marijuana," he said.

I hadn't heard a word about that angle for a long time. I never did hear anything more than that one passing comment last year.

"I wish I knew why that was being whispered around last year, but I don't."

"Really?" TK asked.

"What? Is that some kind of interrogation trick? You say 'really' and I crumble and shout out: Yes! Yes! I know all about marijuana!"

"You really are a smartass, aren't you?"

"I'm not just a smartass. I'm the biggest smartass. The best I know, really. All bragging aside . . . one of my young friends heard a rumor about the marijuana thing last year, but she didn't understand what she heard and couldn't explain it to me. And I haven't heard a word since."

We were interrupted briefly by the delivery of our lunch orders to the table.

"How do you think the vape thing is connected with marijuana?" TK asked. "I mean if there were investors in Madison Properties who thought they were investing in a marijuana venture?"

"Hell, I don't know," I said as I start heading into another trance.

"What do all the ringleaders do apart from all of this?" TK asked.

"They work in monopolies. At least, what I consider to be monopolies. Beer and booze distribution and gambling, you know. They don't like calling themselves monopolies, but that's what they are."

TK took a big bite of his sandwich and looked at me like he wanted me to think for myself for a minute, so he didn't have to tell me what he already seemed to know.

With a shrug, I said, "Maybe this whole system of oversight and jacked up security—or the appearance of it—is just a trial run for a system of oversight if marijuana gets legalized." I add a sarcastic laugh.

TK took another bite and kept looking at me, expressionless.

"You have got to be shitting me," I said. "And you want me to believe that this has been kept secret in the Statehouse by twenty lobbyists and a handful of legislators? No fucking way."

TK corrected me. "I don't know who knows and who doesn't know. At least not yet. I do know that some of the investors in Madison were investing on speculation of control in the marijuana market if one ever happens here."

My God. These guys really had shot for the moon on this one.

"So, we're having lunch here today to see if I can help . . . how exactly?" I asked.

"I'm exploring my options, that's all," TK said.

"Options? What options? What the hell does that mean?"

"Will, I'm interested in busting people for public corruption.

That's my department. That's what I do. I'm looking for the *how* and *why* these legislators did this for Pauly and Karl. It wasn't just a favor. There's too much money at stake."

"Yeah? Me too. We want the same things. So?"

"You want to know how you can help. I'm searching for evidence of how they got Alderman and Miller and whomever else to do this for them."

"If you're looking for a silver bullet or a shiny new car or diamond ring that Pauly gave Alderman, complete with a set of photos and receipts . . . good fucking luck," I said.

"That would be nice. But I'd settle for someone telling you about the car or the diamond. Recorded."

"Aha! I wondered when you were going to ask for that. I don't mind wearing a wire, but I'm pretty sure I'm damaged goods already. I doubt anyone who knows something damning is going to say it to me, or even in front of me. But I'll wire up whenever you want."

TK laughed at that. "Jesus! I have never met anyone like you. You actually want to put your ass out there on the line."

"What do I have to lose?" I asked.

"I don't know, but these guys aren't desperate yet either. They probably think they're home free. Why wouldn't they?" he asked.

"They still won't talk in front of me. I'm going to have to think about who might say something that matters, and to me. You're the damn expert—why don't you suggest a plan, Mr. Special Agent?"

"When we start gathering data ourselves, everyone will know it. So do they think they're home free or not?"

That was an excellent question. There were no visible celebrations or even smiles and handshakes at the end of session. It was as if nothing important had happened. I couldn't decide if that was because they had more to do, or if it was because they were so close to the finish line and a huge payday that they don't want to fuck it up. Probably both.

TK knew he could count on me for anything I was capable of doing for him. We got along, and I assumed his background intel on me and his expert read of my personality had him convinced that I was a friend. I definitely trusted him as a friend, especially since my friends in and around government seemed to be shrinking in every other way.

The act was signed by Governor Pence on March 24.

A couple of weeks passed. It was the beginning of April, and I hadn't heard a meaningful peep about anything—as expected. My client wasn't trying to get licensed, so I had no path to getting behind the scenes. But Ethan Murphy did.

Ethan, what's the latest? I haven't heard a peep in two weeks.

Schulte's is only going to get a deal with two or three companies that I know of.

Total!?

Looks like it. They told one of my guys that they wouldn't be able to help but two or three. And then I heard that two of the guys they were helping were two guys who disappeared from the hallway over the winter.

Who are they?

One owns a liquor store in Evansville, one is in Fort Wayne and is related

somehow to a legislator. And I'm betting
Aarav Patel is in the mix for one also.

That sounds like three deals that were
cut a long time ago to me.

Me too.

So my buddy Jason Farmer with the liquor store association must have set up the Evansville guy. Who knew the family connection from Fort Wayne? I assumed that was worked out at the Winner's Circle with whomever the legislator in play was there. It could be any of three or four suspects. And Aarav and his buddies basically told me they would have a deal when I met with them last fall.

That made one company in the northern part of the state, one in the central, and one in the southern. It was a light version of what I would have told them to implement.

All three of these companies seemed to be Indiana-based as well. I expected Schulte's to contract with at least one company that had facilities out of state—otherwise the interstate commerce violation argument in the federal lawsuit would be enhanced significantly.

If they didn't do an interstate contract, the lawyers fighting in court would be slobbering, like Hooch did in *Turner & Hooch*. Of course, the lawyers on my side already thought they were winning.

. . .

By the time I heard from TK again, it was another Monday morning, April 11. We made plans for lunch again.

I can talk code with the best of them, but I can't think of anything cooler than talking code with a special agent. The cloak-and-dagger act could be seriously fun for a man my age. Especially since I'd never gotten to play that game when I was young.

I pulled up, and he was waiting for me on the sidewalk again.

"To what do I owe the pleasure?" I opened with as I walked up.

"Hey, you started this. Remember?"

"I haven't been sniffing around much, except on who is lining up for licenses," I said.

We ordered, and then he started talking before we escaped the fray around the counter.

"Don't worry, I've been working without you. I just want to bounce some of this stuff off you and see if it gives us some ideas."

"I'm all ears."

"First of all, Karl has a problem in another state that I'm betting no one in Indiana knows about."

"Problem?" I asked. "Legal?"

"Yes. A legal problem worth us spending some time trying to figure out if we can charge him or not."

"Damn! I'd be surprised if anyone here knew anything about that, but again, if they did, they wouldn't be talking about it in front of guys like me."

"I've also discovered that it looks like Karl has some sort of agreement to buy Schulte's."

"You mean Madison Properties does, right?" I asked.

"No, I mean Karl."

"How do these shareholders make money if Karl owns every-thing outright?"

"I don't know that yet," he said. "I need some help with that one."

"And?"

"You're wondering how you can help, right?"

"You got it," I said. "It sounds like these so-called shareholders might be trusting Karl and Pauly more than they should be."

"And that is how you can try and get these guys to talk. You know who is on the list. I assume you didn't tell them to go fuck themselves when you found out. You know they're in the game, but they don't know you know. Right?"

TK had a point there. I could work my way into a conversation with any of about five or six of the lobbyists on his list to find out what they knew about the flow of money. But I wasn't supposed to know about Madison Properties.

"TK, how do I get these guys to talk about a company I'm not even supposed to know about?"

"All I think you should do is find a way to have generic conversations about the whole thing. Don't strain yourself. Just see what you can find out."

"Yeah, yeah. I'll see if I can get some guys talking about it."

After lunch, we headed onto Michigan Street to get into our cars, and he told me what he should have told me an hour ago.

"We are going to start asking to talk to a few legislators soon. Like maybe next week or the week after at the latest. I'll let you know how that goes."

"What!? What the fuck, TK! That place will go bonkers when that first call gets made. You know that, right?" I half yelled.

"Tensions will rise, that's for sure. But they won't say a word. Trust me. They won't want anyone knowing that we want to talk to them, except their partners in crime . . . who, of course, we are already monitoring," he said with a shit-eating grin. "See ya later. We'll talk soon."

"You're goddamned right we will. Jesus."

It was getting real. I'd been the keeper of an abundance of secrets over the years, but these . . . these were the biggest. Everyone I knew in the business would shit if they knew what TK had just said to me.

33

Flip and I didn't get a chance to go on an adults-only date very often, so every one of them was like Christmas morning.

This time she talked me into going to Circle Center Mall to see an excruciatingly cheesy rom-com. It turned out that even Flip didn't like it—but we were so happy to be out and alone, eating a giant bucket of buttered (poisoned) popcorn and sipping from a tub of Diet Coke in the dark that the movie didn't even serve as a decent distraction.

Mal was at a sleepover so we had all the time in the world. It was a burden like no other to keep from trying not to just stuff her mom in the Jeep and race home to my townhouse for some time alone. Isn't that what young parents did when they were kid-free?

But it was supposed to be a night on the town and downtown was my playground—Flip didn't get down there much. After the movie, we went for a stroll.

As we walked through Monument Circle, she said, "I can't believe we let those horses be treated so cruelly, right in the public square," she said.

"Technically, it's a circle," I replied.

She rolled her eyes. "Don't tell me you're okay with this."

"Even if I were, there would be no chance in hell I would admit it to you." I paused. "And no, I'm not okay with it. Don't tell me you want me to go fight this in city hall."

"Maybe Mal and I can fight this one and tell *you* all about it."

"I'm all for that."

Speaking of horses, as we approached one of the spokes on the monument, I realized that we were just around the corner from the Winner's Circle.

"You want to see the scene of the e-liquid/marijuana crime?" I asked, assuming the answer would be no.

"Sure, I'm game if you are."

"I hadn't planned this, but why not. I never go in there with a hot young woman or dressed like I'm getting ready to mow grass. This might be the perfect disguise."

"Let's do it then!" She seemed excited to check it out.

We walked through the door and immediately she looked aghast.

She whispered, "What's wrong with these people?"

"They're gamblers. That's all."

"Are any of your people here?" she asked.

I scanned the room. I had no intention of going into the VIP area, but it was in plain view. There were only three guys in the entire section, all at one table. A young-looking guy looked over his shoulder in our direction. It was Lance Meridian. Junior.

He had the look of a strange combination of a hipster and a friendless nerd. Dark hair that was longer than any businessman's should be and Clark Kent glasses.

He didn't recognize me, as far as I know.

The gorillas sitting next to him drew more of my attention. They seriously looked like they just walked off the set of *Casino*. I'm always amazed at these types. Tough guys. Goodfellas. I have never met a truly tough guy that advertised it like that. But that's the vibe they were sending.

"No, baby. None of my peeps are here. You want to stay for a minute or has this visual been enough?" I hoped we could leave.

"Let's go."

I could tell I had made a mistake for our big date by bringing her there. Her mind was clearly spinning as we walked back toward the mall through the circle.

"Are you all right?" I asked her.

"Oh yeah. I'm fine. Have I ever told you about Mal's dad?"

"Nope. Not in any detail. Did that place remind you of him?"

"Like a slap in the face."

"Why? Did he gamble?"

"He did gamble. And he drank too much. And he chased dreams of all the things that he thought could make him happy. When he realized those things in his dreams were just out of reach, he would change his dream to the next thing and start chasing again, only to find out it was also just out of reach. And on and on."

"Sounds like a miserable way to live."

"I bet you don't spend much time with people who live like that, do you?"

"I used to. I used to be like that in some ways."

"I'm sure you were—maybe you still are in one way. You are a dreamer. It's one of the things that attracted me to you when we first met. You say things like, 'I wish' and 'I hope' all the time. You probably don't even know you do that, do you?"

"I guess not," I said with a smile, scanning my brain to think of an example.

"The difference is that you believe in your dreams. And they don't ever seem to be about you, at least not the ones you say out loud. It's like you don't waste your time dreaming about the things you need for your own happiness, as if that would be beneath you or something, or that you don't need anything for yourself."

"I don't know about all that. I've dreamt about you—plenty."

"I do know. And I know you don't need me to be happy. I think I watch you more closely than you watch yourself sometimes."

All of this sounded wonderfully complimentary, but she also seemed to think more of me than I thought of myself.

"You want to know why I fell in love with you?" she asked.

That question scared me, and she knew it. She continued without giving me much of a chance to stutter.

"Do you remember the night we ate at City Barbecue? The night we first talked about the vapor thing?"

"Of course I do."

"Do you remember the lady you met at the soda fountain?"

"I do," I said with some curious surprise. "And I saw you there, but I didn't know what you heard. What do you know about that?"

"What was her nephew's name?"

I paused for a moment, a little stunned at what she heard and knew before smiling and answering. "Kenyatta."

"Do you think you saved his life when you were his counselor at that reform school you worked at?"

My first job out of college was as a counselor at the Indiana Boys School. Most people would have thought that was a shit job, and it paid like it. But I loved it there—as a former juvenile delinquent myself, why wouldn't I love it there? I worked there for five years, until I thought I needed to make more money. Leaving that job may have been a mistake.

Flip had overheard the thirty-second conversation I'd had with a family member of one of the biggest assholes ever assigned to me. Twenty years had passed.

This punk was seventeen years old, a gang member from Chicago who had moved to his aunt's house in Indy to get away from all of that, and immediately got busted for something. I don't recall what his crime was. There were plenty to choose from, I'm sure. The court in Indy committed him to the Boys School.

He was the baddest ass on the whole campus for a little while before they gave him to me. I worked in the maximum-security unit, and I only got the worst of the worst kids Indiana had to offer. And I didn't take any shit from any of them. At all.

But everyone was scared to death of him and he knew it. The other juveniles thought he was a modern-day Al Capone of the early '90s street gangs, and those who didn't were scared of how big and strong he was. He was built like an NFL linebacker. He had sixty pounds on me.

But he didn't scare me. And even if he did, I was in charge and that was the end of it. He was going to do what I said one way or the other.

It turned out I was the first one who ever made him do anything. And after he realized that there was no other way out, he learned to follow my rules. After a month or two, he started looking up to me like the dad he never had, even though I was only twenty-five at the time. And white, and new to city living.

The two of us might as well have been from different planets.

The only reason he followed anyone else's instructions was also because "Mr. O'Courtney said so." It was the kind of thing that happened for me with a lot of kids back then.

Apparently, Kenyatta was doing well these days. His aunt remembered me when she saw me in the restaurant that night. She wanted to thank me for getting him back on track. I hadn't heard a word about him since he'd gotten paroled. It was good to know he was good.

Flip had heard most of what she said. I didn't notice her standing there waiting to refill her drink until after Kenyatta's aunt walked away. I used to run into family members more often shortly after leaving that job. This kind of thing had not happened in a long while.

"I think his aunt thinks I saved his life," I said with clear disagreement over the thought. "So, that's why you fell in love with me? That's weird, Renee."

"What did you do for that lady's nephew?"

"It's hard to explain," I said as I start to slip into a trance.

"Don't leave me. I want you to hear this. I get the feeling you did what no one else could. Or would. Is that right?"

"Maybe," I said with a shrug.

"That's what I thought. I bet you miss that, don't you?"

"Maybe," I repeated with another shrug and a nod.

"Well maybe that was the last box you needed to check for me. You weren't just someone to giggle at, or flirt and eye chat with anymore. You were someone who had a good purpose for existing. There was something you had that struck people, like that lady who remembered you so vividly so many years later. At least, that's what I thought at that very moment. And now I know I was right. But that's when I knew I loved you."

She did that damn thing with her hand on my cheek and the hypno-gaze into my soul, right there on Monument Circle.

"What else do you want to see downtown?" I asked.

"I've seen enough. Besides, I had plans for you tonight other than a walking tour of downtown."

"Thank God. I don't care what your plans were for me because I'll do whatever you say."

"That," she paused with a nod, "is a challenge I accept. And you can start thinking about how to tell me all of the reasons you fell in love with me."

Off to the mall garage for the car we went, walking a little faster than we had been.

. . .

Monday morning was supposed to be a snoozer, but my phone rang at 8:00. I normally don't answer calls I don't recognize at that hour, so off to voice mail it went. I didn't even listen to it until I got out of the gym about a half an hour later.

"Will . . . this is . . . Amanda Keith . . . uh . . . I don't know if you remember me. I'm on the policy staff in the Senate. I probably shouldn't be calling, but can we get together and talk today? I need to tell you something about that bill you were working on. I'll call you back." Click.

Jesus! Talk about paranoid!

I did know who the young woman was, but that's about it. I assumed she was scared to death about Pauly's scam, though she didn't actually say that.

Hell, she was more nervous than I was. When I asked TK if he could put a wire on me for the meeting with Amanda Keith, he burst into laughter.

"What the hell is so funny?" I asked.

"Just download an app on your iPhone. Jesus, you've been to too many movies."

"What's the fun in that? I wanted to be James Fucking Bond, and you're killing the mood."

"Just go to the app store—"

"I got it, smartass. I'll report back later, and I don't want to hear about this talk again."

"I bet you don't. Hahaha!" Click.

I texted Amanda back on the number she'd called me on, and about a half hour later I walked into Coat Check—again—and scanned the room, but I didn't immediately see her. She'd found a seat down the hall almost to the door to the YMCA. Sitting in a high-back chair, her back was toward the coffee shop area. The place was half empty, and she could have sat anywhere. She must have been thinking she was doing something that mattered.

"Amanda?"

"Yes, Will. Thank you for coming," she said nervously.

"Relax. Please relax."

"I'm sorry, my nervousness is showing. This may not even be a big deal to someone like you," she said.

"Someone like me? What am I like?"

"You're a bigger deal than I am. That's what you're like."

"Let's just see about that. What can I do for you?"

She took a deep breath. "Two years ago, I worked on some language with the legal staff for a senator. He wanted to create a security scheme like the one in the e-liquid law."

"Okay?" I said.

"It is almost verbatim of what ended up in the original version of the e-liquid bill—I mean law—I mean the old law, before it got tweaked last month."

"Relax Amanda. Trust me. There is nothing to be nervous about telling—whatever it is you tell me. You are not taking a risk here. I might ask you to take one later, but I will ask first. Believe me. Keeping secrets is a big part of what I do. Okay?"

"Okay" She took a deep breath. "I'm sorry. Anyway, the senator who wanted it has since retired. But I found out last week that he is going to work for the security firm people in the e-liquid industry."

"What?"

I immediately started thinking as hard and as fast as I could about who had retired recently that would fit that bill.

"You don't have to figure it out for yourself. It was Senator Lawrence."

Damon Lawrence was a conservative Republican, and Amanda worked for the Republicans in the Senate. He was, or is, a lawyer. The one thing he advocated that was outside of the standard conservative stuff was marijuana legalization. It was the only thing that made him normal to me. It took me about two seconds to connect those dots.

"Oh, shit! Were you drafting a bill on marijuana?"

"Yes."

"Was it ever filed or introduced or given to legislative services?" I asked with some serious excitement.

"No. At least I don't think so. I think he got told by leadership to not move forward with it. Maybe. I don't know why he didn't introduce it, but it pissed me off a little because it made my work on it meaningless. And it was one of the first things I ever got to work on. I'm used to my research and other work being thrown away now."

"I didn't know anything about this. But I also didn't know he was going to work for Schulte's. At the same time, I'm starting to wonder who isn't going to work for them." I paused from my stream of consciousness. "Why are you telling me this?"

"Because I heard Senator Billings talking about it. Then when I heard about Senator Lawrence going to work for them, I realized what he was trying to do all along."

"Which is?"

"Monopolize the marijuana market in Indiana. And take a big cut of it."

I sat back in my chair and took a deep breath. There was evidence inside the Senate of this thing. And this thing was bigger than my little sliver of it and the two hundred vape shops they killed in the process. This thing was far bigger.

"Do you have the language or the actual document that you worked on for him?"

She reached into her purse and handed me one sheet of paper. At the top, were the words "security firm defined."

I looked up at her and asked, "Who knows about this?"

"Three or four of us on staff. I did the work for him, but I was so new, I was asking questions every five minutes back then."

"So any one of them could have given this to me?"

"I guess so, yeah."

"Thanks, Amanda."

"And no one will know about me?"

"Not because of this, unless you want them to know."

"I don't care about the position—but I do care about the staff who were just doing their jobs and following orders. The lawyers have attorney-client privilege to worry about. But I don't."

"Don't worry. No one will know we spoke. I don't even know who I would tell about this."

Yeah, right. We parted ways on that note, and I wasn't sure whether I had lied to her or not. Of course, I'd lied. But I was committed to protecting her. Besides, TK was going to find out about this one way or the other. Maybe all I had to do was help him focus on what he should be looking for.

That was what I was hoping.

34

TK was champing at the bit. When I called him to report back, the phone didn't even ring on my end before he answered.

"Well?" was all he said.

"It's good to hear from you too. You want to meet me in my office?"

"I'm on my way."

I went straight there and went to the reception area to secure a meeting room, only beating TK to the building by about five minutes.

I met him in the lobby—and we looked like we dressed each other. Both of us had on shorts and golf shirts like we were playing in the same golf outing later.

Before our asses even hit the chairs in the small conference room, he started in. "What do you got?"

"Easy there, Special Agent. I need to untape the wire from my chest, and it always hurts when I pull it off."

"Yeah, yeah. What did you hear?"

I gave him the story. It was the kind of thing he really wanted.

All TK would need or want now was evidence that there was some kind of payoff in exchange for what the legislators and lobbyists did.

He would scour the documents that had been exchanged and then he would start asking to speak to senators. He already knew more about this whole thing than almost all of them. I had no idea what Charlie Alderman was going to say. Or former Senator Lawrence for that matter.

. . .

There we were in May of a big election year. It looked like it would be Donald Trump versus Hillary Clinton. It looked like it would be Mike Pence in a rematch against John Gregg for governor. And Charlie Alderman was running for another four-year term in the Indiana Senate.

Six months' worth of campaigning and a relentless barrage of nonsense and bullshit about how Alderman was there for the people was what lay ahead of us. He didn't even have an opponent, but he'd be raising money from the hallway as if he did.

Pence would be trying to pretend he wasn't entirely inept. He would also be trying to convince Hoosiers that the whole Religious Freedom Restoration Act debacle that happened last year didn't make him the homophobic, intolerant, and religious zealot we all knew he was.

I would try to spend my summer with my new love and my golf game while TK and his posse rattled the cages at the Statehouse. I didn't know how else I could help right then.

When senators started getting calls from the FBI asking for interviews and it was clear that at least the feds thought something illegal happened, what would the body do? Would the Alcohol and Tobacco Commission go ahead and proceed without a blink?

Nothing would surprise me. Maybe nothing will.

But for most Hoosiers, May is more about the Speedway than politics.

. . .

While TK and his team were doing their work, I was ticket-dealing so that Flip, Mal, and Greg Bryant could join me and my boys for the race. Six together can be a challenge when only seats in one of the penthouses is good enough. Both of my boys had been raised to be ticket snobs, and of course, I wanted to impress my girlfriends anyway.

I worked that out and the six of us were planted right in one of the southernmost sections of the paddock penthouse. There were plenty of bigwigs to see and shake hands with sitting in the area, as was customary.

Even a few of my new enemies were visible that year. So what?

The freshly cut grass in the west side neighborhood smelled just a little better than usual to me. Two of my favorite smells are a mowed lawn and new mulch. Some people think that mulch smells like shit. I don't understand that at all. The homeowners in Speedway, which is a real town all its own surrounded by the city of Indianapolis, have good grass and plenty of new mulch in their yards by race weekend every year. And the 500 doesn't smell like gasoline burning the way the NHRA Grand Nationals do. Those are the drag races that happen every Labor Day weekend a few miles west of Speedway at Indianapolis Raceway Park.

The smells at the Speedway are more like a giant cookout.

Flip and Mal had never been to the race before. It was always a little more fun going with first-timers. It was the 100th running of the race, and the town was a little more pumped up about things this year because of it.

Mal was in awe of the crowds. She had spent her life within three miles of the track, but she'd never really understood what 250,000 people looked like before.

"Will, where do you think all of these people came here from?" she asked as if it were the biggest mystery ever in a fairy tale.

"All over the world—and they came just to visit your neighborhood. How about that?" I asked.

She grinned at the thought. I remember how things like that used to make me feel more special, as if I had some sort of impact on it. I hoped she felt special too.

Mal got to sit with me on her left and Liam and Tomas on her right. She peppered us with questions like a detective interrogating three murder suspects—guilty suspects.

"How long did it take to blow up all of those balloons?"

"Why do they call it 'Taps'?"

"How do you get picked to sing 'Back Home Again in Indiana'?"

"What's a sycamore? A tree? What does it look like?"

"Why isn't Danica Patrick racing today?"

"Why are we eating fried chicken?"

And those were the easy ones.

She and my boys loved each other. She thought they were both the coolest things on two legs, and I never knew how much the boys loved kids until I got to see them with her. Whenever one of them got up, she had to go with them.

"She loves them so much," Flip said to me while the three youngsters were on a Coke run.

"Is this what a blended family looks like?" Greg Bryant sarcastically inquired.

"You ought to be taking notes down there, ugly. This could be valuable training for you. I mean, in case some crazy woman comes along who is into giants that look like convicts."

"I bet I could land one of those T-shirters, as you like to call them," he responded.

"Bullshit. I used to think that was possible, but now that I know them better, I know that they know better."

Sitting between us, Flip rolled her eyes at virtually everything we said. From the time she sat down until the time Alex Rossi took the checkered flag, every time I looked at her, she was scanning the crowd and looking at people. Occasionally, she would tell me to look at something someone was doing. I am a people watcher too, and I have always been one. But she did it differently.

It was like she was looking for the actual reasons that people do what they do. I make up stories to match the stupid behaviors I observe, and I think every one of my stories is hysterical. She, on the other hand, seemed to want to know the truth about total strangers.

"Why does the winner drink milk and throw it around at the end?" was the last of a thousand questions from Mal.

"It's just advertising for the dairy farmers," I said. "And I will explain it in detail after I have taken my post-race nap."

For those of us who go every year, the 100th running of the race didn't turn out to appear noticeably different than any other year. To the ladies, it was the best race they'd ever witnessed.

After the race, Liam and Tomas headed to their mom's house for a cookout, and Greg Bryant went home for his nap. I headed for Flip's couch for one of my favorite naps of the year: the post-race nap. Mal went upstairs to her mom's bedroom to watch a movie. Thank God.

My younger lover got me a blanket and a pillow and sat down next to me to tuck me in like only a mother does. While she was hypnotizing me with her eyes again and running her fingers through my hair, she asked, "Remember a couple of weeks ago when I told you why I loved you?"

275

"I don't have any idea what you are talking about," I joked with her.

"Stop it," she paused. "I want to know why you love me back."

I sat up and said, "Look at me."

As if I needed to tell her to do that, but now I was able to look back at her just like the way I saw her eyes piercing into my soul with that look that she'd been captivating me with since practically the first day I saw her.

"The first night I went to Grace, you were the first thing I saw. I was so curious about you. Your beauty ambushed me. It didn't make any sense why some pretty young thing like you would be there. If I had passed you on the street, I wouldn't have even given you more than a glance. But seeing you there didn't make sense. At least not to me."

"Does it now?"

"I'm not done. That night, you talked about a God that belonged to you. In the time it took you to say those words, I was obliterated. It was like you cast some sort of undefinable spell or power over me. I never thought of any God belonging to me or anyone else. But *you* did. As far as I know, you invented the idea. And because of that, you are the only one who could ever have a God, just for you, and no one else."

"It sounds like I spooked you."

"Of course you did. And then you kept on doing it to me, over and over. God was closer to you than me. He still is. But after a while, I couldn't imagine being alone with anyone else, and then I quit trying to imagine it. Thursday nights became the night I got to look out the window and see the world. My drives home became the beginning of a seven-day marathon without any purpose, until I made it back again the next Thursday to see you." I paused for a second and then gave her some context. "That was all before our first date."

"Now you're spooking me."

"I was looking for a reason, a purpose in life, when I came to Grace. I didn't even know what that was. And then I found you there on the first night. It was like love at first sight, except in reverse. It was love the first time you saw me, really saw me. Do you know what it's like to think God gave you the greatest gift He could ever give anyone just for showing up at church one time?"

"She works in mysterious ways, right?"

"Uh-huh. You got into my soul that night, and I know you will always be there." I paused again, just for a second and looked her up and down. "I wish you would shut your eyes more often though."

"Why?"

"So I could take my eyes away from yours and look at the rest of you a little. Every inch of you is perfect, from your dirty bare feet to that flower smell in your hair. But my eyes can't roam when yours are locked in on them."

"Okay, baby. I believe you. You can take your nap now."

I giggled a bit. "Well, that's part of why I love you anyway. I'll tell you the rest later."

I rolled over toward the back of the couch. I could still feel her eyes surrounding me entirely like a second blanket as I closed mine.

35

June 1 was Wednesday. It was the start of the thirty-day window for the Alcohol Tobacco Commission to issue whatever licenses that complied with the narrow path available to obtain them.

Indiana Government Center South, one of two state office buildings connected underground to the west of the Statehouse, is where the ATC offices are located. I showed up a few minutes before the 10:00 AM start time of their regularly scheduled public meeting. Then I found out that to enter the small hearing room in which they conducted business, I had to sign in.

"Why do I need to sign in?" I asked the receptionist. "It's a public meeting, right?"

"It's our policy that all attendees must sign in," she responded.

"And if I don't, I won't be allowed to attend?"

"That's right," she said with a hint of uncertainty.

I looked around at some familiar faces who were watching me with interest because they knew I had a background in public access matters.

But I didn't want to make a scene about it. At least not yet. Even though I knew they did not have the authority to force people to sign in for a public meeting.

I put on my pleasant charm and said, "I'll sign in today, ma'am. But we may have to discuss it further before I do it again next time. Deal?"

"Deal," she said with a tone of relief that there was not going to be a problem.

The public and I entered the room through one door. There were seats for about twenty people facing a makeshift bench of conference tables shoved together in an L shape where the four commissioners would sit facing the public. There was a door behind this makeshift bench that appeared to lead back to the offices of the agency.

As the clock struck 10:00, the door behind the bench opened and through it walked Pauly James and one of his usual attorneys. Trailing behind these two were all four commissioners and the general counsel of the agency.

Holy shit!

Again, no one batted an eye at this. But it was wildly inappropriate for those who are regulated to be meeting with the commissioners in their offices right before they came to the session where they were to make their formal decisions. The utility commission would explode into a flaming ball of controversial death if a display like that occurred. If some utility executive ushered in the utility commissioners like that, injunctions would almost immediately be filed at the Court of Appeals on whatever the business of the day was. There are both laws and rules that prevent that kind of crazy ex parte communication there.

Here though, no one even noticed it as odd. It's as if people had gotten used to Pauly owning this state agency. Wow!

Pauly and his legal goon took a seat in the corner while the commissioners settled into their seats.

"Hey Pauly, all members of the public need to sign in," I said. "I wouldn't want you to forget that. There's a young lady sitting outside this other door with the sheet."

Half of the room giggled at me and the other half of the room was aghast at what I had just said—loud enough for the commissioners to hear me. Pauly looked back at me and his face immediately turned red. He froze, staring at me as if he wanted to strangle me, but the whole room was watching. He forced a smile and got up and headed for the public door, but his lawyer didn't.

"Don't forget your date over there!"

The lawyer picked up his briefcase and followed Pauly out like a pissed-off little puppy.

Neither one of them came back into the room. And just like that, the rest of the alcohol lobby, and the two commissioners who didn't already know me, knew not to fuck with me. The two commissioners who did know me from their days in the Statehouse already knew that.

The meeting lasted about fifteen minutes, running through a bunch of undramatic bureaucratic bartender and permit renewals. Then right before most people in the room thought the chairman was going to adjourn the meeting, he announced that all the e-liquid permits would be considered at a special meeting on June 29.

That was the actual news of the day. As the chairman adjourned and people stood up to gather their belongings, the two men who were sitting in front of me stood and turned to face me.

They looked like they wanted to say something. I looked right back at them with genuine curiosity. They sort of looked familiar, but I didn't know why. I decided to break the ice. "Yes?"

They acted like they didn't hear me, and then walked out. That's when it hit me. These two were the goons at the Winner's Circle last month! The Goodfellas with Lance Meridian the night Flip and I stopped in.

What the hell was that stare-down about? Were they trying to scare me? Should I actually be scared?

After the typical chitchat with the other guys in the room I knew, I headed out of the building. Leaning up against the limestone walls right outside of the exit were these two goons again, as if they were waiting for me.

I looked straight at them as I walked by without a pause, walking to the east, back toward my office building. They acted like they were going to follow me, and though I refused to look back over my shoulder to see if they were following, I felt like they were back there. It's a five-block walk on an otherwise beautifully sunny day.

I didn't even want to wait to get back to the office to call TK about these tough guys.

"What's up?" he answered.

"I've got goons following me, goddamnit!"

"I know, don't worry about it. We're following you *and* them. Don't worry—you're safe."

"Are you fucking kidding me? Were you going to tell me about this shit?"

"I was going to call you this afternoon. I didn't know you were going to the ATC today."

"Jesus Christ. I'm under surveillance?"

"We are protecting you, that's all. Karl Satterfield has some guys on his team that we are watching for a variety of reasons. Over the holiday, it started to look like they were watching you, so we started watching everyone. We aren't going to let anything happen to you."

"They're trailing me right now, goddamnit."

"No, they aren't. But they were."

"Oh my God!"

"Will, we started calling legislators over the weekend and asking some questions. Some of them are acting nervous and they're making calls to people like Pauly and Karl. We are working on subpoenas right now on about ten people, but until that happens, and these guys realize that we are looking at everyone, we are going to keep you under watch. And them too."

I didn't say anything. I stopped and turned around and glanced back to see that the leg-breakers were gone.

"Will?"

"I'm here," I said as I paused for a second, looking around the sidewalks and the streets for anything that seemed odd. "Are we partners or not?"

"Come on, Will. You know we are."

"You should have told me."

"There are protocols for this, and I was going to tell you this afternoon—the protocol dictated that. And after we contact Karl and Pauly, we're going to warn them about it and confirm that they have backed off before we leave you. I am not going to let anything happen to you, and I'm sure they'll back off when I tell them we have been watching it already."

"Were they at Flip's house this weekend, for fuck's sake?"

"No, they didn't follow you guys there, and we are protecting her too for now, just in case. We have a team assigned to your boys too, but there is no evidence anyone is paying attention to them. I know you don't like hearing it, but this needs to be done sometimes."

"She didn't sign up for this shit, you know?"

"Take a deep breath, man. No one ever signs up for this. They're probably just trying to see who you're hanging around with anyway. But they obviously think you are the one. I wouldn't meet with anyone on this until after we talk to Pauly and Karl."

"TK—they weren't even hiding. They're trying to intimidate me, and you know it."

"That won't last much longer, trust me."

"What do I do about Flip and Mal? Do I stay away?"

"Just act natural—do what you normally do. Trust me, we will take care of this."

Like the day I found out that friends of mine had secretly been on the other team for a long time, now I was looking at everything through new eyes. I hadn't considered that I might not be safe. I sure as hell had never considered that the people I loved weren't.

For once, I needed that penthouse office of mine. I could get back there, shut my door, and hide while I got it together. No one looks for me there, so I could spend the rest of the day there if I needed to and just try to evaluate everything one more time with this added consideration mixed into it all.

I sat there staring out of that big window down onto Indianapolis from thirty stories above and wondered. For the first time, I was scared, really scared. I had spent so much of my time angry about what had happened and driven to correct it. My reluctance had all been about what crossing these lines would mean to my wallet. I had not spent an ounce of energy beyond it.

I had not worried about anyone's safety. Not a thought had been given to my boys or my new girls. Hell, I hadn't even considered my own safety. But there was something shameful about not considering the people I love more carefully.

It didn't take me long to move from anger to fear, and then from fear to shame.

Then a knock on my door broke me out of that trance.

"Yeah?"

The door opened and there stood Jeffrey Wilson, the managing partner of the law firm.

He'd never been to my office before. I didn't even know he knew where it was—in fact I'm certain he had to ask for directions. I could count on one hand the number of times we'd spoken face-to-face. I make a lot of money, for myself and for the firm. But not to him. To him, a lobbying practice is a fringe offering that could be made to the firm's really important clients. That's why he let me occupy space in the firm, for those times at his own cocktail parties when he could say things like "Oh, we know everything that goes on in that Statehouse."

He's a tailored-suit-wearing, slicked-back-hair-sporting, too-much-aftershave-smelling stereotype. Think Gordon Gekko but with only a sliver of the income.

I hadn't had one conversation with him about any of this.

"What's happening under the Dome?" he asked.

"Nothing, thank God. All of those pricks are back home, running for reelection, and if their voters actually knew them, most of them would lose," I said with a chuckle.

"That's not what I heard," he said with a knowing grin.

"Oh, yeah? What have you heard?"

"I had a client tell me this morning that this e-cigarette law was under the microscope, and he was worried that there was trouble brewing with it."

"Well, if you believe what you read in the paper, I guess that's probably true," I said to him. I had no idea why a client would care.

"We have Tobacco America on this issue, don't we?" he asked, knowing the answer.

"Yep."

"What do they think about all this?"

"They think they're going to get the entire law stricken down in federal court. Probably sometime after the first of the year."

"Are we working on that lawsuit?"

"No—a couple of DC firms have that action. Sometimes I get a call to help them with chronology and background, but not much lately."

"Thank God," he said. "I don't think all of our clients would approve of our involvement on that."

"Jeffrey, I ran a conflict check before I took the client last year. Did someone overlook it?"

"No, no. There isn't a legal conflict here. Your name came up this morning from a client we had no way of knowing would even care about any of this. He says you're rocking the boat on all this."

"That's what TA pays us to do, you know?"

"Of course they do, but they aren't our most important revenue opportunity either."

"Uh, I don't know what to say to that. I usually only have the one speed for the clients on my list, and that's full speed."

"I've heard that about you. On this one, though, I think it would be best to fulfill your obligations exactly as the engagement agreement says."

"I think I am doing that, Jeffrey. Can you be more specific?"

"I'm looking at the engagement now. I'll get back to you if we need to revisit our relationship with them."

"Uh . . . okay, I guess," I said, with a distinctly "what the hell does that mean" tone.

"Everything else is good, though?" he asked. I knew he didn't really care what the answer was.

"Absolutely," I said with a dismissive nod.

"Good, good," he muttered as he walked out without closing the door behind him.

That was that. I hadn't given any thought to my family's safety. And I hadn't given any thought to potential ramifications for the firm.

Worse yet, I had made the biggest mistake of all: I didn't leave myself any outs.

Did the whole mafia thing give me a good enough reason to walk away? For a lot of people, I guessed the answer to that would be yes. Should I have trusted TK to keep us safe? And even if I didn't, would the bureau stop pursuing this now, just because I was getting cold feet?

Not a chance.

What happened if all of this worked out perfectly and my boss at the firm knew I was the one who killed a windfall of money for one of his business pals? I would get fired. I assumed I'd get fired if I hurt my ability to keep attracting clients and get things done in the Statehouse. But what he just told me was that he might fire me just to kiss ass with his more important opportunities.

I was all alone.

This couldn't just be about getting the girl for me. There had to be more to it than that. She might tire of me anyway, whether my whistleblowing worked out or not.

There were so many ways for this to end badly for me. And so few ways for it to end well.

36

That same afternoon, I got a call from TK. "You won't see those goons again," he said.

"Oh yeah? You made them disappear like a magic trick?"

"Sort of. We made our first contact with Karl and Pauly. They referred us to their attorney. The first question we asked him was whether or not he or his clients knew those two leg-breakers—because we do."

"And?"

"He asked if we could end the call and call us right back. When he did, he threw some lawyer speak at us for a bit and then said—well, hang on, I'll read what he said. He said, 'I assure you that no subjects of any of your investigations will come into contact, overtly or passively with any associates of my clients going forward.'"

"And that's enough for you?"

"It is, since I told him that if we saw them again, we would arrest them and Karl and Pauly for intimidation. The lawyer seemed to hear that. We're going to keep following them anyway, just to see what they do, but I'm confident that you won't see them again."

"Thanks, man."

We didn't talk about it, but this would also confirm for the bad guys that I was working with the FBI. I wondered who they would tell in the Statehouse world—or how they would do it without divulging they were the ones who were under investigation.

I guess TK's assurances helped some, but I knew the lack of things keeping me busy in my daily life would make the anxiety of it all so much worse.

The rest of the month was all about softball games for Mal and working on my golf game. Sometimes Liam or Tomas would join me on the course, or with Flip and Mal at a game or a romp in the park. In that way, it just seemed like a typical summer.

Except that I could feel myself growing overprotective of my family, suspicious of people, and a little bit sad that all of that was happening to me.

Flip could see it happening, and I would catch her looking at me curiously when I would come out of my trances.

One evening at the ball field, I saw Mal talking to some man I didn't recognize through the fence of the dugout. I watched them talking for what seemed like too long, and it was making me uncomfortable. After a bit, I leaned over to Flip and whispered in her ear, "Who the fuck is that talking to Mal?"

"Relax, baby. That's Marissa's dad. She's on the team. It's going to be all right. Calm down and breathe. I know it's all going to be all right," she said.

. . .

Heading into the ATC public meeting on June 29, Ethan Murphy and I weren't sure who would be getting licenses. We were only sure who wouldn't be.

Licenses were issued to the three Indiana companies we expected, and then three were issued to some companies from Florida that none of us knew anything about. No one from those companies was at the meeting and no one in the room appeared to know who they were. More Google research was ahead for me on all of them.

I send TK a text when I left the ATC meeting to let him know there were no goons and that there were three extra companies with licenses that we hadn't expected.

Yeah, we know who they are.

Why do you know that?

Because they all have
connections to Karl.

What?!

Yeah, this whole thing is turning out
to be blatantly obvious.

Anything coming from the
legislators you're interviewing?

They're all pleading ignorance, and
some of them seem so stupid, it's hard
for me to think otherwise.

You're depressing me.

Any ideas?

Just tell me when you want the world
to know you're investigating all of it,
and I can promise you some media.

Hold that thought. I want to
talk to the team.

I didn't know if I had the patience to let this burn this slowly. I knew that Hanna would crawl through hot lava to do a story about the FBI investigating possible corruption in the Statehouse. Plus, she'd been doing a story every couple of weeks on the licensing process in case something happened.

She was just waiting for some drama on this, and I sensed that the rest of the Statehouse press corps was wondering why the *Indianapolis Business Journal* gave a shit.

A green light from TK was all I needed, and I would leak the whole thing to her.

The next day, on my update call with Bethany, I reported who got licenses and who didn't. She seemed almost uninterested in it. She didn't care about the Florida companies, and had never heard of them. No shock there, after TK had told me that they were plants of Karl's.

She did report that the federal lawsuit was fully briefed and that all we were waiting for was a decision from the court. The lawyers were still confident that part or all of the law would be stricken down as unconstitutional. If that happened, she was going to need me to lobby the Statehouse to either keep any new law from passing or to write one that worked for Tobacco America.

Now that I knew more about this than anyone ever should, I was good with that either way. The news of the FBI investigation would probably rock her world also, if it ever became public.

Later that afternoon, the call from TK came.

"We want to rattle some cages with the legislators and see if we can get some people turning on each other," he said.

"What is that supposed to mean?"

"I thought you could get a story planted."

"Is this the green light for that? Sometimes you have to talk in my code, not yours."

"Yes, smartass. Do your thing with your reporter friend."

"This will blow up right after they publish it, you know?"

"I do know—what are you scared of?"

"Me? I love this shit, since no one's gonna break my legs. Right? No one is going to break my legs, right, TK?"

"That's right, princess."

"Okay then. I'll want to wait till after the holiday to talk to her though, because I don't want her to rush it for tomorrow's deadline."

"Fine by us. We can speed up questioning—give these guys one more chance to tell us nothing, and then the story will hit when?"

"Next weekend, I imagine. Oh, and nothing in it will be attributable to me. I won't even want to be an anonymous source. But I'm sure you guys will get called."

"Perfect."

Tomorrow was July 1—the effective date of the new law. Not the kind of day the State Excise Police would be out in force to make sure the new e-liquid law was being followed. They had bigger things to worry about on a holiday weekend.

The Fourth of July was Monday. Hanna Chastain was about to get a gift when I called her for a Tuesday coffee date.

Flip and all the kids didn't have holiday plans locked down yet, but I felt the need to come up with something. She was not a fan of blowing stuff up with bargain home-use fireworks like the boys and I had done for so many years on the Fourth.

I was having a hard time coming up with any good ideas until I discovered the most disturbing thing about my girlfriends. It came up at dinner on Friday night.

We needed to review just basic summer stuff.

"You don't play golf, you don't camp, you don't set off fireworks. What do you do in the summer?" I asked them.

"We play softball—Leem and Tomas played baseball," Mal objected.

"Yeah, but you don't have any games this weekend, young lady. I guess we could go to a baseball game, but you've probably been to the Indians on the Fourth before."

They both looked at me like they didn't want to admit the sad truth.

"Please don't tell me that neither of you have ever been to Victory Field for a game. Please don't tell me that," I begged.

They looked at each other and then looked back at me and shook their heads.

"Oh. My. God. First year for the race and first year for an Indians game—I don't even know what to say about all of this. Except that we are going to the Indians game on the Fourth. They do fireworks on the field and then we can see the big downtown fireworks from our seats too. You two are unbelievable."

"I want to go the country club pool, too!" Mal said. Flip looked embarrassed that Mal had invited herself.

"You got it then, that's a great plan. We'll go to the pool and eat some cookout food, and then I'll take a nap. And when I wake up, we'll go to the ballgame and stay out late and watch the fireworks. How's that sound?"

"Yes!" Mal announced.

"Should we let your mom come? I have to see if the boys want to come too."

Flip interrupted. "I don't need to come."

"Oh yes you do. I want my friends at the club to meet you in your bathing suit. Those old men will die."

"Why?" Mal asked.

"Because your mom is so beautiful," I explained. "Just like you."

Mal gave me her mom's easy smile and grabbed her phone, and headed out of the kitchen, telling us, "I'm texting Leem to see if he's coming."

I stood there beaming as I watched Mal head down the hall, and then I turned to see Flip looking at me with strong curiosity.

"How are you?" she asked, as if she were asking something more deeply than the words implied.

"I'm great. I love seeing her excitement to do new things. It reminds me of my daddy years."

"That's not what I meant. I've been watching you."

"No shit, baby. I see you watching."

"Hang on," she reasserted. "I've been watching you struggle. I don't know what is on your mind, but I know it isn't my bathing suit or Mal's excitement. So, spit it out."

"It's nothing new," I lied.

"Oh, really? Marissa's dad might think differently if he had met you the other day."

"Sorry about that. I just didn't know who he was."

"Clearly. But that is just an example. I see your mind racing and eyes scanning for something that just isn't there. A lot."

"I don't know, I'm just—"

She came up and put both her hands on my cheeks and forced me to look her in the eye. "What?"

I put my arms around her and hugged her and whispered in her ear. "I will be all right. We will be all right."

She pushed out of the hug far enough to look me eye to eye again.

"I'm going to need more than that. I need it for me, but you need to give me more for you too."

"Don't worry—I'm going to give you everything. Soon. I promise."

"You promise? That sounds weird coming from you. I thought everything you said to me was a promise."

She was so right about that.

37

t didn't surprise me that Hanna Chastain beat me to Coat Check on the 5th. It also didn't surprise me that the place was almost empty. She was sitting in the middle of the room, and I made her get up and move to the table by the window.

"What are you doing out here in the great wide open? We might as well sit outside at one of the sidewalk tables. Good morning, by the way."

"Where am I supposed to sit?"

"Over there in the corner by the window . . . quickly, before someone comes in and snags it. I'll be right there after I order some cinnamon toast."

She packed up her camp and moved while I went to the counter. She was getting settled at her new table when I grabbed my chair.

"You're killing me! What's the big news already?" she half-yelled.

"First of all, I know this place is empty, but we need to bring it down to a small roar while I leak this to you. Okay?"

"Yes, sir," she whispered, and leaned in.

"The FBI is investigating the Statehouse for possible corruption on the e-liquid law."

She wrote "F B I" in big letters on the notepad in her hand, and then looked up at me with the expression of a wild animal about to pounce on its unsuspecting prey. She didn't ask a question or make a sound. I had never seen anyone aggressively listen before, but that's what she was doing.

"Relax," I said to her. "We have all morning to discuss this. I'm going to tell you all I know again, and you're going to keep me out of the story. Right?"

"Whatever you say, Will."

"Goddamnit, Hanna, you are going to keep me out of the story, right?"

"Yes sir!"

"I need to stay anonymous for a little while longer, and I would rather you not even have to cite any anonymous sources. The FBI will take your call, but I want you to call a few senators first and ask them if they have been contacted or questioned by them. Then you can go wherever that leads you."

"Why do you want to stay anonymous?"

"I need people to think I know more than you do, and more than they do—that I know more than anyone. If the Statehouse is convinced that is true, they'll crumble for me on this."

"Is it true that you know more than anyone?"

"It might be."

She resumed her yell-whispers. "So what do the feds have and who do they have it on?"

"They know that this whole thing is a setup to create a monopoly that Karl Satterfield and Pauly James would control for the vape market. They also know that the investors in their company believe that this is—or was—a precursor to a monopoly in the marijuana market in Indiana."

"What! What? When did that enter the fray!?"

"I don't know when. But the FBI seems to know. There's a long list of investors in the scheme that Karl and Pauly set up and you will know about twenty of the names on that list."

"Do you have the list?"

"Not on me, but I can get it. I counted seventeen current lobbyists on it and another six active politico types on the version I saw. Those numbers are minimums. There could be more."

"Fuck," she said, like this might be bigger than she wanted it to be.

"Is this big enough for you? Or is it too big?"

"How long have you known about all of this?"

"It's been coming out a little at a time for the last few months, I guess."

"Why didn't you dump this on the Statehouse before?" she asked. It was an excellent question.

"Do you think if I said all this, the people in charge would have believed me?"

She thought about that for a second.

"These fuckers knew enough to question what they were going along with," I said, "and most of them just didn't care. Well, they're going to care now. Some of them already do, I'm sure. But if they keep claiming they don't know anything and none of them get charged, they still win."

"But if I do a story about the investigation, they'll panic?" she asked like she realized that I was blatantly using her.

"Exactly. What? You didn't think I was partnering with you for no good reason, did you? I've kept up with my part of our partnership. Doesn't that make up for the fact that I have a selfish agenda? And don't tell me you don't want to be part of these bastards crumbling. Please, don't tell me that."

"Take it easy, Will. I'm with you on this one hundred percent. What if the story doesn't turn out the way you want it to, though?"

"Were you planning on reporting something other than the truth?"

"Of course not."

"Then I have no worries. Just call Charlie Alderman first, then the rest of the committee, and ask them if they have been contacted by the FBI on the issue. After you do that, call whomever you want. But if it's not Karl, Pauly, or the feds, I don't know who it would be."

"I'll call them as soon as we part, okay?"

"Fire away, young lady. This is all yours. And remember, the question to them is simple: 'Have you been contacted by the FBI to discuss the e-liquid legislation from the last two years?' And 'Do you have any comment on that questioning?'"

"You think so, huh? I never interviewed anyone before. Thanks for the tips."

I giggled at that a little. "You think so, huh, you think so, huh," I mocked her. "Just call or text if you get stuck. I'll get the list of investors while you're mapping out your big-time interview plan."

I returned to the sit-back-and-wait game. It would be a little different, though, because I thought Hanna would need my help from time to time. I expected her to be reliant on me while she was writing the story. Or series of stories. I hoped TK would be allowed to be the source for the feds on this. That would make things easier on me, though I bet they had someone assigned to deal with this sort of thing.

. . .

I was on the driving range at the country club on Wednesday afternoon trying to learn how to stop snap-hooking my driver, when my back-right pocket started vibrating. It was Hanna.

"These guys are pissed off!"

"Who are 'these guys'?"

"The legislators! They can't get off the idea that the FBI leaked the investigation!"

"What are you telling them about that?"

"That I haven't spoken to the FBI yet, of course."

"Perfect. That probably makes them paranoid."

"Oh my God. They are scared to death."

"They should be. Are they saying anything of value yet?"

"Not at all. It's all denials and ignorance. Even Alderman is acting like he doesn't know how this is all connected in his town with people he knows. It's embarrassing."

"What do you need? Sounds like nothing."

"I need mobile phone numbers for Pauly James and Karl Satterfield."

"I can text you Pauly's number, but I don't have Karl's. Have you called their offices?"

"Yes, but they won't return my calls."

"When you get them, they'll refer you to their attorney, but I'll send you Pauly's number as soon as we hang up."

Then Hanna gave me this nugget. "And you should know that Ethan Murphy went on the record with me, and he had been questioned by the FBI. So he looks like my source."

"That is awesome."

Ethan had given me a perfect cover. I didn't know TK had talked to him.

This story was going to come out on Sunday. Many people wouldn't see it until Monday. The House Republican golf outing was next Thursday. Those guys, especially all the friends of Alderman and Pauly, would be in a froth by then.

I would spend that entire day acting like I didn't know anything about nothing. I would smile a lot. Hopefully I would win the cheap trophy or the long drive contest and just listen to the gossip about the feds looking at all the nasty goings-on in the Statehouse.

I hope I didn't forget to enjoy this.

. . .

I hadn't even gotten home from my Sunday morning workout before the first text message came in from one of my young friends telling me "Holy shit—the *IBJ*!"

The digital front-page headline read: "Federal Investigators Suspicious of Statehouse-Created E-Liquid Monopoly."

Oh shit! The headline implied that she had nailed it—and that she was sitting on the marijuana story. If that were true, she might be elevated to superhero status. I had to stop on the sidewalk on the way home from the gym and read it.

Three or four senators confirmed they had been contacted by the FBI. All of them also claimed they didn't know any differently from the public version of what happened on the legislation. Former Senator Damon Lawrence would not return calls. Pauly and Karl's attorney would not discuss the matter, as they had also been contacted by the feds.

Ethan Murphy was the star. He explained in detail how the scheme worked, how it shut down all his members' businesses, and how Indiana Tobacco and Liquid never had any plans to actually enter the market. It was all a scam. And the legislators who carried it were all in on it.

He had this great quote in the story: "There is no possible way that the legislators and the lobbyists involved avoided committing crimes."

Wow!

The denial from Charlie Alderman was priceless. All Hanna attributed to him in the story was "Nothing illegal occurred on this legislation."

Double wow!

That was the kind of denial that left the reader with a sense of certainty that this guy was dirty—really dirty. This story was the match that got tossed into the Winner's Circle powder keg.

TK also gave her a quote that I loved: "We are not at liberty to discuss the matter at this time." Classic. Like the Boy Scout was unaware of this setup.

And Hanna was keeping some gas in the tank. She hadn't reported on the connection to the gaming company, the OTB, or marijuana. Surely she hadn't done that strategically—not all by herself.

I needed to go to brunch and get ready to work on my "play dumb" act for a little while and learn how to watch these guys squirm, without showing how happy it made me.

38

Bethany got a kick out of the story. Even for someone as all-business as she was, I still thought I might have heard a giggle on the other end of the call.

But I might have imagined it.

I didn't have any cause to be around the Statehouse or Winner's Circle people until the House Republican outing on Thursday. Any time someone texted me or called me about it, all I said to them was "How about that" or "That sure is something."

I heard from dozens of people. Some of them were friends. A few of them were former friends—although they didn't know what I knew about them.

The former friends were trying to find out what I knew for their own good. They weren't getting anything from me—at least not yet.

Hanna had the list of investors and was probably working on that story this week. These former friends may have been contacted by her for comment. She didn't seem to need anything from me, as far as I knew. I hadn't heard a word from her all week.

The golf outing had the potential to be the best damn outing I had ever played. Normally, I am one of those guys who shows up just in time for the shotgun start. But I was ready to go two hours early for this one. I got to Ironwood Golf Club at 11:00, a full hour before the start time, and it was all I could do to wait that long.

I had enough time to get my clubs over to their small driving range and hit some warm-up shots. The range was between the parking lot and the clubhouse, so as the other people arrived, they had to walk past me on the way. It was hard to actually hit any balls, because so many people kept stopping to come down and ask me if I had heard anything.

That same gathering of young people from last year's outing and every other good gossip session was determined to stick around until I gave them something.

"Come on, Will. We know you know all about this shit. Quit acting like you don't," said the young blonde woman who was my true gossip partner.

Her young male counterpart added, "You would kick my ass if I walked away and started telling people you didn't know shit about this. Whether it was true or not."

I had to respond to that one. "Well, you're right about that. And I wouldn't want you people to have to go lie on me, or for me. I'll give you just a little bit, so you can let everyone know you know more than they do. Deal?"

The four who had me surrounded nodded and huddled up, waiting in anticipation for either some juice or a trademark punchline.

"Here's the deal. There will be stories that come out that are worse than the one from this weekend. Way worse. And the next one will probably have more Statehouse people named in it than the last one."

"Statehouse people?" two of them said in unison.

Then my young blonde woman friend pointed out the obvious tell in that description. "Uh, that sounds like more of the hallway is about to get rocked."

I shut down the huddle with this: "I have given you my juice, young people." I raised my hands like Moses parting the Red Sea. "Now go forth and show these old crusty fuckers how you know more than they do. And even though none of you thanked me, you're welcome!"

Heading into the clubhouse to grab a sandwich right before the announcements and the shotgun start brought a very different reception. A shotgun start is when the entire field of players at the tournament all leave from the clubhouse in their carts at the same time, scatter to their assigned holes, and start at the same time. It often looks a little like a social demolition derby if the staff at the golf club doesn't run a tight ship. Ironwood did a lot of outings like this, and they kept the carts in a line like ants marching.

There were a few legislators who actively avoided me. A couple of others said hi and shook my hand as if it were some sort of brave gesture on their part. I could feel the whole room looking at me suspiciously. I just made my sandwich, smiled at anyone who made eye contact, and headed out to the golf carts.

Maybe I imagined the tension.

Pauly didn't usually show up at the golf outings, and he didn't that day. Most of the investors from the list were there, though none of them came anywhere near me as we milled around waiting for the outing to begin.

When the pre-outing announcements started, we went to our carts to listen. The Speaker of the House said all the usual things. No surprises there.

But while I sat in my cart and reviewed the former friends who had avoided me, I noticed something about that bunch. While there were a couple of Democrat lobbyists who invested in Pauly's scheme, there were not any women. It was a classic group of old white guys, a fraternity with obvious exclusivity.

I made a note to remember to point that out later, when it counted.

Hanna called me the next day to give me a heads-up.

"I just wanted to let you know that there will be another story this weekend about the investors," she said.

"I thought that was next. Congratulations that the whole state reprinted last week's story. I'm glad no one else is writing about it."

"Well, what would they write? I'm the only one who has the goods. Thank you for that, by the way."

"What about marijuana?" I asked her, hoping that she wouldn't mention that for at least another week.

"I'm holding onto that for a little while longer. I'm gambling that no one else will come up with that, and I feel pretty good about it."

"I'm with you a hundred percent. No one else is going to get that part without their own leak. I'm looking forward to your next story—I'll pop some popcorn Sunday morning."

I guessed that would explain the tension the day before at the golf outing. Hanna had already called the lobbyists for comment on their presence on the list.

The Sunday morning headline read: "Former Legislators and Lobbyists Invested in Vaping Monopoly."

I scanned the story fast to see that she'd only featured eight or nine of the lobbyists she had info on. She was slow-burning the story. She was torturing them. And it was fucking fantastic.

There was another bomb. For those who didn't have any idea where these stories ended, I'm sure it was scary. Especially if they lacked the confidence in the appearance of their own innocence. Lacking confidence in the appearance of one's own innocence is different than actually being innocent. Although being innocent should help.

Sunday night, while Mal was helping me with the dishes at my townhouse and about twelve hours after the second story was released on the *IBJ* website, my phone rang. It was Senator Marianne Billings. I dried my hands quickly to take the call.

"I'm sorry to call you on a Sunday," she said, "but I need you to join me in a meeting tomorrow in the Senate with the Republican leaders. Can you be there at 11:00?"

"You're the one with the three-hour drive, so if you'll be there, I certainly can be. But I don't know if I want to be there. What's the topic?"

"I'm sure this won't be any surprise to you. They want to know how to fix the e-liquid thing before this spins out of control."

"It already looks out of control to me."

"You got that right. You also warned them, just like I did. But the FBI and these stories coming out of the *IBJ* have really put this place on its heels. They want to know if you're willing to help them fix it."

I giggled at the prospect for a moment. "Senator, I am willing to help make this right for the people who got screwed by the legislature. I'm also willing to help make this right by making sure the dirty bastards who dreamt this whole thing up get shut out. But I'm not interested in helping leadership protect any dirty members of the Senate. Under those terms, do you still want me there tomorrow?"

"Absolutely, I do. I don't know what their reaction will be, but before this is over, I'm sure they're going to need you whether they like it or not."

"Well then, I will see you at 11:00."

Mal was still standing on the "dry" side of the sink and was not excited about the interruption.

"I'm waiting," she said impatiently as I put the phone down.

I glanced into the living room area to see if Flip had heard anything—or everything. She sat there without even looking into the kitchen, like the fifteen feet that separated all of us made the phone call beyond earshot.

"Sorry Mal, oh great princess of the dishes dungeon," I said as I dug in on the last of the dirty dishes in the sink. When I finished rinsing them and put them in the dry zone for her, I looked back at her mom, who was now sitting on the edge of the couch and waiting to hear what was up.

"It looks like the bosses in the Senate want my help getting them out of this jam tomorrow morning," I reported.

"That sounds like good news to me. Is it?" she asked.

"If I trusted them it would be. I'll be keeping my guard up at this first session, that's for sure," I said. Then I added, "But I don't want to forget to enjoy this a little."

"Doing the right thing isn't enjoyment enough for you?" she asked.

"I was just testing you, baby," I said with some fake disappointment.

39

struggled a little with what to wear to the meeting. Normally, wearing a suit and tie was the protocol, but I wasn't asking them for anything this time. They would be the ones asking. I thought about waltzing in there in shorts and flip-flops—but after entertaining the thought, I stuck to the rules. It was a dark suit, white shirt, and red tie for me.

I got there right at 11:00, and I brought nothing with me. No briefcase or backpack. No portfolio or notepad. There were no files. There was no wire. I walked in there without any plan to offer anything or to take instruction.

It was the first meeting. I knew there would be others.

All I wanted to communicate to them was that I knew more than I was telling them.

Andy at the Senate reception desk waved me in toward the President Pro Tem's office before I could say good morning.

"Damn, Andy. Cat got your tongue?"

"All business today, Will. Good luck in there," is all he said.

I walked around his desk and instead of heading up the stairs to the offices of the rest of the senators, I took a quick left turn down a private hall with the pro tem's office on the immediate right.

Through the window I saw Senator Billings and three middle-aged white guys in suits—Peter Jansen, the chief of staff; the pro tem; and the floor leader were all already sitting down. Before I could knock, the pro tem waved me in.

"Good morning, everybody. Don't get up," I said as I took a quick lap around the room to shake hands.

I got nods and serious-sounding "good mornings" in return.

"What can I do for you on a Monday morning?" I asked.

The pro tem took the lead.

"Will, we obviously have a problem here, and Senator Billings believes that you can help us with it. You and I have known each other for twenty years, and I am sure that if you are able to help us you will. I just don't know what a solution is, and more importantly, I'm not even sure I know entirely what our problems are. Again, Senator Billings thinks you might know as much as anyone." He paused for a couple of seconds, and then he asked, "Is she right?"

I looked around the room first to see that everyone knew she was right, and that we were just confirming it.

"I don't know if I can help you with your problem, because I don't know what you think your problem is," I replied. "And honestly, I'm not sure I want to help you unless you are offering to help me simultaneously. But Senator Billings is right. Of all the people who weren't scamming you guys on this thing, I know more than anyone."

"Well, that's a good start," the pro tem said. He would clearly be doing all the talking. "Why don't we start with how we can help you, just so you know we are serious about partnering on this thing. Do you have ideas for that?"

"That's the easy part, Senator. I can get Peter a document, one that he may have already seen, that takes the e-liquid law and strikes about half of it down to a very basic license at the ATC, eliminates the security firm that is the source of the monopoly, and eliminates the clean room and the inspection authority. Ultimately it looks like all my client has to do is register with the state to get back to doing business here."

The pro tem looked at Peter to see if he knew what that meant, and if that was a possible solution. Peter nodded back at him.

"I think we can do that," the pro tem agreed.

Then I threw them my first curveball: "And I want that done on Organization Day."

I knew that was a strong-arm ask, but I hoped that if we could gut this law and replace it with one that let the T-shirters back into business fast, maybe they wouldn't be faced with a total loss. I assumed he would say no.

Fast-track legislation was never done on Org Day. It's a ceremonial day, two weeks after Election Day in November, where no surprises or anything meaningful actually happens.

"How are we supposed to do that, Will?" the pro tem asked, as if I'd asked him for the impossible.

"Oh, I don't know. Maybe you should have a hearing in the Judiciary Interim Study Committee, I'll present the reasoning behind the new legislation to the committee, and the committee will issue a report that shows this is what they recommend to the body. You gavel in and vote on it in November while you're here wasting time on all the ritualistic bullshit and send it to the governor. It's as easy as a veto override vote, which, as you know, you guys handle on Organization Day all the time. That's a solution to *my* problem."

They looked at each other like they didn't have a good reason to scoff at the idea, but it was so unusual that they just couldn't commit to it yet. Plus no one from the House was in the meeting.

The pro tem enjoyed pointing that out. "I can't commit for the Speaker of the House, as you know—"

"Let me stop you there for a moment, Senator, and make sure you know that while his guys haven't been drilled like yours have so far, their day is coming. He'll want the same things you want before long."

That actually made him smile. "I guess you do know more than everyone else."

"This is the best you guys can do to solve *my* problem," I said.

"We'll work on that. Now why don't you tell me what *my* problem is, or what *my* members' problems are."

"Hmmm. Where do I start. First and foremost, crimes may have been committed here."

"What crimes?!" the pro tem asked with some agitation.

"I have no idea, Senator. But do you believe that Senator Alderman convinced you guys to pass this piece-of-shit law and create this monopoly on accident? Do you believe that he just made a mistake? Do you believe that Pauly James had a legitimate legislative package that should have been trusted? Do you think that the two hundred vape shop owners who cannot legally operate in Indiana now deserve to be put out of business by this body? If so, why? I can go on and on. I told you guys this didn't pass the smell test, and none of you wanted to believe me. You believed Senator Alderman's lying ass instead. Well, this is what you get for making that mistake."

"Will, you are describing a mistake, not a crime."

"Oh, really? I've known you for twenty years, just like you've known me. Are you going to try and make people believe that you got snowed by the likes of Alderman, Pauly, and Karl Satterfield and that it was just an honest mistake? That Alderman and possibly others aren't going to make any money off this crooked deal? That will be a tough sell. Especially when you probably don't even know how deep this whole scam runs yet."

The pro tem raised his hands in a demonstrative shrug and asked, "How deep does it run?"

I leaned back in my chair and crossed my legs and calmly answered, "Too deep for you to defend."

A hush fell on the room.

"Will, I am offering to help you and your client, but you don't seem to have much help to offer me."

"I have advice for you, Senator. You need to conduct an internal audit of all the communication your members have had with Pauly, Karl, and their lawyers over the last two years. Then you need to isolate Senator Alderman by removing his oversight of the issue while you fix this. Then you need to cooperate with the FBI as much as is humanly possible and ride out the storm. You understand that by helping me, you are helping yourselves just as much, don't you?"

"How so?" he asked.

"I guess you're just going to have to trust me on that one for now. You may not have known this before today, but I am pissed off about the way my client and friends of my client have been treated here. This time, that actually matters. A lot."

"Are there more stories coming?" he asked.

"If you're asking if there is more to report, the answer is yes. But I don't know if they will be reported."

"What else do we need to know?" he asked, knowing I was not dumping my whole trunk today.

"You need to know that you can't help yourselves without helping me. And that you can't help yourselves and Pauly James at the same time. You might want to lock him out while you get your house back in order."

"Good to know. Thanks for your help. Peter, you and Will can work on the details, right?"

Peter responded in almost military fashion. "Yes, sir."

The pro tem thanked me for coming and dismissed me without letting Senator Billings or the floor leader say a word.

"Thank you, Will. We'll talk soon."

I was shaking when I walked out. They were at least acting like they were caving. And I hadn't even said the word "marijuana." I hadn't even mentioned former Senator Damon Lawrence. They didn't even pin the FBI investigation on me.

But even though they didn't say it, they knew the media coverage was all me.

So what?

By the time I got back to my office, a text came through from Peter Jansen.

> Will, the Judiciary Committee was already scheduled to meet next Wednesday. We want to amend the agenda to add this issue to it, but we won't do that until the end of the day next Monday. Can you be there to present?

I would be there, and I would be brief.

40

TK and his team found evidence of a crime. But not in Indiana and not related to any of this. It was fraud on a land deal in another state that Karl had committed. TK wasn't sharing the details with me and it wouldn't matter if he had.

"What the fuck do you mean, you aren't going to charge him?" I asked him at Coat Check the day before the Judiciary hearing.

"If we don't have cooperating witnesses, it's a waste of time. We aren't giving up on it, but that won't have any impact on what we're doing here anyway," he claimed.

"Oh, yes it will. You and I both know he's dirty—this would be confirmation of that."

"Will, it doesn't matter. Trust me. We are better off continuing to work on a better case, here in Indiana."

"If you say so. I still think you ought to bust them all on the list of infractions and violations of the lobby registration laws and build a RICO case."

"Just keep doing what you're doing and let us do our thing," TK said.

"Okay, smartass, but so far, I'm very disappointed in all of you."

"Noted. I'll even put that in my report."

I had bigger things to tend to. I was the star of the next day's Judiciary Committee. They listed me on the agenda all alone. The entry just said "Indiana e-liquid laws and regulations" with "Will O'Courtney" listed underneath it.

My phone had been buzzing out of control from my gossip club and even some local media. Hanna wasn't bugging me though. She knew that I was only going to offer testimony about everything she had already reported. She was holding back the marijuana part, and I had promised her I would do the same—for the time being.

Without my little agenda item, there would have been ten people there. But because of the topic, the room was jammed. TV cameras, radio microphones, reporters sitting on the floor in front of the testimony table. The whole bit.

Yes, this was the scene right back in my favorite committee room, Room 431.

I'm sure the new judges that were added in Brown County and Knox County appreciated the attention and the noise from the crowd.

No one outside of the inner circle would have understood what this really meant when it came through.

I got an email from the Senate Majority Campaign Committee moving three of their upcoming events to different venues. All three events had been set for the Winner's Circle but were being moved to other places for no stated reason. It seemed Pauly and Karl had been given advice to start lying low—or members were trying to put some fake distance between them and the source of the FBI investigation. I wasn't sure that mattered in any way, but it was fun watching them squirm.

I waited in the hall for the previously scheduled business to be conducted. When they were done, I let everybody shift around and get out of the way before I went inside. Again, I brought nothing.

The chairman announced the agenda item by saying they wanted to review some apparent problems that might have been erroneously enacted on the issue of e-liquid regulation. That was it. Then he added: "Mr. O'Courtney, the floor is yours."

It was a different committee than the one that passed these dog-shit laws. These guys were mostly lawyers. All the members of the ethics committees also sat on the Judiciary Committee. None of them had been on a committee that had heard any of this subject matter before today. And six of the twelve members of the committee had voted against the bills that had passed.

If anyone thought that the law could successfully be defended in this forum—like Pauly or any single one of his high-priced suits—they too would have been on the agenda. But they weren't. It was just me.

It was an easy crowd. The main thing I needed to avoid was going overboard.

"Thank you, Mr. Chairman and members of the committee. My name is Will O'Courtney, and I represent Tobacco America. I'm here today to explain the legislature's errors in the creation of the regulatory framework for e-liquid in Indiana.

"It appears to me that the General Assembly was tragically misled by lobbyists and investors speculating on legislative outcomes that would create a monopoly in this market." I began the story from the beginning.

The lawsuits. The businesses closing. The appearance of improprieties were all highlighted, but there was something I didn't want to forget to say early in my comments.

"I predicted this outcome. I wish I had been wrong, even though I knew I wasn't. That's right. I *knew* I wasn't. The legislature trusted the wrong people this time."

I paused and looked at all of them from side to side. No one seemed interested in interrupting, so I continued.

316

"Here is how this was supposed to work," I said as I explained the functional details to a group that should have known them but likely didn't.

"The three licensees who are not currently operating all have one thing in common. They're all connected in one way or another to Karl Satterfield and a company in Wabash, Indiana, called Schulte's. I will get back to them in a minute.

"I know some of the people who lobbied the General Assembly in favor of these acts. Three people registered to lobby on behalf of a company named Indiana Tobacco and Liquid. That company testified just last year right here in this room that they were building a facility in Indiana to manufacture these products the right way. The safe way. The tamper-proof and child-proof way. They lied to you. There is no manufacturing facility. The company doesn't own any land on which to build a facility. That was never what they planned to do. Never. This year, none of the legislators even seemed to recall that promise."

I actually expected an interruption after that comment, but all I got from the committee was silence, though the crowd in the room burst into muffled laughter at this.

"I apologize for the sarcasm, Mr. Chairman. If I may, I would like to continue. The security firm is the control. No entity can sell this product in Indiana without a contract with Schulte's. The statute requires it. And we have become aware that Schulte's contracts require that companies that contract with it must pay Schulte's with a percentage of its revenue. If that sounds like an old mob-boss requiring the merchants on the street to pay them in exchange for not robbing them, it should.

"So how did these three master lobbyists convince the body to pass such a horrible scheme? As most of you know by now through media reports, it wasn't just three lobbyists. It was more than twenty of them. More than twenty lobbyists, already active in this building, and registered to lobby for other, unrelated companies, had invested in a company called Madison Properties.

"Madison Properties is a company that looks like a pyramid scheme full of investors but with no obvious business purpose or value. Its only asset is a big one, though. That asset is its exclusive right to buy Schulte's whenever they see fit. Presumably, that time is sometime after July 1 of this year, when the monopoly can be effectively launched."

The committee needed to hear about the lobbying strategy, and I gave them the story. I didn't mention any names. I didn't have to. But any Judiciary Committee in history would cringe at what I said next.

"These are all things the criminal investigation, yes, *criminal*, will have to sort out."

Visible anxiety set in on the group.

I gave them my proposed legislative solution, which I had already forwarded to them electronically that morning.

Even though I was a little surprised they let me go on like this without questions, there were a few final things that I wanted to say out loud before I yielded.

"This episode has left a stain on this body. Current and former members of the General Assembly may have been manipulating our state's constitutional processes in this matter in exchange for profit. That would mean something illegal occurred, and that is what the FBI is looking to determine.

"However, there is the possibility that something worse occurred here. Imagine for a moment that no crimes were committed, by anyone. What would that really mean?

"It would mean that our system failed us. It would mean that it can be manipulated in what was an obvious manner, at least it was obvious to me, but the body was unable to recognize it until the embarrassment of the manipulation became inevitable. Like the embarrassment the FBI and *IBJ* have brought. That is a far bigger problem in my opinion."

I paused, took a deep breath, and looked down at the table for a moment to make sure I had my exact words together for my closing.

"In this building, we work hard to clearly establish the difference between what is legal and what is illegal. Sometimes we have to work harder to clearly establish the difference between what is right and what is wrong.

"You guys did the wrong thing here. Some of what you did will likely turn out to be illegal. But there is absolutely no question that it was wrong.

"Fixing this one should be easy. Preventing things like this from happening again will be more difficult. And all of you should be prepared for when the stakes are even higher—like, say, when a public health crisis or the integrity of an election is the thing at stake. Either way, I do not expect to be here long enough to save you the next time.

"Thank you for your time, Mr. Chairman. I would be happy to answer any questions."

Applause could be heard in the hallway through the heavy door. Ethan Murphy had brought some friends to the hearing, but they had to watch on the monitor in the hallway.

The chairman asked the committee, "Do any members of the committee have any questions?" Without even looking, he said, "Seeing none, we are adjourned."

Outside the committee room, while I was getting a range of reactions—from hugs to scowls—the chairman of the committee walked up to me. He put his hand out to shake mine, and I grasped it.

"Damn," he said.

"And there is more," I replied.

He looked at me like he had just seen a ghost and then turned and walked away.

Procedurally, the committee was going to include the proposed legislative fix in its final report that was due on October 31. Election Day was November 8. Organization Day was November 22.

Rarely are bills considered on Org Day, let alone passed. It is extremely rare. I actually don't even know why the idea had popped into my head that day in the pro tem's office.

My expectation was that they would run a bill through that day to show the state that they weren't dirty. And by then, they were probably hoping that the heat would have died down from the media and the FBI, and they would have isolated whatever possible criminal evidence they had on Alderman and whomever else.

All I needed to do was convince Hanna that the marijuana story needed to wait until November. If it ran between the election and Org Day, they would know I still had some gas in my tank, and the fix legislation would end up saying exactly what I wanted it to say.

For the rest of the summer, I did not expect to hear another public comment by a legislator. Except for comments that sounded a lot like "No comment."

I did expect that TK would keep me in the loop—literally. Because I found out the best thing possible about him personally. He happened to play golf.

41

The bulk of my work was done. The pro tem and the Speaker of the House had made themselves available to the press after the hearing and they both publicly committed to fix the law as soon as possible.

They did not disclose that they planned to do it on Org Day, and so that part of it was a secret between the few of us on the inside. Funny. I'd struggled to get out of a circle I didn't want to be in any longer and landed in another one that felt just as bad. This one was temporary, though.

The FBI kept doing their work, and more of it was focused on documents that would be seized and reviewed that belonged to Pauly and Karl and their lawyers. TK and I played golf every week or two as the summer wound down, and he kept me up to speed on the tedious nature of the legal maneuvering that went on between the bad guys and the Bureau.

I wanted to be able to see the legislature take my advice and pre-pare to help the T-shirters who got screwed by what happened. It was obvious that most of their businesses would be gone for good, even if the law was changed with a historic quickness as I expected in the fall.

Most of all, though, I wished the legislature would have punished Pauly and Karl and all their goons by kicking them out of the lobbying business for good. I knew that was a pipe dream of mine, but as Flip had noticed about me, I am definitely a dreamer.

Hanna held the marijuana story. I wasn't sure if she would publish it at the perfect time for me or not, but at some point, I was going to need that story out there. Because while I knew I was getting the e-liquid laws fixed, I wanted to make sure those assholes didn't rally and regain control of a new marijuana market when Indiana legalized it in the coming years. That was the one thing that kept me watching them. I refused to let that happen.

. . .

The election that occurred on November 8, 2016, shocked the planet.

For purposes of this saga, the election actually did matter. The U.S. Attorney would be getting replaced as a result. Almost all the bad guys were Republicans. The Obama appointee was not interested in starting a corruption case around the Indiana Statehouse that he could not finish. And the guys I battled on it had obvious connections to Pence and even a few legitimate ones to Trump.

No corruption case was going to be filed.

But right before the election, a funny thing happened. The Southern District Court ruled that the e-liquid laws were unconstitutional. Even though I had a deal with leadership to gut the old law and replace it with one that made sense, the court finally issued a ruling that reinforced the plan.

Some of Pauly's legislator buddies, especially those not privy to my deal with the pro tem, still wanted to find a way to keep Shulte's legal reason for existence in the space relevant. They should have just slithered back to the hardware business, but they seemed to have been too close to a real fortune to let it go without a little bit of a struggle. I heard rumors from time to time about some members of the House trying to preserve some sort of role for them in the licensing process going forward.

The week between the election and Org Day was when I saw their last gasp to keep the now-obliterated local market from being overrun by big businesses like Bethany's.

The Senate chief of staff sent me the draft version of Senate Bill 1 in an email the week before Org Day on Tuesday, November 15. Peter Jansen's draft was exactly as I'd written it, with one item added for some folks who were clearly friends of Pauly's.

It prohibited internet sales. That was a shot at Tobacco America, since that was a large part of their business model. Seriously, was this a product that would need to be sold in the dying field of brick-and-mortar retail? That little nugget would have to come out of the bill. I set up an appointment with Peter to discuss the matter on that coming Monday.

I then called Hanna. "When were you planning on running your story on the marijuana angle?" I asked.

"Guess," she said, like I should have some kind of clue.

"I guess you will do it this weekend."

"Now why would I do that?" she asked.

"Because I have another leak for you if you do."

"You are truly unbelievable. What's this leak?"

"I said I have another leak *if you do.*"

"Fire away, Will."

"They are going to fix the e-liquid law on Org Day. But they're trying to add a nugget in there to keep big companies like my client out by banning internet sales. No one knows about the Org Day plan yet. So now will you run the marijuana story this weekend?"

"Jesus! Can I put the Org Day fix plan in the story with it?"

"Absolutely."

"Then this weekend it is! Thanks again, Will. But can I let you in on a secret?"

"Of course you can."

"We were going to run it this weekend anyway," she confessed with some truly gleeful laughter. Then she hung up on me.

Damn. That was a good one. She wasn't new here anymore.

. . .

The headline in the digital story read: "E-liquid Scheme Was a Precursor to Marijuana Monopoly."

Peter Jansen had slotted me in for 10:30 on Monday morning with just him and the pro tem. I had my paper copy of the *IBJ* under my arm when my hipster receptionist friend Andy Bauman waved me in.

"Good morning, guys," I said.

"Will, I can't believe you are going to bitch about the internet sales thing after everything we're already giving you," the pro tem said.

"Senator, did you see the *IBJ*?"

"I did. So?"

"So I am not going to stop until I finish this my way. I want that internet shit out of this bill. And you can either help make that happen just because it's the right thing to do, or you can gamble on whether or not I can keep fucking with all of you with the juice I have left in my tank on all this."

"You know, I used to like you so much better before all of this," he said. Then he looked over at Peter, and Peter nodded back at him.

He looked back at me and said, "Deal. Now tell me, are we done here, or will there be more?"

"I will happily leave all of this to you and the FBI, except for one little thing," I said.

"And that is?"

"None of these bastards can have a penny's worth of any marijuana market here. If I hear so much as a whisper about that, I'll be knocking on your door."

"Don't worry about that one. Marijuana won't ever be legal in Indiana as long as I am in the Senate."

"Then deal."

We shook hands and I left his office—and presumably, his circle forever.

. . .

The legislators' families were at Organization Day all dressed up to see their husbands, dads, sons, daughters, moms, and wives get sworn in as a member of the House or the Senate. It was a day of ceremony that featured only speeches of the leaders of each party's caucus.

In twenty years, I'd never paid much attention to the pageantry of the day. And that year, I found myself looking through it more than I was looking at it.

They ran Senate Bill 1 across the desks in both chambers, suspended some rules, and put the bill on the board for votes. Very little was said about it in either chamber. There were no apologies or commitments to higher ethical standards. There was no scolding for the lobbyists who had manipulated them.

It was the period at the end of the sentence in their minds. They were free from it. Some of them probably felt more like they were free from me.

I spent the afternoon in the galleries until the final votes took place. No one voted against it in the Senate. It passed 50–0. The

House had a few hangers-on, and a few voted no, but it still passed in a landslide, 95–5.

When the gavel fell in the House, I grabbed my backpack and headed downstairs to the third floor for what felt like both my last time and my first time. The place wouldn't ever be the same for me.

Coming around the corner, I saw Representative Ben Rizzo standing in the hallway surrounded by family and other lobbyists having a laugh and doing the usual hallway crap. He spotted me and broke camp to come over and congratulate me.

I was distracted for a moment to see that just beyond Rizzo was a crowd of reporters interviewing someone. The TV lights were all fired up and the lobbyists in the hallway were scattering so as not to be in the background of the local stations' shots. I leaned around to see who they were talking to, and there was Ethan Murphy.

I couldn't help but smile to see Ethan giving what I assumed to be jubilant and celebratory comments about his victory. It made me wonder if he knew how monumental the undoing of something like this actually was—and how unlikely he would ever see something like it again. I wondered if he would ever return to the Statehouse.

Rizzo broke my stare. "In the end, these guys shouldn't have bet against you, right?"

"That's right. Though I think everyone lost a little bit of something on this one. Even me. I'm not gonna lie, mainly because I try not to lie any more. I'm pretty sure no one got as much as I did, though. And I don't mean revenge or market share for my client. I mean freedom. I'm free from this shit now."

"How many friends did you lose over this?" he asked.

"Friends?" I laughed at the notion. "Thank you for your help, Ben."

"I didn't do much, but you're welcome. Why do I get the feeling that you're done with all of it?"

"Because I *am* done with all of it. I don't know what I'm going to do right now besides take my boys and my girls to the beach for Thanksgiving. And hopefully when I come back, I'll have a new wife. Then she and I can decide together what my next move is."

"Any ideas?" he asked.

"I thought I might do some writing. I think I might enjoy telling stories."

"What kind of stories?"

"I don't know. Maybe stories like this one."

"God help us," he said with a handshake as we parted ways.

I headed down the stairs to the second floor so I could stroll through the rotunda to take the north exit. I spotted a surprise couple of visitors there. Flip was milling around under the beautiful stained-glass dome in the middle of the building waiting for me and reading the plaques.

She was wearing an old, faded jean jacket, a flowered dress, and, of course, flip-flops. Odd for November, but not odd for her. Her hair was pulled back and from a distance she looked like she did every day. When I got close to her, Mal came running across the marble from the opposite side of the dome.

"Hey Will!" she yelled at me. "You wanna show Mom around? I got to see it all last year on our school trip when I was in fourth grade. Mom's the only one who hasn't seen it."

Flip put her hand on my cheek and stared into my soul again with what seemed like a brighter version of her easy smile. It felt different this time. It was like my soul had something to show her, something clean and worthy enough for her to see.

"Mal and I would give you the tour, but I have had enough of this place. We have a trip to get ready for," I said. "What do you think, Mal? Can we show her the rest of the place another time? We can slide down those bannisters like Liam did when he was your age."

"We can?" Mal asked with new excitement.

I didn't know that day whether it was my last day in the Statehouse or not. But it felt good knowing that I no longer needed the place and all the things that came with it. Not anymore. The old Will was gone, and he was never coming back.

As much as people these days like dropping the mic and walking out of places with some triumphant gesture, that's not how it was for me. The Statehouse actually felt like it belonged to me more now than it did before. I wished more people would participate in this. The self part of self-government was the most important and most fulfilling part of the American experience.

I think I knew that I would be back, and though I'd look the same and some would think I was the same, they would be wrong. I would never be who I once was, and the things I was willing to do would be very different than they once were.

The three of us headed for the door to get on with the rest of our lives together.

I wasn't leaving the arena. I was only leaving the Circle.

ACKNOWLEDGMENTS

An author's purpose for writing a book is often unknown, misunderstood, or both. My purpose for telling this story is to bring light to the types of manipulation or control the American electorate cedes to others by not staying active in its governmental and political processes—at all levels. Corruption in Washington steals that light too easily in the modern media market while consumers, like voters, are the most responsible drivers of that unfortunate reality.

I wrote this book with the hope that it can help improve those things.

The real-life experiences that inspired this story involved far more real people than could be adequately characterized in this fictional account. Many, who are not dramatized in it in any way, contributed to the appropriate outcome of the actual legislative and legal battles that influenced this book. Their efforts were not overlooked, but were purposely omitted to avoid any unnecessary burden on them.

Those contributions to legislative justice and integrity will always be admired and appreciated.

I want to thank Daniel Sandoval and Tyler LeBleu at Greenleaf Book Group for their excitement for and leadership on publishing this book. Thank you to Jay Hodges and Anne Sanow for their editing, specifically for turning a two-year-old manuscript into a coherent story. Special thanks to Lindsay Means and Kevin Corcoran for their early guidance on getting the first draft in the right universe.

Thank you to Cameron Stein at Greenleaf for his cover artwork and to Marina Waters for her expert photography, clearly making me look better than I actually do. And to Geoff Chen, whose Indianapolis photography will be seen in the book's marketing. Thank you for braving the pandemic to get the shots.

My unlimited devotion remains with the secret society of friends who gave me the strength and courage to do so many things that I never would have, or could have, done alone. Your presence in my life for at least the last decade has profoundly impacted all of the things of which I am most proud today. I would name you here, but that's not how secrets work.

Finally, to my wife, Amy. You are the reason, the purpose, and everything else to me. You are the only other person who has read everything I have written, and the only one who can possibly know what a true burden that is. You never complain about my weekly editing needs, no matter how untimely they may come. I love you for many other interesting and unique qualities, but for all you do to make things like this book happen, I am truly appreciative.

Again, this book is for Marlene, Vince and Bryan.

ABOUT THE AUTHOR

Michael Leppert is a lecturer at the Kelley School of Business at Indiana University (IU). He is also an adjunct professor at the O'Neill School of Public and Environmental Affairs at IU, his alma mater. He has a Master of Science in communication (MSC) from Northwestern University.

He spent thirteen years in service to the State of Indiana at two agencies and nineteen years as a contract lobbyist in the Indiana Statehouse. He participated in twenty-five legislative sessions between 1997 and 2021. A prolific columnist, hundreds of his editorials have been published in dozens of Indiana newspapers.

Michael and his wife, Amy Levander, are both competitive golfers, beach walkers, and lovers of live music, comedy, and theater. They live in a historic neighborhood in downtown Indianapolis with their rescue dog, Birdie, and have two adult children, Alex and Jack.

His first book, *Contrary to Popular Belief,* the archive of his editorial writing, and other works are available on his website, MichaelLeppert.com.